The Redemption
of Micah

The Redemption of Micah

BETH WILLIAMSON

KENSINGTON PUBLISHING CORP.

www.kensingtonbooks.com

Prologue

December 1872, Plum Creek, Colorado

The moon hung low in the winter sky, a strange yellowish orange color. Micah stared at it through the window of Eppie's bedroom, wishing the nightmare would end.

The last five months had been hell on earth and he'd endured it, as he endured everything else in his life. There wasn't another choice to be made.

"You need to come down to supper." Orion stood in the doorway, his stooped figure casting a shadow across the silent room.

Micah turned to him, thankful to have the older man in the house to help out. In fact, there was an overabundance of help around the house. No one wanted to leave him alone again.

"Be there shortly."

Orion appeared not to believe him. He stepped into the room shaking his head, the tight white curls nearly glowing in the moonlight. "Sitting up here brooding isn't going to help Miss Eppie. She's surviving and so is the babe."

Micah wanted to snarl, scream and shout at the old man to shut up. He knew exactly what Eppie and their unborn child were doing, every second of every day. He didn't need a reminder.

"Surviving isn't living." He pushed away from the window. "But since you won't leave me be, I'll come downstairs and eat."

"That'd be a good thing." Orion nodded. "Miss Candice brought by some right tasty vittles."

Micah wondered how he'd ever stumbled across people who would give without expecting something in return. Candice had been friends with Madeline Brewster, the woman who had gifted the house to him and helped with Eppie's medical care. Although Madeline now lived in Denver with her husband, others had taken on what she started. Candice now helped with the cooking while Orion helped with the house.

Any man would be grateful for such assistance.

Micah, however, wasn't just any man.

He leaned down and kissed Eppie's forehead, the skin cool from winter's chill. Then he pressed his ear to her burgeoning stomach, and was rewarded with a kick to his ear. The baby was strong, like its mother.

"I'll be back soon, darlin'." He squeezed Eppie's hand and forced himself to walk away from the bed.

As Micah followed Orion out of the room and down the stairs, he barely saw anything but the other man's back. Life was colorless, meaningless without Eppie there beside him. God had seen fit to make her sleep like that princess in the book he'd seen once in Denver. She was sleeping away her life while he endured his.

The smell of beef filled the kitchen and Micah dutifully sat down to eat. Orion frowned at him across the table.

"You know, for a man who has a nice house, a beautiful woman, and everything he could want, you are pitiful."

Micah had to smile at the old man's honesty. Once upon a time, when he'd first come to live there, Orion had acted like the former slave he was. Quiet, reserved, and quick to obey. Now however, free from the yoke the Websters had forced on his neck, Orion had discovered how to use his voice and wield his opinions.

"I know. I'm the most pitiful man in Colorado. Now eat." Micah shoveled the meat and potatoes into his mouth, never tasting a bite. He should have been grateful, as Orion said, but he wasn't. Instead, he felt cheated, resentful, and angry, a perfect combination for misery.

"You plan on drinking your way to the grave?" Orion frowned, a potato halfway to his mouth.

"None of your business, old man." Micah pushed away from the table, unable to eat another bite.

Orion stopped him with a hand on his arm. "She wouldn't want you to do this."

Micah knew a lot of things about Eppie, more than most folks could even imagine he knew. However, Orion was right. She would blister his ears if she saw him wallowing, but he couldn't seem to do anything else.

"But she's not here to stop me, is she?" he snapped. "I'm done eating."

Micah stalked away from the kitchen, heading for the parlor. He had an appointment with a bottle and intended to keep it. Keeping watch over his woman was a hard business and a man had to do what he needed to do to survive.

Much later, he made his way up the stairs, mostly on his hands and knees. The house was eerily silent, Orion long since retired to his room at the end of the hall. Micah crept into Eppie's room, her scent immediately calming him.

He wiped his sweaty face and runny nose with a sleeve. This time when he pressed his ear to her stomach, he didn't get a playful kick from the baby. Her belly was hard, harder than a block of wood.

In his inebriated state, Micah didn't know what it meant, but he figured it couldn't be good. When he put his hand on her belly, it came away wet. He stared at his hand and wondered if he'd forgotten to put the pisspot beneath her.

However, his hand didn't smell like piss at all. It had a unique odor, one mixed with blood and something else. In his limited experience as a man, he hadn't had much occasion to be around women who were expecting a child.

It might have been the whiskey, or it might have been the lack of sleep over the last six months that made him slow to catch on. In either case, he stared at his hand in befuddlement for several minutes. The truth finally slammed into him like a brick wall.

Eppie was going to have the baby. Right then.

Micah almost blacked out for a moment as panic raced through him. When he finally was able to get hold of his senses, he poked his head out of the room and started shouting for help. He couldn't lose Eppie this time; she had survived for so long, had nurtured the baby and stayed as healthy as any woman would be in her situation. Birthing a child was as old as mankind. There was no reason to think she couldn't do it.

Of course, most women weren't in a coma when they gave birth. Micah's heart beat so hard, he could barely catch his breath. Orion poked his head in the room.

"What's all the racket?"

"The baby's coming. Go wake Doctor Carmichael." Micah sat beside Eppie and decided to pray for the first time in a long time. He'd ignored God for years, never trusting Him to help when needed. However, he was willing to try anything.

He fell to his knees beside the bed and pressed his closed hands to his forehead, a penitent pose.

Save her, save the baby.

Chapter One

August 1875, Plum Creek, Colorado

The shovel dug deep into the loamy soil as Micah did his best to fix the mess left by the stupid dog. He shouldn't have kept it in the first place, but the damn puppy had been happily living in the carriage house before he even knew about it. Damn that Candice, anyway; she shouldn't have brought it.

Apparently he couldn't say no anymore.

The breeze cooled his face and for just a moment or two, Micah simply concentrated on his task while the buzz of bees on the flowers surrounded him. He hadn't worked with his hands much growing up. The only things they ever touched were food, women and his horse's reins. God, how things had changed since he'd been a young fool, eager to fight in a war they were supposed to win in six months.

"Good evening." Candice, Plum Creek's shopkeeper and Micah's self-appointed guardian, arrived every weekday afternoon at five to help with supper and anything else that needed doing. She was a forty-something spinster who had shown nothing but kindness, except of course for the puppy incident.

"Evenin', Candice." He spotted the basket under her arm. "Don't tell me you brought another pie."

"Okay, I won't tell you." She looked up at the house. "Any change?"

Micah closed his eyes for a moment and pictured Eppie as she lay on the bed upstairs. He hadn't given up hope, not completely, anyway, but each day grew harder and he often considered what his life would have been like if Eppie had died after being shot, or after she'd gone into labor. A maudlin thought, but Micah never considered himself to be a good person. Taking care of the woman he loved while she slowly wasted away was the hardest thing he'd ever done, and that was saying a lot.

If anything ever did happen, Candice should know he would have been shouting or screaming, yet she asked every day like clockwork. He wanted to tell her to stop asking, but didn't know how without hurting her feelings, and he'd done enough of hurting others for two lifetimes.

"No change, other than the damn dog digging holes again." He kicked at a clump of dirt. "Stupid mutt thinks she's part groundhog."

Candice sat on the steps and shook her head. "She's a bit feisty, I'll admit."

Micah snorted. "Feisty isn't the word and you know it. She's taken over the house like some kind of canine queen."

"Oh, admit it, you like Daisy." Candice raised her eyebrows at him expectantly.

"I'm not admitting anything." Truth was, Micah liked the dog's spirit, but that didn't mean he actually liked the dog.

"Hmph, I don't think you need to." With a tinkling laugh, the redhead stood and walked toward the front door. "I'll fetch you when supper's almost ready."

A black-hearted soul such as Micah never wanted to be beholden to anyone for anything, yet here he was, each day digging himself a little deeper into a hole. If Madeline were there instead of in Denver, she'd likely smack him upside the head and tell him to snap out of it. Fortunately or not, she wasn't there and he continued to wallow in his self-pity.

"Daddy, pick flowers for Mama?"

Micah glanced up to see his daughter, Miracle, standing in the flower bed surrounded by blossoms, with a big grin on her beautiful face. His dark thoughts blew away on the wind. She knew she wasn't supposed to be in there, but the girl loved the feel of the petals on her bare legs. Even her dresses were always in the bright colors of the blossoms that surrounded the house. She couldn't know her mother used to dress the same way, always brighter than anything around her.

"I did it this morning, but if you don't stop walking in those, there won't be any left to pick." He wiped the sweat from his forehead with his handkerchief. "And if Daisy doesn't stop digging in the flower beds, we're going to have to tie her up."

Miracle had been blessed with wavy dark brown hair, her mother's chocolate brown eyes, and the most gorgeous light cocoa skin. The mixture of her two parents gave Miracle an exotic look that made most folks look at her twice. Micah wasn't boastful when he said his daughter was perfect—she was.

Miracle pooched out her lip. "Daisy's a good dog."

He turned to the flowers again, unwilling to get sucked into his daughter's trap to save her dog from a leash. "Yes, she's a good dog." A blatant lie she was the spawn of the devil as far as Micah was concerned. "But puppies need to behave, honey. She's not going to learn if we don't teach her."

When he glanced up again, Miracle's little body was just disappearing around the back of the house. No doubt to go whisper into the yellow dog's ear about how much trouble she caused.

Being a father had taught Micah a great deal of humility,

but he was still working on patience. Although she'd never heard her mother speak, Miracle already had the sassy, bossy quality that always popped out of Eppie's mouth.

"That child needs two proper parents." The Reverend Mathias's voice cut through Micah's peaceful moment like a sickle. The pompous windbag made it his duty to preach to everyone about their sins, shortcomings, and how readily they were headed to hell.

Micah almost snorted at the thought. He'd been in hell for more than ten years. The older man had no idea how much a human being could endure on Earth. Enough so that Micah didn't even think about the hereafter.

"She has two parents." Micah slammed the shovel into the dirt, unwilling to get into another shouting match with the minister. "What do you want?"

"Tomorrow is Sunday. I wanted to come by and personally invite you to services tomorrow." The man bobbed his white-topped head and latched his hands across the burgeoning belly above his belt.

Micah's hand tightened on the shovel. He'd accepted the invitation once. Just once. He'd never do it again. The women in town had treated his daughter as if she had a disease that was catching. No way in hell he'd subject Miracle to it again.

"Until your congregation treats my daughter as a human being, there's no chance in hell we'll come to services." Micah went back to his chores, pointedly ignoring the minister and his judgmental gaze.

"Mark my words, boy, you'll be looking for a Savior and he won't be there when you need him." With that, the man walked away, thankfully leaving Micah in peace.

Two hours later, Micah sat in the parlor and listened to the sounds from the bathing room upstairs. Miracle was singing at the top of her lungs while Candice hummed along. There were splashing, giggles and fun going on, yet he didn't join them. He couldn't.

He ran his hands down his face and looked around at the opulent furniture left behind when Madeline moved to Denver. The room reminded him of his mother's house and how they'd lived their lives in oblivious ignorance, taking whatever they wanted without ever giving back.

Perhaps having Eppie but losing her inch by inch was his penance for such a childhood. Or perhaps it was punishment for his other multitudinous sins. No matter, it was his life and he'd come to accept it, but he couldn't enjoy it. Miracle was everything sweet and good in his life, and he treasured her beyond words. Just thinking about her soft hugs made his throat tighten.

God, he loved that little girl more than life.

With a sigh, he stood and headed toward the stairs. Each night he sat with Miracle as she visited her Mama before bed. Her childish voice would detail every second of her day to an unresponsive Eppie. One day, perhaps, it would be more than a one-sided conversation.

Micah knew exactly how many breaths Eppie took each hour. He watched the rise and fall of her chest, waiting and hoping. The hell of it was, he wasn't sure what he was hoping for. Micah wasn't ready to let her go, but seeing her trapped between two worlds was killing him. He missed her, he loved her, and dammit all, he wanted to see her open her eyes again.

It had been a true-blue miracle the baby survived the trauma to its mother's body; even more amazing was that the child was born healthy and perfect. When she was pregnant, watching Eppie had become a habit because he could watch his child. *Their* child. The baby made from a love that shouldn't be, but was. Miracle had been active, sometimes for hours at a time. During that six-month period, Micah never got tired of sitting by Eppie's bedside and watching, placing his hand on her belly, telling them both he loved them.

Micah wanted so many things, but what burned down deep in his gut was the fact he wanted to convince Eppie to marry him and he wanted to tell her he loved her. He'd been hesitant of revealing his feelings before, afraid of being rejected, of losing what he could have.

Regret was something he knew well, ate for breakfast, lunch and dinner each day. It brought him nothing but misery, yet it was still his constant companion.

He entered Eppie's bedroom and was immediately awash in her scent, that unique smell that always made his heart beat faster. A gas lamp burned on the side table, bathing her in a golden glow. Just being in the room with her made him feel better.

She still looked beautiful, even if she'd survived for nearly three years on broth, milk and water. Micah knew every inch of her body from the adorably crooked little toe to the sweet spot behind her right ear. He ran his fingers down her cocoa-colored cheek, the skin as smooth as her daughter's.

"Hey there, Eppie girl." He sat down in his usual chair and put her hand in his. Squeezing the limp fingers, he started talking of Daisy and Miracle's antics. "That crazy dog actually came back and started digging when I was fixing the damn hole. Miracle wasn't happy about tying her up, but she did it anyway. She's a good girl."

"Who's a good girl?"

Eppie's voice, long since unheard, made the hairs on the back of his neck stand up.

"Jesus Christ." He jumped out of the chair, knocking it backwards a good three feet. Micah looked down into the eyes of the woman who held his heart. "Eppie?"

She blinked and glanced down at herself, then back at him. "Why am I lying in bed? Have I been ill?"

"Are you really talking to me, honey?" His heart slammed into his throat as it pounded so hard, even his bones vibrated. "Eppie, oh my God, tell me I'm not dreaming."

"I'm not sure who you are or why you're in the bedroom with me, but I'm fairly sure you shouldn't be calling me honey." Eppie cocked her head and narrowed her gaze. "Who are you?"

Chapter Two

She had come into awareness slowly over a long period of time. The sounds and smells around her had become familiar as she surfaced from the depths of darkness. His voice had always been there, a soft gentle companion she'd come to expect and wish for.

Now she'd opened her eyes and there he was, a stranger she knew. The shock and delight in his eyes clouded with disbelief when she asked him who he was. She wanted to ask who *she* was, for that matter, but he looked like he'd shatter if she asked that particular question.

"I don't understand." He sat back down in the golden chair with a thump and stared at her. His silvery eyes were wide in sunken cheeks. His brown hair needed to be cut and he was thin, way too thin. She also noted his hands shook as he clasped them in front of him. "Are you saying that you don't know who I am?"

She tried to push herself up to a sitting position but found her arms didn't work well. He seemed to notice what she was doing, because he popped out of the chair and helped her. As he leaned over, his scent enveloped her and she breathed in deeply. That, too, was familiar.

"Here, let's put some pillows back here."

He was skinny but strong, pulling her forward as if she

weighed no more than a feather and getting her situated on fluffy pillows. When he let her go, a small smile appeared on his face.

"I still can't believe you're awake." He ran his hands through his too-long hair and sat back down in the chair. "I've heard stories of folks not remembering things after they got hit in the head, but I never expected it to happen to you. I mean, you were shot in the shoulder."

"Shot? I was shot?" She reached up to feel both shoulders, grateful to find nothing but a cotton nightgown.

"Eppie, honey, it's been three years. The bandages are long gone."

Three years? *Three years?* She understood what a year was, even what being shot or a bandage was, but it seemed she didn't remember anything about herself or how she got there. Three years was such a long time. Had he taken care of her the entire time?

"Who are you?"

His smile was so sad, it could have made an angel cry. "My name is Micah Spalding. You and I, well, we fell in love four years ago. Then something got in the way and you saved my life, got shot, and you've been in that bed ever since."

A very confusing and cryptic response, to be sure. She didn't know if she believed a word of it or understood half of it, but there was definitely an earnestness in his gaze. She tried out his name on her tongue.

"Micah."

He nodded. "Yes, it's me. Do you remember now?"

She didn't want to disappoint him, but she wasn't going to lie, either. "No, I'm sorry, I don't, but I do know your voice."

He seemed to deflate before her eyes. "I've been talking to you since your accident. I took care of you and our da—your daily care. I guess deep inside that hole you were in, my voice must've come through."

"Yes, that's what I remember. Sounds and smells floating

around me." She tried to explain more, but a pounding started in her head. "I'm afraid I don't feel very well." She put a hand to her forehead and could almost feel the pulsing behind the skin.

"Then I think you should sleep." He started toward the night table to turn down the lamp when the door burst open and a little girl came rushing in.

She had hair like Micah, long wavy brown locks that looked towel dried. Her skin was a beautiful creamy tan color with a slight rosy tinge as if she'd been in the bath. Her little nightgown was white with small pink flowers along the collar. When she caught sight of what was going on, she stopped in her tracks, bare feet squeaking on the floor.

"Daddy?" She glanced up at Micah, uncertainty and downright fear on her face. "Is Mama 'wake?"

Eppie's stomach flip-flopped inside her as she realized the little girl was talking about her. The girl didn't look even remotely familiar, but again her voice was. Could she have forgotten her own daughter?

The color drained from Micah's face as he looked back and forth between them. "Miracle, go to your room, honey, and I'll be there shortly."

"But Daddy." She pointed with a trembling hand. "She looked at me. Her eyes open."

The girl was probably no more than three, still struggling to put all the words together to make herself understood. Somehow after waking from a long slumber, Eppie could already do so with ease. She had trouble thinking of herself as Eppie, though, and wondered if it was a nickname.

"Miracle, go to your room now." Micah sounded like a daddy right about then, using a firm tone that signaled he meant business.

Miracle stuck out her lower lip, but she minded her daddy and stomped out of the room. A red-haired plump woman stood in the doorway, her mouth open.

"Sweet Jesus." She looked at Micah with wide blue eyes. "Is she awake?"

Micah ushered the red-haired woman out of the room. "I'll be there in a few minutes, just put Miracle to bed, please."

The little girl protested all the way down the hallway, at the top of her lungs, but she went just the same. Micah leaned against the doorway and took a deep breath before he went back into the room. As he closed the door he looked at Eppie and shook his head. His gaze roamed her up and down, sending a shiver through her. There was much more than emotion coming off him and it confused her.

"If you weren't sitting up in that bed right now I'd think the whiskey had done its job on me." He came back to the chair and sat down, taking her hand in his. "I am fairly certain you're scared right now, confused and in need of a break from the insanity of our home. Before I let you sleep, tell me if you're hungry or thirsty."

She didn't know exactly how she felt, but it wasn't thirsty or hungry. "No, I'm not." She pointed to the quilt at the end of the bed. "I'm a bit chilly, though." Anything to get the sad-eyed man out of sight so she could think clearly. Something about him confused her.

He jumped up as if someone had pinched him, pulling the quilt up and over her in seconds. She didn't know whether to be flattered or afraid of him. He was obviously as confused as she was.

"Better?"

"Yes, thank you." The warmth of the quilt settled over her and tugged her toward sleep.

"Even the way you talk is different. You know, you sound just like me now." He frowned.

She didn't understand what he meant, so she didn't answer. Instead, she closed her eyes and listened as he set the room to rights and lowered the lamp. Then sleep claimed her.

*   *   *

Micah leaned against the door outside Eppie's room and tried to catch his breath. Blood thundered through his veins as he controlled the nearly insane urge to run back in the room and shake her. Make her recognize him and remember everything. She loved him, he loved her. They were supposed to be together.

Yet she didn't remember him and it was a knife in his already battered heart when he should be rejoicing and shouting. Micah had so many dreams about what would happen when she woke up. This was not one of them.

It wasn't the worst possible thing that could happen. She might never have woken up, or woken up and been unable to speak or function. However, having her there but not there hadn't entered his mind. She looked at him as if he were a complete stranger and when Miracle came in, she'd looked horrified.

He slid down to the floor and wrapped his arms around his knees, then pressed his eyes into them. Stars swam behind them, giving him something tangible to grab on to as he flailed around inside.

She didn't remember him.

She didn't want her daughter.

She looked at him as if he were crazy.

He'd been holding out hope she'd wake up and everything would be perfect. Maybe it would take some time for her to get completely well, but it was supposed to happen. Instead, it was a nightmare he hadn't imagined would happen.

A small hand patted him on the head. "Don' cry, Daddy."

He opened his arms and Miracle filled them. Her soft baby scent surrounded him, giving him the strength to get himself under control. Her little arms wrapped around his neck and hung on.

Micah definitely had an unusual family, but it was his and he vowed to hang on to it and make it all right. If he loved Eppie, it was a forever kind of love, one he would stay true to forever, through the good and the bad. Or the unthinkably bad.

After a few minutes of absorbing his daughter's goodness, he felt control returning and patted Miracle back. She was natural medicine to a man caught in the throes of a shattered soul and a broken heart.

"Let's get you to bed, sweetheart." He stood, scooping her into his arms, and carried his daughter to bed.

Her room was decorated in yellow because she loved sunshine. The ruffled curtains Candice had made blew gently in the breeze from the window. Miracle snuggled into the fluffy bed, barely making a lump under the blanket, her long hair displayed on the pillow beneath her. Her brown eyes looked up at him, so much like Eppie's.

" 'Night Daddy," she mumbled on a sigh.

"Good night, Miracle." He sat on the edge of her bed, his hand on her back feeling her breaths, her heartbeat. Once again, he would likely not sleep that night, particularly when he knew Eppie had finally woken from her endless sleep.

After an hour of watching Miracle, he finally rose and left her room. The house was eerily quiet with only the sound of ticking clocks and the squeak of the floorboards beneath his feet. He slipped off his shoes and left them by his door. The urge to check on Eppie grew too strong and he couldn't wait any longer.

He pressed his ear to the door and listened with his eyes closed. No sound, not even a peep, came from within. He should let her sleep, leave her in peace, but he couldn't. His heart thumped with a regular rhythm and it still whispered "Eppie."

With his hand on the knob, he waited again while perspiration dotted his brow. After a few minutes of wrestling with his conscience, he finally gave in and opened the door. The moonlight coming through the curtains dotted the room, painting everything a silvery glow.

He'd entered her room so many times over the last few years and the same sight always greeted him. Eppie lay on her back, still, yet alive. This time she lay on her side with one leg out of the covers and her right arm flung over her head.

The vision made his knees wobbly and he sat down in his chair while he drank it in. She really had woken up and spoken. Even if she didn't remember him, she came back to the land of the living and survived almost being dead. That meant more to him than losing her. A truly unselfish person would revel in the fact that the woman he loved hadn't died.

Micah wasn't that unselfish, unfortunately. He wanted all of it—the woman, the child, the marriage and the future. As the moon moved across the sky, he sat and watched her sleep. As he watched her, she moved in the bed, shifting positions and sighing, occasionally even grinding her teeth. Each sound was like music to his ears because she was sleeping normally, not caught between life and death.

As the first rays of the sun crept into the room, Micah rose with his stiff body and stretched. Although she hadn't needed them, her clothes hung in the armoire in the corner, waiting for her. He took out her favorite purple dress and underclothes and laid them on the chair by the bed. Then he tiptoed out of the room to make breakfast.

Today had to be the day she remembered him.

This time when she woke, it was instant. The fog of yesterday's wakening had cleared and she saw everything clearly. The same room, the same bed and even the same skinny body beneath the covers. The man, Micah, was gone, however, giving her a chance to get her bearings.

A lovely purple dress lay on the chair, almost blinding in its vibrant color. He must have laid it out for her while she slept, a fact that didn't please her. No matter what he thought, she didn't remember him, and he didn't need to be sneaking into her room while she slept. When he appeared, and she had no doubt he would, she could give him a piece of her mind about it.

When she swung her legs around and gingerly touched the floor, her feet felt odd, almost spongy. It took a few minutes to get herself upright and she was tired almost immediately. She sat back down and tried to get her breath back. Maybe he'd been telling the truth and she had laid there for three years. No wonder her body felt out of sorts; it didn't remember how to work.

She might not know who she was, but she did know she was no quitter. No siree. After a few minutes of rest, she stood again and raised her arms above her head, stretching until muscles screamed at her. Then she bent over, trying to reach her toes, but that was even harder. She could only do that for a minute before she had to sit again with her head swimming.

At this rate, she could make it downstairs by supper.

A small knock at the door had her grabbing for the quilt to hold in front of her. She was still in her nightclothes and had a sense of modesty even if Micah didn't.

"Mama?"

The little voice certainly didn't belong to him, but the girl scared her more than the man did. She decided not to answer, a cowardly thing to do, but perhaps the child would go away. After a few moments of holding her breath and watching the door handle, the pitter-patter of feet walked away. She took a deep breath and let it out.

It was going to be a very long day.

Miracle appeared in the kitchen doorway, a forlorn expression on her tiny face.

"Mama sleepin'." She plopped down in her chair and looked up at Micah.

"Do you want a biscuit?" At her nod, Micah took the biscuits out of the oven, still amazed at how much he'd learned about cooking from Candice. He put one on a plate and blew on it before placing it in front of his daughter. "Let that cool a minute before you eat it."

"Mama waked up yesterday." She was obviously not going to drop the subject until he acknowledged what she already knew.

"Yes, she did." Micah sat down and thought for a minute on how to explain to a three-year-old that her mother didn't remember her. Not an easy task. "Your mama was hurt very badly. She was sleeping very deeply, but her body took care of you until you were born."

"She got a owie?" Miracle picked at the biscuit, popping tiny pieces in her mouth.

"Not anymore, but her head had an owie we couldn't see. It made her forget some things." Micah cupped his daughter's chin and looked into her chocolate brown eyes. "She didn't know you were inside her when she was hurt, so Mama doesn't know you yet."

Tears rolled down Miracle's cheeks. "Mama don't know me?"

"No, sweetheart, but that's okay because she doesn't know me, either. It's our job to help her remember and then she'll know how much she loves you." Micah's throat closed up, unwilling or unable at the moment to consider the possibility that Eppie might not ever love them. He wasn't ready to entertain that notion.

" 'Kay. Can I give her hug?" She swiped at the tears, showing Micah that his baby was growing up, way too fast in his opinion. She was always a strong-minded girl, and independent to boot.

"Not yet, but soon. Maybe we can just help her by bringing her warm water to wash and good food and drink. What do you think?" He pointed to the invalid tray on the top shelf. Madeline had used it with her father when she owned the house. "There's a tray up there we can take upstairs."

Miracle clapped her hands together. "I carry it!"

"No, sweetie, I'll carry it because you have to go pick some flowers and bring those."

She scrambled off the chair so fast it fell over backwards. Still dressed in her little nightgown, Miracle ran outside to pick flowers for her mother. Micah took a deep breath and thanked God again for such an amazing child. Even he didn't understand what was happening, but Miracle accepted it at face value. It was a lesson she could teach most adults.

Micah got the tray down and washed it off before Miracle came bounding back inside, with muddy pawprints on her nightgown and a handful of flowers.

"I pick flowers for Mama." She held them up for inspection. "See?"

"They're lovely. You did a wonderful job." Micah pointed to the half-eaten biscuit. "Now put the flowers on the counter and wash up so you can finish your breakfast while I get Mama's ready."

Miracle did as she was bade, and climbed up the little steps he'd made for her at the sink. She ended up getting more water on the floor than her hands, but she was clean enough to eat. Micah buttered a few biscuits and put a pot of jam and a cup of coffee on the tray. He wasn't sure what Eppie was up to eating, but it was a start. After he put some warm water in a pitcher, the tray was ready to go.

The girl practically inhaled the biscuit with crumbs hanging all over her chin and announced she was done. She grabbed the flowers and the vase from the counter. Micah saved the glass vase before it hit the floor by snatching it out of her pudgy little hand.

"Let me get the water for you." He pumped it full, then let her stick the flowers in there, so full they barely squeezed in the narrow neck.

"I carry."

"Be careful, honey." He wanted to take it from her, but

didn't. It was damn hard to let your child start growing up. He'd had no idea just how hard it was until he had to stop himself from doing everything for her as he had all her short life. She was smart and capable for a child and he had to let her make her own mistakes, no matter how hard it was on him.

He picked up the tray and followed her as she climbed the steps, the vase firmly stuck under her left arm and hugged to her chest. She made it up the steps with only a small trail of spilled water behind her.

Miracle stopped with her hand on the knob and looked back at Micah.

"Knock first."

She frowned, but knocked twice and waited, her face alight with anticipation.

"Who is it?" came the voice from within. It unnerved him to hear his accent, his inflection, and his vocabulary coming from Eppie. The only explanation he could come up with was she listened to his voice while she was in the coma. Perhaps with her memory of things gone, it was the familiarity of his voice that she did remember.

It still made him wish for her bossy, sassy voice to come bursting from her mouth.

"It's me, Mama." She turned the knob and peered through a small opening in the door.

"We brought some breakfast, Eppie. May we come in?" Micah found his palms sweaty and his heart slamming against his ribs again, as if he was taking a test—which he really was since she didn't remember him. He hoped she approved of their offering.

"I suppose." Not an enthusiastic answer, but he could live with it.

After he nodded at Miracle, she pushed the door open and ran in with the wildflowers out in front of her like a trophy.

"Hi, my name's Miracle. Brought you flowers!" She thrust them into Eppie's face before Micah could stop her.

"Oh, my." Eppie was sitting in his chair, the purple dress hanging on her like a sack. She was half the size she'd been three years earlier and it made his heart ache for what she'd had to endure. Eppie had always been thin, but now she was almost emaciated.

"They're lovely." She took the vase and held it at arm's length and squinted at them. "I don't remember their names." Panic flashed across her features, but she shuttered it quickly and smiled at Miracle. "Thank you kindly."

Miracle turned to look at Micah. "She sound like you, Daddy."

So he wasn't the only one to notice. He inwardly winced at the truthfulness of children—they never thought of other's feelings or consequences. Life was so simple to them.

"Scoot out of the way so I can set this tray on the side table." Micah stepped fully in the room, breathing in Eppie's scent, and felt an immediate calm settle over him. Even if she didn't sound like herself, she was still there talking, breathing and living.

"It smells delicious." Eppie peeked at the biscuits. "I wasn't hungry before, but those biscuits have riled my hunger."

She looked winded and a bit sweaty as if getting dressed had drained her. Likely it had, but he understood why she hadn't called him even if he wished she had. Micah was still a stranger and no woman would ask a strange man for help to get her clothes on.

"I was considering getting back into bed, but the chair is quite comfortable." She gave him a wan smile and he read between her words.

"Allow me." He scooped her up, the flutter of her heart against his as she squeaked.

"What are you doing?"

"Bringing you back to bed." He laid her down on the quilt, fluffing the pillows behind her. "I've been taking care of you for almost three years, Eppie, there's nothing I haven't done or wouldn't do for you."

He couldn't look her in the eye or he might embarrass himself by begging or something equally as stupid. Instead he went back to the table to retrieve the tray. By the time he turned around, he was more in control of himself and managed a smile.

"I wasn't sure what you might want to eat, so I brought only coffee and biscuits." He fitted the tray onto her lap and handed her the napkin. "There's some warm water in the pitcher."

She took it from him hesitantly, her eyes guarded. "What's my full name?"

Micah was so startled he didn't answer her for a full minute. It was worse than he suspected. It wasn't just him she didn't remember, Eppie didn't remember herself. Sweet Jesus.

His mouth went cotton dry but he was finally able to find his voice. "I'd have to ask Madeline, but I believe it's just Eppie. I don't think I ever heard a last name."

Miracle was busy arranging the flowers and thankfully didn't notice the exchange between them.

"Who's Madeline?"

"Madeline Brewster. She's your best friend and one of my closest friends. This house used to be hers, but she deeded it to us after your accident." He pointed to the food. "Why don't you have something to eat and when you're done, we can talk." He inclined his head toward Miracle.

"Of course, that sounds like a good idea. Thank you for the food." She looked at Miracle. "And thank you again for the lovely flowers."

"Welcome." Miracle stared up at her mother, still apparently trying to gauge who she was.

"Go get dressed now, honey, and let Mama eat in peace."

He ushered his daughter out of the room, not daring himself to look back at Eppie. If he did, he might not be able to leave himself. "I'll be back in a little bit to check on you."

The biscuits smelled heavenly and her mouth watered at the remembered taste. It was frustrating to know there were inane things she remembered without effort, but she couldn't even think of her own name. She tried to focus to remember and the pain in her head roared at her.

Leaning back against the pillows, she closed her eyes and took a deep breath. After a few minutes she realized her life was nothing but blackness and the last twelve hours in this room. It was a pitiful excuse for a life if it was all she'd ever remember.

Self-pity reared its ugly head, but she beat it back, with considerable effort. She put a bit of butter and jam on a biscuit and gingerly nibbled on it. After only a quarter of the biscuit, she felt full. No matter how good it tasted, if Micah was telling her the truth, she hadn't had solid food in three years. The last thing she wanted was to make herself sick.

The coffee was hot and strong, and she must've preferred it that way because she drank the entire cup. It helped her feel a bit stronger, definitely warmer. The dress told her she had been much bigger, either that or he gave her someone else's clothes. Either way, she was very thin, too thin.

Now what she wanted was to get cleaned up. However, she realized the tray prevented her from getting out of bed. It appeared she was stuck until Micah came back.

As if she'd conjured him from her mind, there was a knock at the door.

"Eppie, may I come in?"

"Please do." She found the long-haired man's appearance to be less shocking. In fact, she could now see the kindness and concern behind his silver eyes. He gave her a quick smile when he opened the door wide and came into the room.

"I'm glad you ate something." He pointed to the tray. "And my coffee isn't too bad?"

She found her own smile tickling her lips, but she didn't want to let it out just yet. Much as the man was being nice, she didn't know him or herself well enough yet. "The coffee and biscuit was wonderful. Thank you for your kindness."

He waved his hand in dismissal. "No thanks are necessary. Are you finished?"

At her nod, he took the tray away, freeing her lap, but she found herself not ready to move yet. What she really wanted to do is remember something, anything, aside from the fact she liked biscuits. When he turned to leave the room, she found herself asking him to stay.

"Wait, please. I . . . can you stay for a few minutes?"

The surprise on his face was only matched by the hope. "Absolutely, honey—I mean Eppie." He fluttered around a bit, putting the tray on the floor by the door and arranging the chair by the bed. He smiled tremulously as he sat.

"Tell me what you know about me." She felt heat creeping into her cheeks, but she didn't drop her gaze. Micah was her only link to who she was, who she was supposed to be.

"You moved to town and met Madeline about five years ago. I think you were originally from North Carolina." Micah settled back in the chair, his posture relaxing.

She knew North Carolina by name, but try as she might, no picture came to mind. "Where are we now?"

"Colorado, in a little town called Plum Creek, maybe fifty miles from Denver. That's the capital." He pointed to the window filled with bright sunshine. "It's Monday morning, August sixteenth, eighteen seventy-five."

"Who owns this house?" The more information he gave her, the more she felt stupid and helpless, but she had to know.

"I do. Madeline gave it to me right after the accident almost three years ago. Before that you lived here with her. You were friends, best friends." He looked away as his throat moved. "We've been here together since then."

She wished she remembered Madeline, her best friend, but nothing was familiar at all. "How old is the girl?"

His face softened at the mention of the child. "She's almost three. Her birthday is in a few months."

Apparently she could still do simple math, because by her estimate, if the girl was her daughter, she was born when Eppie was unconscious. Suspicion replaced panic.

"And she's my daughter?"

"Actually, she's *our* daughter." His smile was crooked. "Once upon a time you and I loved each other, Eppie, and we were going to be married." His eyebrow twitched when he said it, so he was lying about something.

"And she was born when I was sleeping?" Her voice started to gain in volume.

He seemed to realize she was getting angry, and his posture was suddenly ramrod straight. "It's called a coma, a type of very deep sleep while a body heals. I don't know the exact medical particulars, but you'd been hurt and it took a long time to heal."

"I gave birth in this coma?" She was sitting on the edge of the bed, full of enough energy to stand.

"Yes, you did, with help, of course. The doctor practically lived here the last two months of the pregnancy. He was the best money could buy, all the way from St. Louis." Micah stood, stepping behind the chair using it like a shield.

He'd better hide if he was lying to her.

"Who paid?" she nearly snarled as she stood, her head banging like a drum while her legs shook beneath her.

"Madeline paid for everything. She loved you, loves you, just as I do. Sweetheart I—"

"Don't think for a minute that I believe everything you're telling me. I'm not a fool to be toyed with. It's going to take more than your explanations to convince me of what's happened. For all I know we're not even in Colorado." She pointed at the door. "I appreciate your kindness, Mr. Spalding, but until I see proof of your cockamamie story, I'm reserving judgment on exactly what's going on."

His mouth dropped open and his eyes widened as she spoke. When she finished her diatribe, he shook his head and sadness crept back into his eyes.

"I see your fire in there still, a bossy, sassy woman who's been sleeping for so long." He turned toward the door. "No matter how much you don't believe, I believe enough for both of us." When he reached the tray, he picked it up but didn't look at her again. "I just hope I have enough love for both of us."

His words sent a chill up her spine and she sat back on the bed, breathing as if she'd run a country mile. She didn't know up from down, but she did know that man believed everything he said. That fact scared her more than anything.

Micah held himself together by force of will. It was either that or break into a thousand pieces in front of his daughter. As he closed Eppie's door, she stood five feet away, her red-haired dolly clutched in her hands, fear and confusion in her gaze.

"Mama mad?"

"Yes, honey, Mama's mad. She's confused and unsure of what's going on. We're going to have to give her time to get to know us, remember?" He walked down the stairs with Miracle at his heels.

Unfortunately for Micah, he forgot about the water she'd dropped and his shoes found the biggest puddle. As his feet went out from under him, all he could think of was, please God don't let her lose both parents.

Chapter Three

Eppie had just gotten herself settled in the chair when she heard the crash and the girl screaming. She jumped up with more energy than she thought she had and darted out the door. The sheer size of the house made her eyes goggle and she wondered if he'd been telling more truth than she realized.

She spotted him at the bottom of the steps, the tray of food scattered around him. The girl sat beside him smacking his cheek.

"Daddy, wake up."

Eppie made her way down the stairs, clutching the thick mahogany banister. When she made it to the bottom, the little girl looked up at her with tears in her eyes.

"Daddy sleep?"

"I'm not sure, honey." Eppie's fear was that he'd died before she figured out if he was telling the truth, or worse, that he was truthful and didn't get a chance to tell her everything about herself. She'd be trapped in a house she didn't know with a child she didn't know in a town that was as unfamiliar as the people around her.

She knelt down and put her hand on his chest, and felt the steady beat of his heart. A breath of relief whooshed out of her. He must have just knocked himself unconscious when he fell. She didn't think she knew much about being a doctor, but she did feel for any broken bones and was glad to find none.

"He bumped his head and went to sleep."

Instead of reassuring the girl, she started screaming and shaking Micah by the shoulders. "No, Daddy, wake up!"

Eppie didn't know what to do to calm the girl down. Her reaction made no sense.

"He'll wake up in a minute or two. Why don't you get a pillow for his head?"

The girl sobbed even louder, but she nodded her head and stuck her doll under his neck. The sight made Eppie want to laugh, but she swallowed the chuckle. She started picking up the broken plate and the pieces of biscuits. Without being asked, Miracle helped clean up even as she continued to cry.

Eppie didn't know if that was common for her, but she knew it was unusual for a girl that age to have such a sense of responsibility. After they'd picked up the mess, Micah still hadn't roused. Eppie wasn't really worried, but she was getting concerned.

"Where is the kitchen?"

The girl pointed to room down the hall.

"Can you go get a glass of water for your daddy?"

"Why?" Precocious little thing.

"To help him wake up."

The child looked at her as if she'd sprouted horns, but went to the kitchen just the same, frowning fiercely and crying all the way. It gave Eppie an opportunity to study Micah up close without feeling self-conscious about it. She could see the resemblance between him and the girl, a glimmer of his cheekbones and chin. The hair, of course, was identical.

He had a terrible scar that ran from his jawline down his neck. It was deep and made by something sharp. He had a whisper of whiskers on his cheeks, and shadows permanently etched below his eyes. There were very light brown baby hairs around his hairline. Without even thinking about it, she reached out to brush the hair from his forehead.

"Don't touch."

Miracle's stern admonishment made her heart skip a beat. Eppie turned around and managed a small smile.

"I was making sure he was okay."

The doubtful expression didn't leave Miracle's little face. She thrust the cup of water forward, splashing some on both of them.

"Thank you, Miracle." Eppie's stomach was jumping around like crazy, but she put her hand behind his neck and trickled water into his mouth. He swallowed, thankfully, then he sighed, the smell of lemon tickling her nose.

His eyelashes fluttered and her relief knew no bounds when those silver orbs peeped up at her.

"Eppie?"

"You fell down the stairs and knocked yourself silly." She set the glass down and let his head back down onto the doll.

"I did? Oh damn, the water, I forgot." His eyes widened. "Is Miracle okay?"

"She's fine. A little upset." An understatement, but she didn't want to scare him.

"I here, Daddy." She inserted herself between them. The warmth of her little body seeped into Eppie's. It startled her and she shifted back to escape from the sensation. She definitely wasn't ready to be physically close to anyone, much less a child calling her "Mama."

"Thank God." Micah took Eppie's hand in his. "You have my gratitude."

She wanted to snatch her hand away, but at the same time, his dry slender hand felt comfortable in hers. A shiver ran up her spine at the thought.

"It's not hard to be kind to people in need." She managed to extract her hand and sat back on the step above him. "Do you think you can get up?"

He frowned and shifted, wincing as he did. "I think so, but it's going to take me a few minutes. I think I bruised my back."

Although she didn't want to touch him, she helped him to his feet. Even if her head and her heart didn't remember him, it appeared her body did. She wasn't sure if it was just being close, his scent, or something else entirely. Whatever it was, as soon as her arm went around his waist, her body warmed to his and heat flowed between them.

To her astonishment, her nipples even hardened. She hoped to God he didn't feel those against his side. She'd be absolutely mortified if he did. It was hard enough to forget everybody she knew, but to have no control over her body made it even worse.

"I help." Miracle jumped around to the other side of her father and together they steadied him.

"Where is your room?"

"Upstairs next to Miracle's. It's the largest room in the house and Madeline insisted on me taking it." He smiled sadly. "I think perhaps she thought you and I might use it together."

Eppie wanted to let him fall on his head for trying to manipulate her. He had to understand she didn't forget him on purpose. She'd give anything to remember one shred of who she was. If he kept pushing her, eventually she would shut the door on any possibility of a relationship with him. One thing she did know about herself was she didn't like to be forced into decisions.

She'd been doing a lot of thinking since she'd woken up. There were a lot of decisions to make and she wasn't done making them. Micah would just have to be patient.

Somehow they made it up the stairs and none of them fell back down. Micah straightened and took hold of the banister and Eppie let him go. Her body yelled at her to grab him again, but she listened to her head instead and crossed her arms, stepping away.

"Thank you." He took a shaky breath. "I'll be okay. I'm going to splash some water on my face." He laughed. "Although I might have had enough water for the day."

Eppie couldn't help the smile that escaped. His charm was a surprise. "I'll be in, well, in my room I suppose." She ducked away and escaped before he could call her back.

She leaned against the door and pressed a hand to her chest, trying to will her heart to slow down the blood as it raced through her. Since she didn't even feel comfortable being in the house with him, it made no sense that she tingled just being next to Micah.

Winded and exhausted from too much so fast, she climbed into bed and pulled up the quilt. Within minutes, she closed her eyes and drifted off to sleep.

"You fell down the stairs?" Candice stared at Micah with wide eyes. "Do you need the doctor?"

"No, no, I'm fine." Micah felt the twinges from the fall all over his body, particularly in his knee where he'd been injured during the war. Fortunately nothing had been broken, just bruised, including his pride.

She set the basket on the counter and turned to him, hands on her ample hips. "Now we need to talk about what's happening upstairs. I saw her awake and talking. Have you wired Madeline and the doctor in Denver?"

Micah eased himself onto a kitchen chair and picked up the mug of coffee she'd set down for him. The bitter brew felt wonderful sliding down his throat.

"No, I haven't wired the doctor and I especially haven't told Madeline. So please do not tell her what's going on." He let out a sigh of frustration, longing and pain. Being close to Eppie, feeling her body against his, had stolen his breath. She felt wonderful. More than that, she felt perfect—as if she belonged there.

Too bad she didn't remember him from the next man she saw.

"What is going on?" Candice glanced at Miracle outside playing with her puppy in the sunshine.

"She doesn't remember."

"The accident? I don't blame her. No one wants to remember being shot." Candice visibly shuddered. "I still can't believe she survived losing all that blood."

"No, not just the accident. She doesn't remember *anything* . . . or anybody." He took another swallow of coffee, the burn taking the sting away from his words.

"What do you mean? She doesn't remember you?" Candice's expression would have been comical if he'd have been in the least ready to laugh. Her mouth formed a perfect "O" and her eyes were like blue saucers.

"She doesn't remember me, this house, Madeline, or anything other than how to talk, walk and do all the normal things people do. Jesus, Candice, she doesn't even remember who she is." He ran a hand through his hair as his friend gasped. "I wanted to give her a couple of days to see if perhaps she remembered something, anything, but so far it hasn't happened."

"What are you going to do?" She put her hand on his, giving him a lifeline he desperately needed.

"I don't know. Funny thing is, she sounds like me." He barked a laugh without a smidge of humor. "No more Eppie sass, just my stupid southern drawl with a mixture of highfalutin' vocabulary words."

"I never heard of such a thing. It's like she isn't herself anymore." Candice seemed to realize what she said and she squeezed his hand in apology. "I'm sorry, Micah. I'm not helping at all, am I?"

"It's okay, I know what you mean. I felt like I've been in a hurricane the last twenty-four hours." He ran a hand through his hair. "She's proper, soft-spoken and a complete stranger to me, but I still love her. Eppie's still in there somewhere."

"I know you still love her. You're the most devoted man I've ever met." Candice tsked. "It's a shame what one group of men did to this town, to Eppie, and all for revenge and greed."

"If that bastard Jackson Webster wasn't in jail, I'd have already killed him." Even Micah was surprised by the venom in his voice.

The ex-sheriff and his partner, the former judge Earl Martin, were serving prison time for embezzling funds for years from Madeline and the bank in town. They'd done their best to destroy her, but hadn't succeeded. Instead she'd turned the tables on them and Eppie got caught in the crossfire, literally. Jackson had been attempting to arrest Madeline and found Micah instead. During the struggle, Eppie'd been shot in the shoulder, taking a bullet meant for him.

That fact alone haunted his dreams, each time reliving the nightmare of her lying in a pool of blood, unresponsive and dying. Now he wondered what was worse—her near-death years earlier or her rebirth as a different woman who didn't know him or love him.

His heart was breaking all over again and there was nothing he could do about it.

"Micah, you need to fetch the doctor in Denver. He knows all about what happened to her and perhaps he could help. Please, we can ask him not to tell Madeline what's happened, but we need to get him here as soon as possible." Candice made sense, but that didn't mean Micah was happy about it.

"What if he says it's permanent? That she'll never remember?" His voice cracked on the last word, unwilling to accept that the woman he loved didn't exist anymore.

"We'll cross that bridge when we get to it. We need to make sure she's not suffering any other ill effects from waking up after so long." Candice stood. "I'll get pen and paper and we can write the wire. After dinner I'll take it to the store and get it sent off."

Candice owned the general store in Plum Creek. She'd inherited it when her brother died and with Madeline's help had become a successful, savvy businesswoman. She also owned the only telegraph station in town.

Micah nodded, knowing she was right. Eppie was so thin and weak. Although she did help him up the steps, he'd been using the banister for support. Truth was, he helped her up the stairs more than she helped him. When she disappeared into her room, her face had been pale and her eyes a bit glassy. No doubt she was exhausted from everything that had happened. Going up and down the stairs would have exhausted her, much less taking care of an idiot that fell down them.

He sipped the coffee and watched his daughter play. She was truly a miracle and perhaps he ought to follow her example and simply introduce himself to Eppie. They obviously had to start over since the accident had erased what they'd had, and the best way was to start at the beginning.

In another hour, he'd check on Eppie and vowed to be a perfect gentleman, just as his Mama had taught him. Maybe if he stopped acting like a lovesick calf and more like a man, she'd see who he was, even if she didn't know him.

Eppie slept for a while after getting back to her room. The walk up the stairs had sapped her energy completely. The truth was, she was getting more frightened by the minute. She obviously couldn't remember anything and the world was not so forgiving to a memoryless nobody. After she woke, she rolled over and stared out the window.

Despair was a hard emotion to push aside and it settled over her like a scratchy blanket. She pressed her fists into her temples, willing her brain to remember something.

"Please don't hurt yourself."

Eppie whirled around to find Micah in the doorway with a steaming mug in his hand. He moved so silently she hadn't heard him even open the door. Or perhaps her own self-misery had prevented her from hearing anything but her own inner wails of pain and frustration.

"I don't plan on hurting myself." She sounded petulant even to her own ears.

"Good." He smiled gently and held up the mug. "I brought you some tea with honey. You used to like it sweet, so I thought it was a start to try and remember."

Eppie appreciated his thoughtfulness, truly she did, but being told how she used to like things just drove the nails of frustration in harder. She tried not to unleash it on Micah. "Thank you. Please put it on the table there."

He came in and set it on the small table next to the bed. When he glanced at the chair, then back at her, she knew he was asking permission to stay. She was tired, but wide awake, and her own company was obviously not working well.

"You can stay for a few minutes." She sat up slowly, while he stood beside the bed, obviously waiting to help. It shouldn't annoy her, it should make her feel better. "I really wish you wouldn't do that."

He froze and his eyes widened. "Do what?"

"Hover over me like I'm an invalid. I know I'm ailing, but I'm trying to get better. It makes me feel, well, like an old woman who can't get by without a man when you hover." She hoped she hadn't hurt his feelings, but she had to be honest with him. At this point in her short existence, he was the only person she knew she could count on, strange as that was.

"I'm sorry, it's an old habit. I'll try to stop." He backed away to the chair at the foot of the bed and sat down. "I don't like people to fuss over me, either. My nanny used to—" He stopped himself and glanced down at the floor.

Eppie, however, had her interest piqued. "You had a nanny?"

His lips tightened into a white line. "Yes, I did."

"If you think I'm going to let you stay in here and keep quiet, you've got another thing coming. I am tired of the silence and my own company. Tell me something about yourself I don't know." Her attempt at humor made the corners of his lips twitch. "What was your nanny's name?"

He let out a rather frustrated sounding sigh. "Eleanor."

"Am I going to get this information one word at a time?"

His gaze met hers and those silver orbs were completely unreadable. "Perhaps."

Eppie chuckled, which made him smile. "I'm waiting for the next word then."

"I was a baby when Eleanor was brought in to be my nanny. She was barely sixteen at the time, but had experience with five younger brothers." He glanced out the window, back into another time. "I think it was because she was still a girl that we had such fun. She would play games with me, not just watch over me. But if I got sick or hurt, she would hover just like I was doing. As a young boy with a head bigger than the house I lived in, I hated having my nanny fuss over me. It wasn't manly."

"And you were very manly?"

"Don't sound so surprised. I was a prince in my past, given the best of everything and the substance of nothing." An ancient pain echoed in his words and she felt it reverberate in the room.

She'd meant to pass the time with Micah and get to know him better, not to make him step into darkness.

"The tea smells heavenly." She picked up the tin mug, surprised by how much her hand shook just holding it.

"It's a tea blend Candice ordered for Madeline all the way from China. I don't drink the stuff, so it's been waiting for you." He met her gaze and a shiver flew down Eppie's skin at the emotion in those silver eyes.

She took a few sips of the tea and stared at the pattern on

the quilt. Micah was a very intense man, and he made her jumpy. She wasn't sure yet if that was a good thing or not. The warmth of the liquid seeped into her bones and her eyelids began to droop.

Micah had obviously been watching because he took the cup from her hands and helped her slide back under the covers. She wanted to protest, to say something, but instead she closed her eyes and felt a peace steal over her. The last thing she remembered was a kiss on her forehead and then sleep claimed her.

The next week passed by with Eppie sleeping quite a lot. Each day she recited the date because she didn't intend on missing another day in her life. She'd developed a routine of sorts and when she woke, she practiced walking and stretching, under the watchful eye of Micah. He simply told her to let him know if she needed help, although he hovered outside the room almost all day. It was as if without Eppie to take care of, he didn't know what to do with himself.

She felt as if she'd been asleep one hundred years instead of three. Each time she rose from bed, it was an effort simply to stand upright. However, even as her body screamed for mercy, she pushed herself harder and longer each day. Eppie was determined to be strong for herself, as the only thing she did have control of was her body. She could regain some of her life by regaining her strength.

It was Monday again and raining so hard the drops sounded like rocks on the window outside her room. Although she wanted to roll over and go back to sleep, she pulled the quilt back and swung her legs over to the side of the bed. The door opened just an inch and a little eye peeked through the opening.

Eppie inwardly sighed. She'd done her best to leave the girl alone and allowed Micah to keep her away. However, the girl had called her Mama and hovered around in the hall many times during the day. The rain would keep her inside, which meant she'd be looking for things to do. No doubt, Eppie would be on the top of her list.

"Good morning, Miracle." Eppie stretched her arms over her head as her muscles groaned in protest.

"Come in?" came the little voice through the door.

"Yes, you can come in."

The door squeaked open slowly and Miracle shuffled into the room. She wore a white and pink nightdress with pretty lace on the collar. In her arms she clutched the rag doll with red yarn hair. Her beautiful curly brown hair was sticking out every which way as if she'd just rolled out of bed, too. She rubbed her eye with her fist as she got closer to the bed.

Eppie stood up and tried to touch her toes. Miracle's tiny face appeared upside down next to her.

"Whatcha doin'?"

"I'm trying to get stronger."

Miracle dropped the doll on the floor and bent over just like Eppie. "I be strong too."

Eppie smiled at the little girl's imitation of her. "It's important to be strong, but I think you're already strong. Your daddy takes good care of you."

She didn't know how much Micah had told her and didn't want to give her any information she might regret later.

"Love Daddy." Miracle plopped onto the floor with her legs splayed out in front of her.

"I'm sure your daddy loves you."

The girl cocked her head as Eppie rose to her feet and started stretching her arms out to the side. "Mama love me?"

Eppie's stomach dropped to her knees. This is what she was afraid of. She didn't know how to answer the question, and she had hoped Miracle wouldn't ask it, yet she had.

"Did your daddy talk to you about my, um, sleep?" She felt so uncomfortable, as if Miracle's gaze could see through her silence and find the scared woman hiding.

"Mama had owie and sleeped a lot." Miracle brushed her hair away from her face.

"My head was hurt, too, and I'm trying to remember things." She felt like an idiot trying to explain to a little girl that she couldn't remember her name, much less a child who hadn't been born yet when she lost her memory.

"Uh huh. It's okay." Miracle stood and patted Eppie on the cheek. "You be okay." With that, she picked up her doll and headed for the door. "Love you Mama."

Eppie sat back on the bed in disbelief, her heart beating hard and her mind completely bewildered. With one tiny gesture of acceptance Miracle showed her what it meant to simply allow things to be as they were. The child didn't care that Eppie didn't remember her or that she spent time in her room avoiding her. To the girl, Eppie was her mother and she loved her. Simple as anything could be.

She wasn't ready to be a mother yet, but when she was Miracle would let her slide into her life without a hiccup. Eppie didn't know what she'd had prior to her accident, but apparently God had seen fit to give her a ready-made family, complete with a devoted husband and loving child. Too bad she wasn't married and she didn't remember being pregnant. It was a cruel twist of fate.

Micah stood outside the room with a tray for Eppie. He listened to their conversation and realized again how much he loved both of them. Eppie was so strong and Miracle, well, she was just amazing. The child looked at life with her simple view of the world and reminded the adults of it. He'd twisted himself into knots over the last week trying to please Eppie and make her feel comfortable and welcome.

He'd been doing it all wrong.

The best thing for him to do was give Eppie time to get used to him, the house and everything it entailed. He'd been pushing her to heal, to remember, and to shake off whatever ghost had stolen her memory. Perhaps he should have realized sooner he was making a mistake.

Without Miracle, he might have gone on for weeks going the wrong way. He could have smacked himself. Instead, he knocked on the door and took a deep breath when she answered.

"Who is it?"

"I brought you a breakfast tray. I'll leave it by the door in case you're hungry." He swallowed the urge to enter the room as he set the tray on the floor. "I'll be working outside if you need me."

After two beats, she answered. "Thank you, Micah."

That was it, but in her voice he heard relief and knew he'd done the right thing. With his pride, if not his heart, intact he walked back down the stairs alone.

His hands were smooth and cool as they slid up her legs. The small hairs on her body stood up as tingles raced through her. She knew the hands as well as she knew her own. They'd been on her body before, giving her pleasure. She reached up and pinched her nipples, prolonging the tingles and turning them into waves.

"My love, my life, my heart," he whispered. "You are exquisite."

She arched her back as his thumbs reached her nether lips, spreading them. He blew onto her heated flesh before his mouth descended.

Eppie woke with sweat coating her body, her heart pounding and her pussy moist with arousal. The dream had been so real, it felt more like a memory. She tried to grab hold of it, but it slipped away so fast she couldn't. Frustrated, she punched the bed, making her dress slide up against her nipples. She realized they were still hard and so sensitive it was as if he really had been there with her. Had it been Micah?

She didn't know, but her body's reaction the week before to being close to him gave her a clue to the answer. However, it scared her since she didn't seem to have control over it. She rubbed her eyes, grainy from sleeping too long and thinking too hard about why she was dreaming about a man's touch.

The rain had stopped and the sun in the window looked as if it were late afternoon. She sat up and realized she wasn't alone. Micah sat in the chair at the foot of the bed. After that morning when he'd finally given her time alone, she thought he was through coming in the room uninvited. Yet there he was and he'd been witness to her dream, maybe even watched as she writhed on the bed in arousal. Her cheeks heated with embarrassment, and she opened her mouth to tell him to leave when she heard a snore. He was sound asleep, thank God.

What she wanted to do was yell at him for not listening, again, but instead, she crept out of bed and slowly opened the door. It was bad enough her body still had the last vestiges of the erotic dream coating her like a haze. She didn't want to go through it with Micah watching.

Although it made a few tiny squeaks, the door opened easily and she left the room. It was time she explored the rest of the house and gave herself some time away from her mini-prison and her strange guard.

From what she could see, it was an opulent mansion with numerous rooms, and everything appeared to be expensive and ornate. It didn't fit with what she knew of Micah, but he did say Madeline had given him the house. Perhaps she was the one who liked fancy things.

Eppie walked down the stairs slowly as she drank in the glass chandelier and the paneling on the walls. The main hallway was wide enough to fit a wagon and there were more doors than she could even count.

She was at a loss where to go, and a sense of hopelessness washed over her. What was she doing here? This place didn't feel like a home at all. There was no warmth here, only things that someone took the time to buy to make sure people knew a lot of money had been spent.

Just as she was about to turn around and head upstairs, she heard a giggle from the end of the hallway. Then another. Plain as day, they were the girl's giggles. She hadn't given the child a chance, so she decided to take another leap of faith and go find little Miracle.

The mirror surprised her, or rather her reflection did. Set in the hallway above a marble-topped table, the mirror was unobtrusive until Eppie walked past it. The woman stopped and turned, staring openmouthed.

There were many things she didn't know about herself; one of them was apparently how she looked. There was no looking glass in her room upstairs and she could obviously see her body and hands, but still, seeing herself for the first time was a shock beyond measure.

She raised her hands and touched her gaunt cheeks, sunken into her face as if someone had pushed them in. Her skin was a light cocoa color at best, but appeared more gray than anything. Her nose was slender and pointy, while her cheekbones were quite prominent.

Her hair was cut quite short. It couldn't be more than an inch or two long and it stood up as if someone had frightened her. The worst, however, was her eyes. They were like chocolate buttons in her face, topped by thick, curly eyelashes staring at her.

Fear shook her bones when she remembered where she'd seen those eyes before—in Miracle's face. A small moan bubbled up in her throat and she put her hand over her mouth to contain it. Sweet heavens, she had no idea how hard it would be to look at herself in the mirror and realize she was a stranger.

A complete stranger.

As she watched, the stranger's eyes filled with tears and spilled down her cheeks. She felt so lost, so completely alone, and didn't know what to do. Who would help her? Micah seemed to want to, but he pushed too hard, harder than Eppie was willing to let him. Miracle was barely out of diapers, which left no one as far as she could tell.

Except, of course, herself.

However, she had no idea if she was strong enough to re-acquaint herself with everyone and everything. She had to be willing to accept some things on faith, and be willing to try to trust others, and herself. There was no other option.

Eppie leaned her elbows on the table and stared deeply into her own eyes, trying to find the woman somewhere in there she'd lost. Her heart ached with the knowledge that she was no one and nothing. *Nothing.*

God must have decided she was a strong person, strong enough to be born for a second time, only this time without a mother or father to nurture her, to help her grow up. Eppie swiped at the tears and took a shaky breath, desperately trying to get control of herself and swallow the enormous lump in her throat.

No matter who she was when she was injured and fell into the coma, she was a different person now. She would have to understand and accept that. She expected it to be a very long, rocky road ahead with no easy answers. Life was a gift and she was grateful to have been given it twice.

It was time to have a little faith.

Giggles sounded again from the kitchen. The pure sound of the girl's laughter was evidence that life went on around her, ready or not to face it. Eppie wiped her face with her trembling hands and did her best to chase away the haunted look in her eyes.

Her legs still felt as weak as a newborn calf, but she made her way to the kitchen just the same. By the time she got there, the strain from everything forced her to fall into a chair as soon as she arrived. The red-haired woman and Mir-acle stared at her with shock on their faces.

"Eppie! Land sakes, you look as if you're about to expire." The woman dropped the potatoes she'd been peeling and worked the pump to get some clean water. She grabbed a glass from the shelf above the sink and filled it with water.

"Mama, okay?" Miracle's little chin wobbled as she watched her carefully.

Eppie didn't want to be rude and not answer, but still didn't feel comfortable with responding to "Mama," either. Thankfully the red-haired woman saved her from answering.

"Give her a minute to catch her breath, child." The woman brought the glass to Eppie's lips and put her hand on the back of her neck while she drank. The woman's skin was nearly as cool as the water and strangely comforting.

"I know you don't remember me. Micah told me everything." She smiled and her bright blue eyes shone. "I'm Candice Merriweather and I own the store in town. I've been helping out here since your accident."

"She makes cookies." Miracle piped up.

"Yes, I cook and help with the chores so Micah can take care of you." She brushed the hair from Eppie's forehead. "You've lost so much of yourself, child. I'm sorry for that."

In the depths of her round face, Eppie saw true sympathy. For the first time since she'd woken up, she felt as if someone understood what was happening to her. She decided she liked Candice a great deal and the round woman with the kind eyes would be her first friend. Lord knows she sure needed one.

"Thank you, Candice. I appreciate your help." She sucked in a much-needed breath and took the glass, surprised by how heavy it felt. "I didn't realize how parched I was. It's still hard to believe I lay in that bed for three years."

Eppie waited for confirmation of what Micah had told her, but it didn't happen. The room was quiet as death again with Candice staring at her openmouthed. She cocked her head and then shook it, the red curls bouncing.

"He said you didn't sound like yourself anymore, and he

was right." She smiled a wide, toothy grin. "I think you sound like a right sophisticated lady."

Miracle giggled and popped a piece of cookie in her mouth. Eppie had the choice to be upset again or laugh, too.

She chose the latter and it felt wonderful.

"Yes, I remember the day it happened. Hard to believe how much time has passed. That awful Jackson Webster and his cheating partner. I knew those two were up to no good, always poking their nose into everyone else's business. Jackson's wife is still walking around town as if she owned it." Candice went back to the potatoes, all the while chatting away, which made Eppie more comfortable, oddly enough.

"Who's Jackson Webster?" If she had to relearn everything, she might as well start with the past before she could move forward into the present.

Candice glanced at Miracle, who sat there with a wide-eyed expression as she absorbed everything like a little sponge.

"Miracle, sweetie, I think Daisy probably needs some fresh water."

Like a magic wand, mention of Daisy catapulted the girl off the chair. She headed for the door, her little shoes clacking on the shiny wooden floor. Just before she reached the back door, she skidded to a halt and turned around.

"I forgot." She ran back into the kitchen and threw herself at Candice's legs, giving her an effusive hug, much to the older woman's delight. Her giggle sounded as young as the girl's.

To Eppie's astonishment, Miracle turned around and eyeballed her. She chewed on a fingernail for a moment before she walked over and gently wrapped her arms around Eppie's neck and gave her a squeeze.

"Mama's hurt, gotta be careful." After a soft, dry peck on the cheek, Miracle skipped to the door and out into the evening light.

Eppie shook with the force of that hug and kiss. She knew what Micah had told her about the parentage of the child, had seen the resemblance in the mirror, but to have the girl show affection with no encouragement or acknowledgment was astounding. It was completely unexpected and turned the world a bit sideways.

"She's a loving child." Candice smiled as her gaze followed the girl out the door. "That's Micah's doing. He's an amazing father."

Eppie had already been witness to Micah's parenting skills, and from what she'd seen, she agreed with Candice's observations. However, knowing Miracle considered her Mama without reservation, judgment, or expectations humbled her. Things were very simple for a child her age and much more complicated for Eppie. More than she could think about at the moment. If she thought any harder, she might lose control again. Right now she had all she could do to think about the next ten minutes, much less the next day or even week.

"You were going to tell me about Jackson Webster." She tasted the name on her tongue, but it wasn't familiar at all.

"He was the sheriff of this town, grew up with Madeline he did. I'm sure Micah's told you about her?" Candice cut up the potatoes with a small paring knife into a pot of water.

Eppie nodded. "Yes, he's told me a bit. I have to be honest, knowing there's someone out there who considers me her best friend, and I don't know her, is rather frightening."

Candice's eyebrows went up. "I'm sorry if I seem surprised. It's not what you said, but rather how you said it." She smiled. "It's going to take us all time to get to know each other again."

Eppie was glad Candice felt that way, because things were confusing enough without being expected to know exactly who she had been or how she should act or speak.

"It's okay, I understand. Things all sound different to me."

The older woman laughed. "I'll bet they do. Now, let me get back to Jackson. He was always a blowhard and never failed to brag about everything to anyone who would listen. He finagled his way into becoming sheriff. He and the local judge, Earl Martin, did their best to steal Madeline's money, make it appear as if she'd done it, and put her in jail."

Eppie was astounded. "This was the sheriff and a judge? That's, well, that's just awful."

Candice shook her head. "It was just that. The town wanted to believe the worst of Madeline, but you stuck by her and so did Micah."

It was comforting to know she had been a loyal friend, but there was still so much she didn't know. "You know he hasn't told me about the accident where I was injured and how I came to be in Micah's care." Eppie sipped the water, her curiosity screaming at her to find out more about herself, like a story unfolding, and she was the young girl waiting for the next page.

"I'm not sure that's my place, Eppie." Candice put the pot of potatoes on the stove and stoked the fire within. "Micah was there when it happened, and he's the one who should tell you."

Eppie told herself not to be annoyed with the other woman, but it was hard not to. She had been so close to an important piece of the puzzle of her life.

"I understand, but I hope you change your mind. This is, well, important to me."

"Then you should tell him. What he had with you was much more than I know about. It wouldn't be fair or right to talk to you about it." Candice sat down and patted Eppie's hand. "That man loves you so much, and I know that's hard to accept right now. I've never seen someone so devoted."

Eppie wanted to squirm in her chair at the subject of Micah's love and devotion. *That* topic she didn't yet want to hear about. "What about the house? It's enormous and so fancy. Did Madeline really give it to Micah?"

"Oh, now that is a story." Candice peered at Eppie's face. "First let me get some milk and a snack for you. I think you need something more than water."

While the red-haired woman puttered around slicing off bread and slathering it with honey, Eppie felt a hominess to the tasks. She was familiar with the place and the feeling. It helped her relax a bit more.

When Candice set the plate in front of her, the smell of honey and yeasty bread filled Eppie's nose. A wave of longing raced through her and she wished for so many things at once her throat closed up. She struggled to keep her emotions hidden, not yet ready to share them with a woman she'd known for fifteen minutes.

"It's okay, sweetie, take your time. I won't expect anything else." Candice sat down with a steaming cup and looked at Eppie with sympathy in her gaze. "I drink chamomile tea every day in the afternoon just to keep away what could ail me. Now eat up, or I'll think you don't like my vittles."

Eppie nodded and took a hesitant sip of milk. The cool creaminess of flavor exploded in her mouth. Her stomach howled with pleasure as the milk slid down her throat. It tasted so good, she drained the glass before she realized it. As she stared at the empty glass in astonishment, Candice chuckled and handed her a cloth napkin.

"Well, it's good to know you have an appetite. Milk's good for you."

Eppie glanced at the bread as the milk landed in her empty stomach. It almost filled her up, attesting to the fact it had been a while since she'd eaten. "No, I'll just nibble on the bread, but thank you."

"Of course, I'm your friend, whether or not you remember me."

It appeared Candice was exactly as she appeared, an honest, kind woman. Eppie was more than thankful to have her around, although she wondered if there was anything more than friendship between the older woman and Micah. If she had been taking care of the little family, as a wife and mother would, it wouldn't be unusual for something to develop.

The thought made her stomach cramp and the milk felt like a rock. It was a strange reaction, and she didn't understand it, but there was a great deal of things she didn't. What made the prospect of Micah and Candice together so unquestionably wrong to her? Maybe he was right and she and Micah were in love, but since she didn't remember him, that meant the love had died.

Her body, however, told her a different story.

Chapter Four

Micah woke with a start, jumping out of the chair as the vestiges of the nightmare fell around him like ashes. He'd been in the woods at night searching for Eppie. Although he could hear her crying, he couldn't find her, no matter how hard he searched. Branches and brambles tore at him, yet he continued looking for her as panic latched its claws into him.

He rubbed his face with both hands, trying to dispel the utter despair he'd felt when he couldn't find her. The rasp of his whiskers sounded loud in the room and when he peeped through his hands, he realized he was alone. Eppie had woken and left him alone.

First of all, he shouldn't have fallen asleep, that wasn't his intention. Secondly, he was embarrassed be in her room without permission again, and the fact she caught him made it worse. And last, she'd obviously left him sleeping on purpose, to escape him or to allow him rest, he wasn't sure which.

It didn't matter, of course, because he'd made a mistake again. He blew out a frustrated breath and left her room, leaving the door open behind him so she'd know he was gone.

The house was quiet enough he heard the tick of the clock

downstairs in the parlor. Miracle was probably outside playing with Daisy with Candice watching over her. He'd been blessed with such a good friend and didn't know how he would ever repay her for everything she'd done.

Without his friends, Micah would still be a drunken Confederate soldier with nothing for company but pine trees and squirrels. Sometimes he wished for that simplicity again, for all the pain and confusion to go away. But then he wouldn't have Miracle or Eppie, and life would be as gray as his uniform had been.

He walked down the steps, trailing his hand on the mahogany banister and feeling sorry for himself. It wasn't as if life had been cruel to him, but it hadn't been kind. When he'd retreated to his mountain cabin ten years earlier, he fully expected to live his life alone. Madeline changed that when she saved him from drowning in the river and showed him what a friend was. He blocked out the memory of the river and its deadly current because then he'd have to remember why and how he ended up in the river.

It was lost in a haze of whiskey and tears, and if he tried too hard, he might discover he intentionally ended up in that current, never expecting to feel pain again. For a man with so many ghosts riding around on his back, death was a blessing he had yearned for. The weight of his past sins was a load no man would want to bear. He'd done it for so long at that point, years since the war ended and he'd returned to find—

He cut off the thought before it could form as he stopped at the bottom of the steps. Leaning forward with his hands on his knees, he squeezed his eyes shut and forced the memories back with a sharp stick. He was unwilling to relive his nightmares during the day when he could control them.

After a few minutes, the urge to vomit had passed as had the horrific memories he refused to acknowledge. He did, however, feel very thirsty. It was a thirst he'd been able to keep at bay for quite a while. Working himself from morning until night until he'd literally passed out, too exhausted to drink.

Perhaps to prove to himself he wouldn't drink even if tempted, he'd left the bar in the parlor fully stocked and for the last almost three years, the bottles had yet to be opened.

Demons cackling in his ears, his body buzzed with rampant thirst as he walked toward the room. It had been the room where Madeline had hosted guests, one of her least favorite rooms because of all the frippery her father had insisted on. It stood unused most of the time because the population of Plum Creek didn't come visiting very often.

His feet had a will of their own and he felt caught up in an urge so powerful, it made his bones shake. By the time he entered the parlor, he was breathing as if he'd run to the end of town and back. Tears stung his eyes as he closed the door behind him. What was he doing? He shouldn't even be in the parlor, much less with the door closed.

He leaned on the door and tried to tell himself to leave, but it was no use. The bottles sparkled in the late afternoon sun that crept through the gauzy curtains. Myriads of light bounced around them as he approached as if they welcomed him, asking him where he'd been. If it had still been raining, the shadows in the room would have hidden the bar. Instead the sun had come out and he was helpless to stop himself.

Micah watched as he grasped the neck of the whiskey and pulled the cork out. The woodsy scent of the amber liquid filled him and he breathed in deeply. His entire body screamed in utter delight and his mouth actually watered. He swallowed hard and picked up the bottle and a glass.

As he walked over to the settee, he told himself to put the whiskey back, to run like hell and find his daughter. Yet he didn't. The demons inside exploded from him, filling the room with dark magic as he sat down and poured himself four fingers of liquor.

His hand shook so bad, it spilled onto his fingers and he

leaned forward to lick it off. At the first taste of whiskey, he closed his eyes in nearly sensual bliss as his body jerked in reaction. It had been so long, so long since he'd given in, since he'd found peace. Perhaps just this once he could lose himself for just a little while.

Micah let the tears flow unchecked down his cheeks as he raised the glass to his lips.

Eppie sat in the kitchen for the rest of the afternoon, talking with Candice and watching her make dinner. When Miracle came in looking like she'd rolled in mud, Candice tut-tutted and sent her back outside to wash up. The girl obeyed without question, but her feet dragged a bit. She obviously was raised well and did as she was bade, but was a very typical three-year-old.

How Eppie knew anything about a three-year-old's behavior escaped her, but she had apparently been around children enough to understand. It comforted her to know that she wasn't completely without knowledge to be a parent, particularly given the resemblance she saw between her and the girl.

Wanting to help, Eppie was shucking peas at the table while Candice hummed and added meat to her stew. It smelled heavenly in the room, especially after she started making dumplings to cook on top of the stew. Miracle came back in, this time with a face scrubbed until it shone with a pink glow and water spots all over her blue dress.

She sat down on the chair with a humph and stared at Candice as if she'd ordered her to do something terrible.

"You know you needed to be cleaned up, so you just need to cut that out," Candice admonished with one dough-covered finger. "You can suck that lip back in where it belongs."

Miracle sighed and moved her gaze to Eppie. "Mama better?"

Eppie swallowed and tried to find a way to ask the girl not to call her Mama, but couldn't think of one. The word made her skin jump but judging by what she saw, it was true. Who was she to judge a little girl when she'd obviously been told all her short life that Eppie was her mother? Eventually the name might not make her uncomfortable, but for now she would have to simply accept it. After all, the girl accepted her without question.

"Yes, I do feel better. Thank you for asking." She smiled at the girl. "Miss Candice is a good nurse."

"Daddy's good." She snatched a handful of peas from the bowl. "He fixed you."

The idea that Micah had fixed her hadn't entered Eppie's mind, but given Candice's comments earlier and Miracle's pronouncement, perhaps he had fixed her. If she'd been so grievously injured as to be in this "coma" for almost three years, he had done his best to take care of her, to fix her.

It had been a week and she hadn't taken into consideration that Micah had given up all his time, his life even, to care for her. Did that show devotion? Perhaps it did, and she would do best to recognize that. Micah might be like her constant shadow, but he may have good reason to be. She didn't know if she was ready to open her arms to him, but she was ready to give him a chance.

Suddenly it seemed important to talk to him, to ask him what had happened and find out more about how she ended up in the coma. She'd left him sleeping in her room, but since it was close to supper, he'd need to wake up anyway.

Her decision made, Eppie focused on finishing the peas. Candice chatted with Miracle about Daisy, who Eppie discovered was a puppy, and apparently one with a mind of her own. She tried to focus on the stories about the dog and its proclivity for digging, but her mind kept wandering to Micah.

The sad-eyed man was thin to the point of gauntness, yet

he managed to take care of her and his daughter. Candice told her she only came during the week usually at five, but today she wanted to come early because Eppie had woken. She knew there'd be more to do and wanted to make sure she was there to help. Micah had said hello, asked her to watch Miracle, and disappeared upstairs.

"I was surprised to see you, actually, since he said you were sleeping. Where is he, anyway?" Candice took the bowl of peas and put it in the stew. As she expertly dropped the dumplings on top, Eppie watched with envy. She hoped she knew how to cook, too.

"He was sleeping in the chair in my room." She glanced at the doorway to the hall, as if she could see him around the corner, up the stairs and through the door.

"Ah, that chair became his bed." Candice shook her head. "No matter how many times I told him not to sleep in it, he usually did. The man hasn't had more than two hours of sleep at a time since, well, since the accident." She looked away, likely still respecting Micah's right to tell Eppie what happened.

The need to talk to Micah overwhelmed her and she got to her feet slowly. The lightheadedness wasn't so bad anymore. The milk and food must have done her a world of good. Her legs still felt as shaky as they had, but she did feel stronger.

"I'm going to talk to Micah." Once she said it, she immediately felt as if she'd made the right choice. It was time she found out exactly what had happened.

"Take it slow now, Eppie. No need to rush around when you're still getting better." She pointed at Miracle. "You help your Mama now."

"That's not necessary." Eppie wasn't sure the girl was ready to hear what her father had to say. It likely wasn't fit for a child's ears.

"Oh, pshaw, she'll come right back when you get where

you're going. I won't hear of you walking around alone anymore. I don't want you to get hurt." Candice was like a mother hen, clucking around Eppie as if she was one of her chicks.

"I help, Mama." Miracle hopped up and ran over, tucking her arm around Eppie's waist. She smiled up at her and Eppie knew a moment of sweet innocence. Perhaps it wouldn't be so hard to love the girl, after all.

Eppie put her hand on top of the girl's head. "Okay, I give in. You can be my helper."

"Yea!" Miracle squeezed her just a bit, then looked serious as Eppie started walking.

Together the two of them made their way down the long hallway to the foot of the stairs. The effort made Eppie winded, so she sat down on the bottom step to catch her breath. Miracle scooted next to her looking up with wide eyes.

That's when Eppie heard the crying. Someone sobbed in a room nearby, but it was muffled, as if they had a pillow over their face. She glanced at the girl, but she didn't appear to be bothered by it.

"Do you hear that?"

Miracle nodded. "Daddy cries."

Daddy cries.

Those two words echoed through Eppie's mind, repeating over and over. He cried because he was sad or for some other reason perhaps. Obviously to the girl, it was commonplace, and she recognized it easily. It bothered Eppie that he cried because it meant it was likely because of her.

This man who had apparently sacrificed everything to take care of her and his daughter was regularly torn up enough inside to let tears flow. She might not remember much, but a man crying was not a common sight. Apparently it was in this house.

Fatigue forgotten, she wanted to find him and get the truth

from him. She didn't want him to cry about her anymore. Eppie rose and hung on to the banister for a few moments. Miracle got to her feet and readied herself to help Eppie again.

"Where is he?"

Miracle's brows furrowed as she listened, her head cocked to the right. "Fancy parlor." She pointed at the closed door closest to the enormous front door.

It was made of dark wood with a paneling that looked too ornate for someone's house, but the entire place was like that. The parlor was a fancy name for a room, and she was sure it meant it was where rich folks entertained visitors. It was usually at the front of the house with lots of windows.

Eppie must have either lived in this house long enough to know that or had brought the knowledge from wherever she'd come from prior to arriving here in Plum Creek. No doubt the "fancy" part came from the furniture in the room.

She approached the door with a little trepidation, not knowing what to expect. If he was crying, did he really need her to intrude? Regardless, she knew she wanted to talk to him and it was as good a time as any. She looked down at Miracle.

"I'm going to talk to your Daddy now."

Miracle nodded sagely. "Needs a hug."

Eppie pinched her lips together to stop the smile from spreading. The girl was really a precocious little thing and seemed to understand a great deal about what was going on around her. It was a skill someone far more mature than a three-year-old normally had. At least that's what her mind was telling her.

Shaking off the confusing thoughts, Eppie knocked lightly on the door. As she waited, her stomach jumped around as if an army of frogs had taken up residence. Miracle's little hand slid into hers, and Eppie squeezed it, absurdly grateful for her presence.

There was no sound from the parlor.

Eppie knocked again and heard a shuffling sound from within the room. Then what sounded like glass clinking against glass. What could he be doing in there?

She raised her hand to knock a third time when someone else knocked on the front door beside them. Eppie jumped about a foot, startling herself and Miracle.

"There's someone at the front door, Micah." She called through the parlor door.

"Don't care," came the muffled, slurred response.

Was he drinking? It sounded that way to her, but she didn't know Micah well enough to know what he did or didn't do. The knock at the front door sounded again, even louder this time.

"Hello? Anyone home?" trilled a woman's voice.

Miracle wrinkled her nose. "Miz Webster."

Mrs. Webster? Was this the wife of the infamous sheriff Candice had told her about? Eppie couldn't stop herself from answering the door if she wanted to. She had to know more about the infamous woman. With her will firmly in place, Eppie walked to the large front door and turned the knob.

She didn't know what to expect, but the appearance of three nearly identical blond women surprised her. Each one had a slightly different hairstyle and wore a fancy dress of varying shades. They also had identical expressions of shock upon seeing who answered the door.

Eppie told herself she shouldn't feel a sense of perverse satisfaction for shocking the three ladies. It wasn't kind of her, and she pushed the feeling to the depths of her heart.

"Eppie?" the middle woman asked, her face as pale as milk.

"Good morning, ladies." Eppie put a smile on her face. "What can I do for you?"

"I, um, well, I can't believe that's really you. I mean, it looks like you, but, well, I don't know what to say." The blonde in the middle appeared to be the spokesperson for the group.

"Did you ladies come calling for Micah? He's not accepting visitors at the moment, but I'd be happy to let him know you came by." As soon as she figured out who the heck they were.

Miracle peeked out from behind Eppie and all three of them looked down, then back up at her.

"Why, she does have your eyes, doesn't she?" The one on the left had a nasally voice.

"Virginia, I told you Micah was telling the truth. He wouldn't have guarded the house like an attack dog if she wasn't." The middle one pasted a smile on her face that didn't even come close to reaching her eyes.

"We're so happy to see you recovered, Eppie. May we come in?" While she spoke, the three of them stepped across the threshold, their combined bodies forcing Eppie to step back. "If you'd be so kind as to let Micah know we're here, then fix us some lemonade. We'll be in the parlor."

They turned right like a school of fish and stepped toward the parlor. Before Eppie could stop them, Miracle slid across the floor and blocked the door with her little arms across her chest and a scowl on her face.

"No."

The ladies stopped in their tracks and looked back at Eppie as if waiting for her to do something. Eppie didn't want her first impression with these ladies to be a sour one, but she couldn't allow them to intrude on Micah's privacy, especially considering the haunting sobbing she'd heard not ten minutes earlier. She pushed aside the fact that they'd considered her hired help and ordered her to provide refreshments. That particular battle could wait.

"I'm afraid Micah is not accepting visitors at the moment. He's come down with a terrible cold and is sleeping in the parlor so as not to get anyone else sick." Eppie smiled and pulled Miracle to her side. "I will be sure to let him know you stopped by."

"You're very different, Eppie." The middle one cocked her head and frowned. "You sound, well, you sound like you're educated, which is impossible."

Eppie's face felt hot with embarrassment and anger. This woman was pushing her too far, but she didn't want to ruin the day by slapping her, especially in front of Miracle. Later on she'd think about how the urge to let her temper fly was troubling.

"Perhaps being in a coma for three years was education enough." Eppie gestured to the front door. "Again I thank you for coming by to visit."

Although they were pushy, they were apparently still ladies and understood a dismissal when they heard one.

"Of course. Do you know when Madeline might be here for a visit? I mean, after all, you are awake now." The blond spokesperson raised one eyebrow and waited.

"Madeline will be visiting soon." Eppie was lying, of course, but she kept her face neutral.

"Thank you for the hospitality. Beatrice, Virginia, let's depart. I hope next time you'll feel well enough to complete your ablutions, Eppie." With that parting snide comment, the three of them filed out the door.

Disbelief, anger and hurt swirled around as she stared at the backs of their pretty blond heads. Eppie controlled the urge to slam the door, but just barely. They were like a pack of vicious dogs, biting and snarling with shiny bows in their fur. She shook with the emotional upheaval their short visit had caused. If the spokesperson was Mrs. Webster, Candice had been right about her walking around town as if she owned it. She certainly owned her two little blond accomplices.

Eppie wanted to ask the woman who she was but wasn't

about to let on that her memory was gone. That would no doubt be a terrible mistake.

"Mean ladies." Miracle frowned at the closed door.

"They weren't very polite, were they?" Eppie put her hand on top of the girl's head. "Why don't you go help Candice while I talk to your daddy?"

Miracle frowned and stomped down the hallway, but she went just the same. Eppie took a deep breath and wondered how she'd woken up in such an odd little family in an odd town. If she didn't feel so sore and tired, she'd think she was still sleeping. This time she decided not to knock on the door. It was a parlor, after all, which meant it was meant for everyone to use.

She didn't know what she expected, but it wasn't to find Micah sitting on a window seat, a bottle of whiskey in his hand. He'd removed his shirt and sat only in his trousers.

She closed the door behind her and leaned against it, as the scent of booze and despair washed over her. It appeared as though she was right—he did have a dark side that he hid in front of her and Miracle. The dark side should frighten her, but somehow, it didn't. It drew her in.

"Micah?"

He didn't move but a sigh bubbled to his lips. "Eppie, love, I made a mistake."

A shiver crawled up her spine at the word "love." It was the same as in her dreams, the same inflection and depth. Perhaps she'd been remembering rather than dreaming as suspected. Did that mean she and Micah had been intimate lovers? Had she truly been in love with this broken man?

The setting sun made a halo around him, making his light brown hair into a fiery mass of gold and orange. She couldn't quite make out his expression, but no doubt it was as sad as the atmosphere in the room. As she stepped closer, she started to make out details, such as the scar on his left arm and the larger one on the right side of his chest. He appeared to be a mass of scars, both inside and out, although muscles crisscrossed his thin body, belying the appearance of thinness.

"What mistake?"

He turned and smiled, relaxed for the first time since she'd opened her eyes. "I forgot why I didn't drink."

Eppie had been afraid she'd find him a sobbing mess; instead he seemed calm and approachable. It knocked her a bit sideways and she wasn't sure what to do, so she sat down on the cream-colored settee.

"And why didn't you drink?"

Micah chuckled low in his throat and held up the bottle. "I never knew when to stop. You see, I started drinking to forget the memories that plagued me. Unfortunately I would drink too much and the I'd fall into nightmares of what I was trying to forget."

She sorted through his confusing answer. "You mean, you wanted to forget, but you'd drink too much and end up having worse nightmares?"

He took a long tug from the bottle. She watched his throat work as he swallowed, as a drop trickled out the side of his mouth and down his chin. He obviously had a high tolerance for liquor, because half the bottle was gone and she had a feeling he'd been the one to open it.

"Exactly." He finally turned to look at her. His smile was sexy and did funny things to her. A throb echoed through her lower body and whispers of her erotic dream floated through her mind. He was drunk and she was having sexual urges for him. What was wrong with her? It did not seem to be the right reaction, but as before, her body wasn't listening to her head.

"So stop drinking."

He held the bottle up to the light, the sun turning it to liquid gold. "If only it were that easy. You see, it becomes my mistress, my lover, my best friend."

Eppie's heart pinched at the thought, and she couldn't explain why. "So what do you need me for? You can live your
life and never need a wife."

It sounded petulant to her ears, but it must've sounded
very serious to him. He snapped his gaze to hers and all color
drained from his handsome face.

"Don't ever say that." He jumped off the window seat and
ran around to the settee, sliding on his knees until he reached
her. Up close, the scent of whiskey was so strong it made her
eyes water. Underneath the booze, however, was another
smell, one that was familiar. "You and Miracle are the reason
I wake up each day. Without you I wouldn't be here."

He took her hand in his, and she knew a moment of fear.
She didn't want to be the reason he woke up in the morning.
It was too much responsibility for any one person to bear.

"Micah, that can't be. I don't even know you and I don't
think you know me."

"Oh, I know you." He cupped her cheek and brushed his
thumb across her cheek. "I memorized every square inch of
you from your toes to your crooked left ear. I know the lines
in your palm, the beautiful sweep of your hip, the curve of
your collarbone, the softness of your mouth. I *know* you."

He lowered his head as Eppie's body grew heated and the
air charged so much it made the small hairs on her body
stand up. His silver eyes glittered with many emotions, from
arousal to sadness to despair.

She didn't know him a week ago. She didn't know herself
a week ago. Eppie knew she should pull away, tell him to
stop, push against him, do something.

Yet she didn't, wouldn't, or couldn't. She didn't know
which. All she knew was that she wanted to feel his lips
against hers, to remember them or perhaps see if they were
the same as the dream lover who had visited her.

His hovered over her as he gazed deep inside her, searching
for something. Whatever it was, he must have seen what he

was looking for, because he let loose a whiskey-soaked sigh and finally lowered his head to hers.

Soft and gentle, his lips skimmed over hers like a butterfly sipping on a flower. He didn't touch her anywhere else, although her body leaned toward his, seeking his touch. She seemed to have no control over her reactions. Eppie wanted to turn and run, yet she knew deep down there was no way that would happen. It seemed her body remembered him, after all, judging by the way she reacted.

He kissed her again, from one end of her lips to the other, sweet nibbling kisses that left her wanting more. Micah's tongue snuck out and lapped at her, making her gasp. The sensation shot straight down her skin and spread through her, raising goosebumps and her nipples. She hadn't been as aroused during the erotic nocturnal meanderings of her mind as she was at that moment.

To her mortification, a moan bubbled up in her throat and escaped.

Micah swallowed her moan and responded with one of his own. The sound went straight to her cunt. It started to throb in tune with her galloping heart. Eppie felt herself falling into a deep chasm of heat, arousal and animal urges. That scared the hell out of her.

She pulled back, sucking in a shaky breath. He followed, chasing her lips, but she threw up her hand to stop him. The feel of his hot breath and wet mouth on her skin sent a pulse through her. She knew she was heading into unknown territory and had to stop right then or risk more than a few stolen kisses.

"Stop, Micah, stop." Her voice was breathy and high.

"God, Eppie, please, I can't." He grabbed her hand and pressed it against his forehead. "You smell so wonderful."

His reaction scared her almost as much as her own. Perhaps it was the liquor in his system because he hadn't even remotely acted as if he couldn't control himself around her. Yet she felt the heat in his skin, the rapid thump of his blood beneath, and the sweat trickling down his temple.

"Let go of my hand." She pulled, half-expecting him to hang on to it, but he didn't. After rising to her feet, she swayed, lightheaded and dizzy.

"Please don't go yet." He looked up at her, so much pain in his gaze, she sucked in a breath.

"I can't be who you want me to be, Micah." She turned to leave the room as fast as her shaky legs would move.

"I really do love you, Eppie," he called after her.

Eppie didn't stop. She couldn't. When she emerged from the parlor, the stairs seemed twice as long as she gazed at them. She knew she wasn't up to climbing them and probably wouldn't be until she recovered from kissing Micah. The front door beckoned, fresh air and a bit of late-day sunshine.

When she opened the wide oak door, a whoosh of air caressed her face and she breathed deeply. Yes, that was what she needed. Not knowing where the house was situated or even what was out there made her hesitate a moment.

However, the lure of being outside the house beckoned and she stepped out onto a beautiful long porch. A swing hung in the middle, rocking gently in the breeze. The house itself was a bright blue color, which she knew was a unique color for any residence. It cheered her, though, and helped her feel a bit better.

She walked toward the front steps and stopped, amazed by what she saw. Beautiful flowers covered nearly every square inch: yellows, oranges, reds and even blues. The wind brought the scent of them and it infused her with a sense of life, of hope.

A small head popped up from the middle of the flowers and startled her. The yellow dog had floppy ears and big brown eyes. Eppie smiled, realizing it must be the puppy, Daisy. She disappeared back into the blossoms, leaving Eppie to wonder if she imagined the dog.

She settled on the top step of a very well-kept set of stairs. The paint wasn't chipped and the boards were all in good shape. She looked around the yard, noting the big elm trees and the pines lining the side yard. In the near distance, she heard rushing water, like a river.

Birds sang merrily while squirrels chattered and the world looked amazingly peaceful and normal. These were two things Eppie hadn't remotely experienced in the last week, which was for all purposes, the first week of her life. Like a newborn discovering everything around her, Eppie watched each bee as it landed on the flowers, the sun glinting on the surface of the rocks on the path, and the clouds drifting across the sky. Life surged around her.

For the first time, she felt alive, as if she had truly woken up the moment she walked outside. What happened inside the house wasn't necessarily life, more the trials and tribulations of people. Mother Nature showed her what she'd been missing.

Eppie dismissed the melancholy and upset she'd brought with her out the door. She sat on the front steps for quite a while, until the sun had nearly reached the horizon. Carriages, people and horses passed by about a hundred yards away at the end of the road, but no one came to the house. Maybe it had something to do with Micah, or maybe it had something to do with her. It didn't really matter, either way.

It seemed to Eppie as if this enormous, fancy house lived in its own world. The town in the distance almost didn't, or wouldn't, see and acknowledge it. Granted, the three women had ventured into the realm of the house, but she figured it was more morbid curiosity that drove them to visit. None of them had been particularly friendly and they'd all been a bit snooty.

Sitting outside in the real world gave Eppie a helping of strength she needed. The situation was so intense inside, she couldn't be happier being away from it, even if it were only for an hour. She made a promise to herself to find time each day to get a dose of fresh air and sunshine.

"So there you are." Candice walked out the front door with a smile. "I was wondering if you'd run off."

Eppie shook her head. "No, just hiding." No need to pretend with the older woman; she seemed to understand quite a lot about what Eppie was feeling.

Candice sighed and sat down next to her. "He's been in the whiskey."

"I'm guessing this is not a good thing? He didn't appear to be drunk, just sad and different." Eppie tried to find another definition of what she felt and saw, but that seemed to be the most appropriate one.

"Micah can consume quite a bit of spirits and still appear normal. He unfortunately already had a high tolerance before he arrived in Plum Creek." She glanced up at the branches of the big elm tree in the front yard. "It only got worse after your accident. I'm afraid he has trouble coping sometimes."

Eppie nodded. "I can already see that. Do you know how his problem began?"

"No, and I've never asked. I'm not one to pry." Candice scratched at the dried dough on her apron. "He's got a lot of ghosts, though. You should know that."

"I think I've already met a few of them," Eppie said dryly, thinking of the many faces of Micah.

Candice laughed. "I'll bet you have. Micah is, well, he's one of the most selfless, giving men I've ever known, just like Madeline's Teague."

"Madeline's Teague?" She had no idea there was a man in her best friend's life. "Are they coming soon?"

"Oh, well, I don't know about that. They live outside Denver now and with two little boys, their lives are so busy." Candice's eyes widened and she clapped a hand over her mouth.

"What is it?" Eppie grew alarmed at her pale complexion.

"Good afternoon, ladies."

Eppie whipped her head around to find an older white-haired man wearing a minister's collar. His cool blue gaze was sharper than any knife and it was aimed directly at her.

"I see Matilda was correct and our sleeping daughter has arisen. I must send a quick prayer up to God for his mercy." He inclined his head at Candice. "Miss Merriweather. Glad to see you are still helping Mr. Spalding."

"Pleasure is all mine, Reverend. I've got bread to take out of the oven, if you'll excuse me." Candice rose and disappeared faster than Eppie thought she could move. She left Eppie with a stranger who by her estimation was not a soft-spoken man of the cloth.

He leaned against the side of the house and scrutinized Eppie, so she did the same to him. Probably close to sixty, the man had sagging jowls, a scary pair of eyebrows, and a paunch that had likely seen many free Sunday dinners. It was the disapproval in his gaze, however, that caught her attention. Obviously the good reverend did not like what he saw when he looked at her.

"Did you come by for a visit?" She might as well get the conversation moving. It might prompt him to be on his way sooner.

"Just wanted to check on you, Miss Eppie, and of course, Miracle. You two have been in my prayers for nigh on three years, since the stormy night she was born." He shook his white head. "Shame you were sleeping for the last three years and missed seeing her grow."

The comment stung as it was intended. Eppie wondered why he'd only started praying for her after Miracle had been born. Everyone in this town she'd met so far was not nearly what they appeared, except Candice.

"I'm sure God had a plan in mind when he allowed me to heal during those three years." Eppie planned on keeping her memory loss a secret from everyone but those closest to her. "Micah has been telling me everything I need to know."

A half-truth, or perhaps quarter-truth.

"You realize, of course, that God does not plan for a good Christian woman to have a child outside of the bonds of holy matrimony." His frown grew deeper along with Eppie's discomfort. "Perhaps your long illness was punishment for your sins."

Eppie took a deep breath and absorbed the arrows he slung at her with each passing moment. This was Plum Creek's spiritual leader? He was an ass and a bully, in her not-so-humble opinion. Was there anyone in town who wasn't mean?

"I would hope that God recognizes the inherent good in all of us, even if we do make mistakes."

"You sound different, Miss Eppie. I don't believe I've ever heard you use a word such as inherent." He folded his hands in front of his belly, looking at her with suspicion. She hoped he wasn't thinking she was a witch or possessed by the devil. Actually it wouldn't surprise her.

"Perhaps Micah reading to me for three years helped with my education." Truth was, Eppie didn't know if Micah had read to her or not, but she suspected he had. Since she didn't remember herself prior to last week, there's no way of knowing how different or uneducated she'd actually sounded.

"Preposterous. You were in the land between the living and the dead. You couldn't have heard a thing because God had shut you in there for a purpose." He nodded as if he was agreeing with himself. "You were being punished, plain and simple. I'm sure you can understand that."

Eppie resisted the urge to hug her knees and curl up in a ball. The reverend was a frightening man, one who obviously kept people on edge and uneasy. Bullies usually backed down when confronted, or at least that's what her brain was telling her.

She rose to her feet and scowled back at the minister. "I refuse to believe God was punishing me for anything. I had an accident and needed to heal, plain as that. Good day, Reverend."

When Eppie turned on her heel and left him standing there, she hoped he wasn't going to start throwing more insults at her. Her nerves were popping like oil on a hot pan as she opened the door and stepped in.

"I'll pray for you, Miss Eppie," was the last thing she heard before she shut the door behind her.

God willing, the prayers would be good ones. Eppie had the energy after all to walk up the stairs. Her gaze wandered to the parlor door, but it was still closed and she wasn't ready to open it again.

Chapter Five

The knock on the door startled him, and he fell off the settee, landing on his head. Fortunately the thick Persian carpet broke his fall, but stars exploded at the contact. He clutched his head and rolled onto his back.

"Jesus please us." He pried his stinging eyes open and glanced around. It was dark in the room and no light burned. Through the gauzy white curtains he could see the gray light of what could be dawn. If it was, he'd lost a day somewhere. The last thing he remembered was the parlor and the whiskey. His mouth was dry as cotton and tasted as if he'd been eating dirt.

Somewhere buried deep in his memory was Eppie's scent and the feel of her lips on his. Had he kissed her? Had she kissed him back? It was all fuzzy and grainy, and with the pounding in his head, there's no way he'd remember clearly for a while.

The pounding continued and he realized it wasn't in his head but at the front door. Micah got to all fours and used the coffee table to bring himself to a standing position. The room swam around him as if it had been dipped in a lake. He put out his arms to steady the movement when his stomach decided to join in the fun. A rather noxious burp traveled up his throat, leaving a burning path of bile in its wake.

He felt as if he'd been dragged behind a horse. Every muscle in his body ached, right along with his head. Hell, even his nose hurt, but that could have been from the tumble off the settee.

The pounding started again at the front door and Micah took a tentative step forward. It was slow going, but he made it across the room and out into the hallway without falling down or vomiting. A victory of sorts.

"Hold your horses, I'm coming." His voice sounded as rusty as an old bell and clanged just as much in his poor skull.

By the time he made it to the front door, the banging had grown louder, sweat poured down his face, and he was afraid he would faint on the floor before he got there. Somehow, some way, he didn't collapse.

His hand was slippery with sweat and it took three tries before he was able to grasp the knob and pull it open. Micah lost his balance and fell forward, only to be caught by a rather strong pair of arms.

"Good catch." He slurred as unconsciousness beckoned.

"Oh Micah, not again." Madeline's voice permeated his pickled senses and he smiled.

"Madeline, oh my dear, I've missed you." He smiled crookedly at the wooden planks on the floor.

"Pick him up, Teague, and bring him up to his room. Doctor, can you wait here a few moments?" Madeline, as always, took control of the situation, and Micah was glad for it.

He didn't want control and giving it over to someone who would take it was his fondest desire. As he was flipped over a large shoulder he realized Teague, Madeline's dark-haired giant of a husband, carried him as if he were a sack of flour. Micah was about to protest when the world went black just after he realized he'd vomited on Teague's legs.

*   *   *

"He retched on me." A loud male voice boomed outside Eppie's door, making her jump.

She'd heard the pounding on the front door and at first thought it was part of a dream. When strangers entered the house, she realized she wasn't sleeping and quickly pulled on her clothes. Cursing, stomping, and general shouting went on as she tried to determine who was there and what they were doing.

"He didn't mean it. You know how he gets when he drinks." This one was a woman, and she sounded cultured, very educated.

Eppie pressed her ear to the door and listened hard, trying to catch every word they said. Her breath came in small bursts as she struggled to be as quiet as a mouse.

"It smells." The man sounded like a complaining little boy now.

"Now you sound like Henry and he's only two. Just bring Micah in here and we'll clean him up." They walked past her room, still talking, and apparently entered another room.

She assumed they were talking about Micah and wondered if he was okay. Obviously he'd vomited on the man, so he was alive, but that didn't mean much if he was truly sick from the liquor. She wanted to open the door, but unease kept her from following through.

Five minutes passed while she listened to thumps, quiet murmurs and not-so-quiet curses. Finally, footsteps sounded down the hallway again heading for her room.

"Don't be such a baby. I'm just going to check on Eppie, then make coffee." The woman's voice grew closer. "Now be quiet before you wake Miracle up. She doesn't need to see her papa like that."

Before Eppie could get to the bed and pretend to be sleeping, the door swung open and she jumped back. In the doorway stood a very tall, curvy woman with reddish brown hair wearing a gray suit. Her skin was the color of cream and her eyes were dark as pitch. However, on her face was the most astonished look Eppie had ever seen.

"Eppie!" she shouted as she ran into the room and wrapped Eppie in a hug.

The woman's scent surrounded her, like the flowers outside the house, and suddenly Eppie knew exactly who this was. It must be Madeline, the best friend she couldn't remember and was afraid to see. No matter if her memory didn't work, because the hug was like a magic wand. Suddenly Eppie's eyes filled with tears and her heart felt as if it were in her throat. This was genuine affection from someone who obviously loved her.

She knew right then Madeline must have been someone special in her life, someone who knew her secrets and shared her dreams. There was a bond there, a connection that couldn't be severed by a forgotten past. What she felt when she was with Micah was confusing and frightening, unlike this, which felt as if she'd truly woken up.

"Oh my God, I can't believe it." Tears streamed down Madeline's face as she pulled back to look. "You're awake! I knew something was wrong when he wired the doctor asking him to get here as soon as possible. How could he keep this from me? Oh, Eppie, I've missed you."

Madeline kissed her cheek, then hugged her again. Eppie was so overwhelmed she didn't know what to do, so she just hung on until a large shadow filled the doorway.

"What is it? What happ—holy shit." The man who'd complained about Micah vomiting on his trousers was enormous. More than that, he had to duck to get through the door. With shoulders as wide as the entire frame and a shock of wavy brown hair, he stood at least a foot taller than Eppie. His sheer size should have scared her silly, but the softness in his brown gaze when he realized she was in Madeline's arms chased away any ill thoughts.

"Is that really you?" He smiled, and Eppie saw how handsome the big man really was. "My little curmudgeon is finally back?"

Curmudgeon? Was that what she had been like?

"Teague, can you believe it? I still can't." Madeline put her arm around Eppie's shoulders and squeezed. "Our Eppie is back. Let's go have coffee and biscuits. I'm sure Candice left some from last night."

Eppie let Madeline lead her downstairs as Madeline chattered like a magpie, never letting anyone else get a word in edgewise. It was a good thing, too, because Eppie had no idea how to tell her she couldn't remember a thing.

Another man stood downstairs, wearing a bowler hat and a natty brown suit. His black eyebrows rose when he spotted Eppie walking down the steps with Madeline.

"Holy Mary and all the saints. She's come back." He took off his hat with a shaking hand. "Micah should have told me and I'd have come sooner. I can hardly believe it. How are you feeling, Eppie?"

"I'm feeling just fine, thank you kindly." She attempted to smile, but the chaos and confusion made it hard. "I believe I'd like to sit down, though."

Madeline stopped in her tracks, Teague turned to look at her with widened eyes, and the doctor stepped back a pace.

"You sound like Micah." Madeline squeezed her arm. "That sweet drawl of his is unmistakable."

Teague shook his head. "It sure as hell isn't sweet on him, but it's definitely odd coming from her."

"Interesting. You know he read to her quite a bit while she was in the coma. This would make an excellent case study for a journal article." The doctor reached into his pocket. "Where did I put my pencil?"

Eppie pulled away from Madeline, resisting the urge to simply cut and run. "I appreciate the fact that you're all concerned about me and my welfare. However, I am a person,

Eppie grabbed her arm. "For right now, just sit with me and tell me about our friendship. I need—" she swallowed "—a friend more than anything. Micah scares me and Miracle confuses me. Please, Madeline."

Madeline leaned down and wrapped her arms around Eppie and gave her a small squeeze. "I am your friend, Eppie, always." She wiped at her eyes and Eppie was surprised to see tears on the taller woman's cheeks. "Let's have that coffee now."

Grateful for the reprieve from the constant confusion in the madhouse, Eppie sat with Madeline for the next hour and sipped coffee and nibbled biscuits. She found her new friend to be funny and extremely intelligent.

"How did we meet?" Eppie found she liked two spoonfuls of sugar in her coffee. It made the hot, bitter brew just perfect.

"Well, about five years ago, my father died and I lived alone in this big house. It was too much for one person, so I started letting folks stay here. Those who were passing through town and didn't have money for a hotel." She smiled as she stared off into the distance, apparently remembering. "You arrived on my doorstep, a sassy-mouthed sixteen-year-old who had a chip on her shoulder the size of Texas."

"So I'm twenty-one?" Eppie gobbled up the bits of information like chocolate.

"About that, yes. You never told me much about your life before you arrived in Colorado, but I do know you came from North Carolina originally." Madeline took a bite of biscuit and frowned into her coffee. "I'm afraid you didn't talk about your family, either."

Eppie tried not to be disappointed. "Do I have a last name? Is Eppie my first name?"

"From what you told me, you were born Elizabeth Archer, but you'd always been called Eppie."

Eppie took the information and pulled it close, holding on to it as if she'd been given the best gift in the world. Elizabeth Archer. She had a name, a real name, and it felt wonderful.

With that name, she finally felt like a real person, not just a ghost who'd entered someone else's life.

"Thank you." She swallowed the lump in her throat. "I can't tell you how much it means to me."

"I'm glad to help you in any way I can. Even if you don't remember me, I am your friend, Eppie. I hope you come to believe that."

"I think I already do." Eppie took Madeline's hand, comfortable with the long fingers and smooth skin against hers.

"He finally stopped stinking up the place and is sleeping now." Teague entered the kitchen like a brown-haired hurricane. "The doc is settling into the room next to Miracle's. She woke up and is bouncing off the walls." He stopped and stared at both of them. "Aw, shit, you've been crying, haven't you?"

Madeline burst out laughing, and so did Eppie. It felt wonderful and freeing. He shook his head and left the kitchen.

"Don't understand 'em, never will."

That made them laugh harder, and Eppie reveled in the sweet joy of the moment. It felt good to be alive for the first time in her short life.

Micah was wide awake in an instant, no hangover or sleep cobwebs around him. He sat up and realized he was in his bed and it was the middle of the day judging by the sunlight streaming in his window.

He wondered just what stupid things he'd done, starting with drinking whiskey, and ending with vomiting. The stench in the room attested to the condition of his body. He climbed out of bed and padded to the pitcher and basin on the washstand.

After he stripped off the stinking clothes, he poured water into the basin, surprised to find it lukewarm. Someone had brought him hot water at some point, and that fact touched him. He washed quickly but thoroughly, then shaved with trembling hands, ignoring the red-rimmed bloodshot eyes staring back at him.

He knew he'd made a mistake, a huge one, and wallowing in his stupidity wasn't going to help matters. A thousand questions fluttered in his brain, starting with how he got to his room and exactly why he had an image of Eppie crying burned into his mind.

Thankfully, he had a set of clean clothes hanging on the hook, and he dressed with the intention of looking like a respectable man instead of a raving lunatic. He was just fastening the buttons on his trousers when the door burst open and of all people, Teague O'Neal stood there.

The big man and he had been at odds since they met. A Johnny Reb and a Union Blue were always going to be somewhat enemies. They both loved Madeline and had developed a tentative bond because of it. However, Micah doubted he would ever be friends with Teague. Too much blood had been spilled during the War Between the States and the memories of those battles haunted both their dreams. He didn't need to hear it from Teague to know it was true.

What surprised him the most was that Teague was actually standing in his room, hand on the doorknob and a scowl on his face.

"About time you got your lazy ass up. I was going to dump a bucket of well water on you in another hour."

"Hello to you, too, Teague. I can see your manners are as impeccable as always." Micah used a strip of leather to tie his hair back and considered himself ready to face the world. "I'm assuming Madeline is here as well."

"You know it's always bothered me the way you say that. Madeline as if it's a long vowel." Teague folded his arms across his massive chest. "She's mighty upset with you."

Oh hell, that meant they'd seen Eppie and likely talked to her as well. Micah wanted to avoid all this, which is why he hadn't wired Madeline in the first place. It appeared the doctor was loyal to the woman who paid his bills instead of the patient he was treating. Dammit all.

Micah stepped toward the door, but Teague, like the tree he resembled, didn't move.

"It would help if I could leave the room and find Madeline to speak to her. However, with you in the way it makes it difficult to do that." Micah's drawl always deepened when Teague was around, as if it hadn't been ten years since he'd left Virginia behind.

"If you make her cry, you and I are going to have a set-to." Teague moved out of the way, but Micah swore he heard a rumbling from the other man's throat, like a dog warning a potential threat.

Micah really didn't know exactly what Madeline saw in her husband, but love could be a strange thing. He and Eppie had met four years earlier and against all odds and proper society, had found something more precious than the biggest diamond in the world. He'd tried to stay away from her, truly he had, but once he'd had just one moment in her arms, nothing could stop him.

Madeline had no idea the lengths they'd gone through to keep the relationship a secret. For almost a year, they'd met every week down by the river. Sometimes they'd barely speak, so great was their hunger for each other. Many times they'd sit and talk for hours about everything and nothing.

It had been Eppie who refused to marry him. That argument had led to a rift between them and they'd stayed apart for a month, until Madeline had asked him to help her. All of that led to the fateful day when Jackson Webster tried to force his way into Madeline's house.

And Eppie had stepped in the path of a bullet to save Micah's life.

He felt dizzy with the memory of her lying on the wooden floor, her blood seeping out through her dress. It was a nightmare that replayed itself every day and every night for more than three years. Even now just thinking about how close she came to dying, how close Miracle came to never being born, made his stomach cramp with pain.

"You plan on walking down the stairs or counting 'em?" Teague gave him a little shove with his finger. "Let's go, Spalding."

Micah hadn't even realized that he'd stopped at the top of the stairs. "Where are they?"

"Out back with the girl and that crazy dog. Damn mutt tried to steal my hat and use it to chew on."

Micah smiled and decided he would keep Daisy just because she annoyed Teague. He walked downstairs and headed for the kitchen. Lightheaded and weak, he knew he had to eat something before confronting the two women he adored. When he stopped at the table to eat a piece of bread with honey, Teague threw up his arms in disgust.

"What the hell are you doing?"

Micah held on to his temper by a thread. "I need to have some sustenance before I lose consciousness again. I'm sure you'd prefer I walked on my own two feet."

"Damn right. Fine, then, but make it fast. They've been waiting for almost six hours for you to wake up." Teague, fortunately, left him alone in the kitchen.

It gave Micah a chance to catch his breath and gather his thoughts before facing the women. Funny how the fairer, weaker sex could tie a man into knots. No doubt Madeline had some choice words for him since he hadn't told her Eppie had woken up.

Who knows what Eppie would say about his drunken binging the previous day. He couldn't think of a single reason she would accept that didn't involve him being selfish. That's what it was—a purely selfish escape from his problems.

The coffee on the stove was still moderately warm, so he poured a cup and gulped it down after the bread. It helped him feel better, more ready to face the confrontation he knew awaited him outside.

After making sure he had no crumbs on his face, he went out the back door and found Madeline and Eppie sitting under the big oak tree by the carriage house on a blanket. Miracle rolled in the grass, playing with Daisy. Teague was nowhere to be seen, thank God.

Madeline didn't see him at first, but Eppie's gaze snapped to his immediately. He pretended she was glad to see him, but from a distance he couldn't quite see her expression.

The heat of the day settled over him as he walked across the dusty ground to the lush greenery in the shade. Summer had truly taken hold of Plum Creek. He was glad he had taken the time to wash and shave because he was already sweating—a combination of nerves and the temperature.

Eppie sat up straighter and watched him approach, her dark eyes unreadable. Madeline, however, was not so hard to understand. Her lips tightened into a white line when she spotted him, and he knew he'd hear more than a hello.

"Good day, ladies. It's lovely to see you, Madeline. You are looking as beautiful as always." He turned to smile at Eppie. "Hello, Eppie, I'm glad to see you outside. The fresh air agrees with you."

"Micah, sit down." Madeline pointed to a spot on the blanket in front of them. "We need to talk."

With no small amount of trepidation, he lowered himself to the blanket. The previous day's activities left their mark on his body and he felt as if he'd already been trampled by a horse.

"Why didn't you let me know?" Madeline wasn't angry, she was upset and hurt. "Micah, you know I love her as much as you do. Why?"

Micah took a moment to gather his thoughts. He glanced at Eppie's face and saw the same questions Madeline had just voiced.

"I'm sorry I've hurt you, Madeline. You know you are in my heart for good." He smiled sadly. "When she woke, I wanted to shout it from the rooftops, believe me. Then I realized she didn't remember me and then, even worse, she didn't remember herself. I panicked. Candice convinced me to wire the doctor to have him examine her. I was afraid of overwhelming her with people and confusion when she had trouble even knowing who she was."

He searched for the right words. "I thought perhaps if she could just be left alone, her memory might return. I've heard of men losing their memory after being hit on the head, but she was shot in the shoulder."

"That story I'm still waiting to hear." Eppie finally spoke, as distant and cool as the river that lay behind the house.

"I will tell you, I promise. Eppie, honey, I didn't tell Madeline to protect you for just a little bit longer. I was going to wire her after the doctor had examined you. You must believe me, I had good intentions, just didn't make the right decisions." He knew that now and regretted his stupid choices, but he couldn't change them. Micah could only try to right the wrong he'd caused.

"I believe you, Micah." Madeline touched his hand. "But you are the dumbest smart man I know."

Micah chuckled rustily. "I'm not sure if I can ever change that."

"You can't fix stupid." Teague took that particular moment to appear and make his sarcastic self known. His big feet were visible on the left, which meant he'd been in the carriage house.

"Not funny, O'Neal." Micah didn't even bother to look at him but kept his gaze on the women. "Eppie, honey, I'm sorry for all of this, for everything. I really thought I was doing the best thing."

Eppie glanced down at her hands as they fidgeted in her

lap while Micah held his breath. "I believe you are sincere, Micah."

It was a start, a small one, but he grasped on to it as if it were much larger.

"Thank you, honey."

"For now I'd prefer you didn't call me honey." She raised her gaze. "I know you mean well, Micah, but this is going to take time."

Micah swallowed the protest that rose to his lips. It would take time, a lot of time, and that's what he feared the most. With time came more opportunity for her to choose a different path in her life, a different man to love. It was what he dreaded most, but he didn't say a word for fear she would simply get up and leave.

At least she had said "for now." It could've been worse. She could have left with Madeline for good.

"Now that you're awake, we can talk about what the doctor found." Madeline gestured to the house. "He's taking a nap now."

"What do you mean what he found?" Micah frowned. "Did he already examine her? Why didn't you wake me up?"

"You were passed out, not sleeping. We thought it best for Eppie to be looked at as soon as possible. Doctor Carmichael agreed with me." Madeline nodded and dared Micah with her gaze to question her.

"I think you did the right thing, Maddie, so don't let Micah tell you any different." Teague glared holes in the other man.

"I still would like to have known what was going on."

Eppie surged to her feet. "I'm sitting right here, you know, so stop talking about me as if I'm still upstairs in that coma." Eppie's sassy spirit emerged in front of his eyes. "I get to make my own decisions now, not any of you."

She walked away, leaving Micah to wonder if he'd ever get close to Eppie again. He needed to find a way to explain why he acted like such an ass. God knows he deserved a tongue-lashing and he was prepared to let her yell at him all day, if only she didn't leave him. He couldn't live without her.

Eppie walked toward the sound of water. Daisy barked behind her, but she ignored her. Madeline and Micah meant well, but they did speak of her as if she were an inanimate object rather than a person with a brain and feelings. Eppie had allowed the doctor to examine her, not under anyone's orders or to please someone else.

She wanted to know what had happened and he was the closest thing to a solution she could find. The young doctor was apparently the best in his field and treated Eppie at Madeline's request. No doubt there was a great deal of money involved. It appeared these people threw their money around as if it were dandelion fluff on the wind.

Anger was better than self-pity and fright, and Eppie welcomed it. Being angry meant she was learning to be a person again instead of an empty shell. None of them understood what it felt like and she refused to keep trying to explain it.

When she reached the river, the sound of the water rushing past soothed her frayed nerves. She sat on a large rock and watched the sun sparkle on the liquid dancing beneath her. After a few moments of self-righteous anger, she started to calm down and began to regret her outburst.

Her new friends meant well, even if they were heavy-handed. Candice seemed to be the only one to allow her to make mistakes on her own.

"I'm sorry, Eppie." Micah's voice came to her from behind; however, she didn't turn around.

"I'm not ready to talk to you yet." She ran her fingers along the moss at the edge of the rock.

"I know, and that's why I came to apologize. Eppie, hon—I've made so many mistakes in my life I've lost count. You were the first thing I didn't regret."

Eppie hadn't doubted Micah's sincerity since that first day when she'd woken. He was a man with a lot of shadows in his past, but his present was see-through. There was no question he loved her, somewhat desperately in her opinion, and that fact alone scared her and thrilled her.

She wasn't sure which feeling was winning the battle.

Eppie sighed. "You might as well come over here and sit down, so I can tell you what Doctor Carmichael said."

He was beside her in seconds, likely flew across the grass to get to her. In the shade of the pine trees, he smiled at her and Eppie saw the handsome man beneath the layers of sadness. With his hair back and his face shaved, a dimple peeped out from his left cheek, making him look young.

"How old are you?"

"I'm thirty-five." He looked startled by the question.

"I'm twenty-one, according to what I told Madeline." She tossed a few pebbles into the river. "The doctor says he's not sure why my memory is gone, but he thinks it might have something to do with the blood I lost."

She heard Micah swallow. "About that, I was guarding the house so Madeline and Teague could go to Denver and get the evidence they needed against the sheriff and the judge. Webster tried to force his way into the house, and I stopped him, or tried to anyway. When he pulled out his pistol, you jumped in the fray, and the gun went off." She heard him swallow hard. "Webster ran like a goddamn coward, and I took care of you with Candice's help until a doctor could get here. I'm sorry for keeping it from you. I meant to tell you what happened, but I wanted to go slow, to allow you to heal physically before you were bombarded with all the details you forgot."

"I can appreciate that, but I had a right to know. Thank you for telling me." She shot him a sidelong glance. "I expect if you want to be around me, you had better wear your honest cap at all times. If I find out you're keeping secrets from me or lying, there won't be another chance. Do you understand what I'm saying?" Eppie had enough of the overprotective nature of the man who would be her lover. He had to give her room to breathe.

"Yes, ma'am." He smiled and reached out to touch her cheek with the back of his hand. "The sunlight makes your skin glow. You know this is our spot?"

Eppie couldn't help but be startled. "Our spot?"

"Where we met every week for almost a year." He looked to the left toward a group of aspen trees. "I'd bring that big blue blanket and we'd lie out under the stars. When I saw you come here, I can tell you my heart started beating a mile a minute. Maybe somewhere you do remember deep down."

Eppie's heart joined in and beat right along with his. Was he right? Could she remember things by instinct? She had no idea they'd met for a year before she was injured, but the fact that they were so different should have given her a clue their relationship wasn't the normal type.

"Why did we meet here?"

He jerked a thumb toward the house. "You didn't want Madeline to know. I always hoped it wasn't because you were embarrassed by me, but rather that you didn't want to marry me since I'm a crazy hermit from the mountains."

She shook her head in disbelief. "You're a crazy hermit and you asked me to marry you and I said no?"

"Oh, you sure did. Let me see if I can remember your exact words. 'I might love you, you crazy fool, but that don't mean I am crazy enough to marry you. I ain't got to this point in my life to marry the first man to ask me.'" He shrugged. "I've thought about that night for the last three years. It was the last time we, well, were together. I think it was the night Miracle was made."

Eppie's throat tightened, and she knew a moment of panic. Had she spoken like that to him? Who was she to throw away a chance at happiness with a man who obviously loved her? She was already intimate with him, that couldn't be debated, so why didn't she want to marry him?

"I'm sorry if I hurt you."

Micah chuckled, sounding half in pain, half amused. "Ah, Eppie, love can bring a mountain of hurt and an ocean of happiness. I accepted one and embraced the other."

The silence between them stretched into an uncomfortable one. Eppie didn't know what to say, so she let the quiet continue until he finally spoke.

"What else did the doctor say?"

A safe topic, thank God. "He said I was in good health, but underweight and needed lots of fresh air and exercise. My muscles hurt because I haven't used them in so long, but he also said someone had been caring for me by stretching them regularly. Was that you?"

"I did everything he told me to. I wanted to make sure you came back to me." Micah's simple explanation told her a great deal about his motivations, which were selfless and selfish at the same time.

"He's going to consult with a few other doctors in New York and Chicago, then do some reading in a journal for doctors. I don't know how much Madeline is paying him, but to be a doctor's single patient is a bit odd. I told him I didn't want to become an experiment." She already felt as if she were on display and it would only get worse if he used her to study on.

"I won't let that happen. I've kept you safe for three years. Please let me continue." His silver eyes glittered in the dappled sunlight and Eppie felt odd for a moment, as if the world tilted beneath her.

An image flashed through her mind of a younger Micah, with fuller cheeks and longer hair, smiling and tickling her nose with a feather. She yelped and scampered backwards, scared and unsettled.

"What is it? What happened?" Micah looked as worried as she felt.

"I think I just remembered you."

If she had given him the keys to a golden city, he couldn't have looked more thrilled as his eyes danced with joy. "Really?"

"I think so. It was here, only you were younger and you were tickling me." She tried to swallow, but her throat was so dry, she couldn't.

"With a white feather?"

Eppie stared at him in astonishment. He'd confirmed what she had suspected. She'd *remembered*.

With a squeal she threw herself into his arms and lost herself in a tight embrace as they celebrated the minute taste of her previous life. Her heart beat so hard, it knocked against her ribs, and she felt the answering throb of his.

When she pulled back, she was close enough to count his eyelashes. His pupils had dilated and she felt an answering arousal growing within her. Her body felt as if she'd been hit by lightning.

"Please?" He didn't beg or take, just asked politely.

Eppie couldn't refuse him, her body wouldn't let her. She nodded and closed her eyes as his head lowered. This time the kiss was more intense because their bodies were touching. Her nipples pressed against his hard chest at the same time his hands roamed up and down her back. Sweet, sweet heavens, kissing Micah was like nibbling on the most decadent dessert.

She forgot where she was and what was around her. Diving into Micah was like diving into a pond on a hot day. It felt wonderful, exhilarating, and like exactly what she needed.

He leaned back and touched her cheek, rubbing his thumb along her cheekbone. She stared up at him, waiting and wanting, what she wasn't sure. It could've been sex, it could've been confirmation she was desirable.

Judging by the stick of wood in his pants currently pressing against her hip, Eppie was definitely desirable.

"I don't want to rush you."

She shook her head. "You're not. This is my choice." She swallowed the lump of fear and uncertainty. "Show me."

He smiled then, a sweet, beautiful smile that lit up his whole face and Eppie knew then what he looked like when he wasn't wallowing in the depths of misery. Micah was exceptionally handsome and for some reason, God decided to give him to her.

For the first time since she'd woken, Eppie took a chance on something other than what to wear or eat. She took a chance on Micah.

"My pleasure." He ran his hands along her breasts, her nipples screaming for more than the light touch.

She closed her eyes and allowed herself to feel what he was doing. He made quick work of the buttons on her dress. The warmth of the sun and the cool breeze tickled her bare skin as he spread the dress open. Micah nuzzled her breasts. The softness of his lips made her want to beg for more, but she beat back her impatience with effort.

By the time his mouth closed over her nipple, lightning bolts of tingles shot through her. He laved and nibbled at her while his fingers tweaked and rolled her other nipple. It was heaven and hell rolled into one. She arched into him, wanting more, needing more.

His hand meandered down her stomach, raising her short hairs as it progressed. Moisture coated her cunt as it heated in anticipation of his touch, of the pleasure he could bring.

Eppie couldn't say it was a memory of being with him that allowed her to let go of her inhibitions, but she did feel comfortable doing it, as if her body had taken over and whispered "It's okay" in her ear.

His fingers skimmed her nether lips, teasing and tickling.

She moaned and spread her legs, eager for more. His teeth closed around the nipple as his fingers landed in her slick folds. He'd obviously done it before, because he knew exactly how to bring her to a panting mess.

"You're so wet, darlin', and you feel so good." He whispered against her breast. "I need to taste you."

The very thought of his mouth on her made her skin sing. She had no idea what to expect, but obviously her body did.

"Yes." She couldn't possibly say no considering how much she wanted it.

Micah released her nipple with a pop and the cool breeze kept it as tight as a diamond. He ran his tongue along the seam of her lips and kissed her, fucked her with his tongue even as his fingers did the same to her pussy. She vibrated with arousal as he built her closer to the ultimate pleasure.

When he let her mouth go, she sucked in a breath and he chuckled. "I'm glad I'm doing something right."

"Mmmm," was all she could manage.

He kissed his way down her body until he reached the opening in her drawers. It felt naughty somehow to still have on underthings and be almost naked beneath the boughs of the trees. That naughtiness added to her arousal. She'd had no idea how much it would. The fact that anyone could come along and see them, perhaps watch them, made her shudder. She didn't have the mental wherewithal to figure out it was good or bad because Micah had reached the juncture of her thighs.

"You smell delicious." He took a deep breath through his nose. "Like a banquet waiting for me to feast on."

Oh God, his words did almost as much as his talented hands and mouth. She pulled her knees up, opening her legs as far as she could, waiting.

"Please," popped out of her mouth on a whisper.

"Always, my love."

He spread her nether lips, just as he had in the dream, and

blew on her heated flesh. She shivered and dug her fingers into the soft moss around her.

The first swipe of his tongue made her nearly fly off the ground. He held her down with both arms and licked her again. This time she mentally nailed herself to the ground and allowed herself to let go.

His tongue was rough as he lapped at her pussy, sweet, long strokes from top to bottom. He stopped to tickle the sensitive nub with each pass. Every time the stop grew longer until his thumbs began entering her and he latched onto that nub and sucked.

The sensations buffeting her were akin to a twister. Sweet ecstasy flooded her as he expertly licked, nibbled and sucked her nub while his fingers teased her below. She heard herself moan but didn't care who heard her. In fact, she cared about nothing but what Micah was doing to her.

"Touch yourself." His soft command shocked her, but she did his bidding since she couldn't do anything else.

Her hands grasped her breasts and she pinched her own nipples. She gasped from the dual sensations as they rocketed through her. His thumbs switched positions with his mouth, and soon his tongue was entering her like a small cock, even as his fingers continued to pleasure her nub.

Eppie knew her body was near to exploding and she welcomed it. She started moving against his thrusts, naturally following the rhythm set by him. The wave of absolute ecstasy began somewhere near her feet and traveled up through her so fast it stole her breath. He sucked at her nub as she bucked and writhed from the liquid sensations buffeting her body.

Heaven and Earth and the stars collided, and she floated above it all. When his mouth left her pussy, she felt his cock nudging her entrance. She should tell him no, to stop before it went too far, but it was already too far. Eppie wanted him inside her.

He went slowly, as apparently was his style, going in only an inch, then withdrawing, then two inches, then three. By the time he'd fully penetrated her, she was panting again for what pleasure was to be found with Micah.

"Look at me, love."

Her eyes popped open and he smiled.

"You are exquisite when you come. I want to see it again."

Eppie didn't think it was possible, but as he thrust into her, the kernel of pleasure began to build again into a wave. She still pinched her nipples and his pupils had dilated into dark pools as he watched her hands.

"That's it, love, let me join you."

His mouth closed over her hand and his tongue joined her fingers. The hot wet mouth combined with her own ministrations, and suddenly she found herself nearly ready to reach her peak again.

"Tight, so tight." He mumbled against her. "I'm so close, so close."

Eppie closed her legs around his hips, bringing him deeper inside her and that was apparently the way to open the gates of heaven. Pure joy, ecstasy and everything in between poured over them. Micah thrust into her as she closed around him like a fist. Life, death, and love pulsed through both of them as they reached their peaks in unison.

She couldn't get a breath in and stars floated in her vision. It was so much more than sex, and she knew it. Two people who didn't love each other couldn't possibly find such amazing pleasure together.

When he raised himself up on his elbows and looked down at her with that beautiful smile, Eppie was terrified. She didn't know what scared her more, the fact that she wanted to find it again with him or that she'd acknowledged there was love between them, lurking in the shadows.

Chapter Six

The morning sun streamed through the kitchen window, illuminating the table and the solitary figure who sat drinking coffee. Micah stared at the pattern of sunbeams on the table as he thought about Eppie.

Their encounter in the woods a few days earlier left him hungry for more of her. Eppie appeared to want to forget it happened, yet there was nothing on earth that could make him forget it.

It was the first taste of paradise, of happiness, he'd had in years. He wasn't going to let Eppie take that away from him, even if she was confused about it. However, he wasn't going to be a bully, either, and force her to repeat it if she wanted to keep her distance.

The truth was, he loved her enough to give her more time. It was killing him to wake up each morning with sweat covering his body, the strong urge to drink on his tongue, and the memory of her nude form burned into his brain.

"I didn't realize anyone was here."

Eppie's voice startled him and he spilled coffee on his hand. With a hiss, he set the cup down and blew on the burn.

"I'm sorry." She pumped water into the sink and wet a rag. "I always seem to be causing you pain."

He choked on a laugh. "I don't even know what to say to that."

Eppie seemed to realize what she said because her cheeks reddened. "I also seem to suffer from an abundance of awkwardness around you."

"That was a mouthful." He closed his eyes against the sensation of having her hands touching him. "I don't mean to scare you, make you feel uncomfortable, or chase you away."

She stopped and stared down into his eyes. "Then what do you want from me?"

He smiled. "That's easy. I want to spend time with you, to talk and perhaps, even spark a memory or two."

"That's all?" She looked suspicious, and she probably should. He wanted much more than that, but it was what he would settle for.

"That's all. It's all I could expect. Now if you'd care to join me, I'd love some company. Breakfast is a lonely meal around here." His breath caught in his chest as he waited for her answer.

"Okay, I will have breakfast with you." She set the rag back on the wooden sink and turned around to face him. "You mustn't push me, Micah. I am doing this all based on how I feel."

"I know, and I am willing to give you all the time you need. I'm not going anywhere." He couldn't help being anxious for much more, much sooner, but he'd been patient enough to wait for her for three years. He could be patient some more.

"Then let's have breakfast." She turned toward the stove, then glanced back at him. "I'm not sure if I can cook."

Micah laughed and stood. "Then let me show you how to make eggs."

The next morning, when Eppie woke, she wasn't sure if she would go to the kitchen or not. Micah had challenged her to spend time with him and she'd accepted the challenge.

She'd be a coward if she didn't go downstairs for breakfast. Eppie didn't want to be that person, so she got herself washed and dressed.

When she opened her bedroom door, her stomach did a funny flip as nerves did their best to stop her. She took a deep breath and told her feet to move.

Fortunately they listened to her and she went downstairs to the kitchen. The smell of coffee wafted past her and she breathed in the scent. If Micah did anything right, it was coffee. If nothing else, she would have a good hot cup for breakfast.

Petty thinking, she knew, but Micah kept her on edge. She didn't know if it was his behavior or simply her reaction to him. Probably a combination of both.

When she walked into the kitchen, she half expected Micah to jump up and hug her, but he didn't. In fact, he barely glanced at her from his perch at the stove.

"Good morning." He gave her a small smile. "Have a seat and I'll pour you some coffee."

She had built up so much dread for what she'd find, all of it suddenly deflated in an instant. "Thank you," she managed to get out before she sat down.

"I've asked Brenda Monahan, the seamstress in town, to come by and alter your clothes for you. She does wonderful work." He chatted as he cooked, the smell of bacon making her stomach rumble.

"Thank you again. I didn't realize I was so hungry." There were a lot of things she didn't realize. For example, how adept he was at cooking. The day before, he'd made two fried eggs and a piece of ham in a frying pan.

From what she saw that morning, he'd made fresh biscuits and cut bacon and cooked it, along with the coffee. Micah was self-sufficient in the kitchen.

Eppie felt odd sitting while he did the cooking. Even if she didn't remember her name, she did remember women were supposed to do the cooking, not the watching.

"Can I help?" She wasn't sure exactly what she was could do.

"No, just sit and relax." He turned and met her gaze. "Did you sleep well?"

It felt like an odd conversation, as if they were a married couple having breakfast together.

"Micah, tell me about yourself." She was satisfied to see him twitch, breaking the strange domestic feeling in the room.

"What do you want to know?" He picked up the pot of coffee with a towel and poured her a cup, avoiding her gaze.

"Where are you from?" She held the tin cup in her hand, grateful for its warmth.

"Virginia." His voice was tight and she realized questions about himself made him uncomfortable. He filled a plate with bacon, eggs, and a biscuit, then set it in front of her. His answers about his past were apparently going to be as sparse as the food was bountiful.

Her stomach rumbled again and Eppie decided she was going to eat what he'd prepared. After all, she was hungry and he was nice enough to make it. She decided to try a different topic for conversation.

"You're a very good cook." She put a forkful of eggs in her mouth and the explosion of flavor made her groan. "These are delicious."

He chuckled as he set the plate down across from her. "Why, thank you. I didn't used to be able to even boil water, but necessity made me learn in a hurry. I couldn't let Miracle starve."

Eppie's opinion of Micah went up a notch. A father who wanted to take care of his child, even to the point of learning to cook for her, couldn't be a bad person deep down.

"I'm impressed," she managed to say between bites. "You learned well."

He met her gaze across the table. "You want me to teach

you? Well, not really teach you, just remind you. You used to be the best cook in the entire state."

Eppie couldn't stop the smile from spreading across her face. "Really? I was a good cook?"

"Oh, the best. Your green beans? They were so good I used to dream about them." He took a gulp of coffee. "I'm sure if you started, you would remember as you went along."

She considered his idea, recognizing she would have to spend time with him. Micah was giving her the opportunity to turn their morning breakfast into a cooking school. It might make her feel more comfortable with him, and that, above anything, was what convinced her to say yes.

"Okay, that sounds good." She nibbled the biscuit. "Provided you teach me how to make these biscuits. They melt in your mouth."

He laughed, and for a second, Eppie saw the man beneath the brooding, sad exterior. That man was handsome, smart, and funny—a combination she knew would appeal to her a great deal more than learning to cook breakfast.

"Those I learned from Candice. She specializes in pies and cookies, but oh, how she can make bread and biscuits." He raised one eyebrow. "Are you enjoying the breakfast, then?"

She shook her head. "You know I am, so don't tease me. This is hard enough as it is."

Micah immediately raised his hand in surrender. "You're right. I, well, it's just that I've been waiting to eat breakfast with you for a very long time. We never had a chance to. This is almost a dream come true, as corny as that sounds."

Eppie saw honesty in the depths of his gaze. She trusted her instincts, which told her he was telling the truth.

"I believe you." She realized the odd, uncomfortable feeling that had been plaguing her since she woke up was gone. Micah's cooking, and his honest responses, had chased them away.

Eppie was glad she'd made herself come downstairs. It had brought her to the next stage in her new life.

"I can't tell you how glad I am to hear that." He grinned over his mug. "Maybe tomorrow I'll put out jam and really make you smile."

His silliness made her laugh. He must've been a charming young man before he ended up in Plum Creek. The path between Virginia and Colorado must've been a long, hard one. She wondered just what forces had shaped him into the haunted soul he was now.

Eppie wondered if she would be strong enough to find out.

The rest of breakfast was like time with a friend for Eppie. Before she knew it, the food was gone and he was clearing the table. She wanted to help him, but she felt sleepy and so comfortable at the table.

He came and kissed her on the forehead, surprising her. "You should go upstairs and nap. I'll clean up."

Eppie nodded and left the kitchen, tired, full, and strangely content.

The next week passed by quickly. Eppie was almost happy until she had to leave the house. "I don't want to go." Eppie folded her arms across her chest and stared at Micah. "There's no reason for me to go."

He sighed and put his hands on his hips. "We've already talked about this. Madeline wants you to sign the papers giving you half the house. You never had a chance, since you were in a coma, but she did give this house to both of us."

It had been eight days since Eppie and Micah had made love in the sunlight. She'd tried to forget it, pretend it never happened, but each night her dreams were full of Micah and the feeling of his body on hers. They had begun sharing breakfast together, alone, talking as friends would. He even kept to his promise and was teaching her to cook.

She looked forward to each morning with a spring in her step. Micah was charming, intelligent, and very tempting. She shook off the thoughts with effort and focused on what he was saying about the house.

Eppie didn't feel comfortable taking half a mansion from anyone, even if she'd been her best friend. She had no idea what the house was worth, but by her estimation, it was entirely too much to give to anyone.

"I can't accept it. It's too much, Micah. I mean, look at it. She'd be giving away so much." She pointed to the ornate rug in the parlor. "That rug alone must cost more than an entire house."

"I don't know how much it cost, but I agree, there's a lot of money in this house. It doesn't matter because, you see, Madeline can't live here anymore." He sat down and took her hands in his, rubbing his thumbs on the backs of hers. It was a pleasant, arousing sensation, and she decided she liked it.

"Why not?"

"Her father was not a nice man. In fact, he was a bit of an ogre if the stories she tells are any indication. He treated her like an object, someone to do his bidding and keep his house. That's nothing compared to how he treated the people of Plum Creek. Rufus Brewster kept the town in his pocket and didn't hesitate to do whatever he had to to keep his money and his power safe." Micah toed the carpet. "This was his, all of this was his, except for the sitting room. Madeline wanted to start her life over when she married Teague. She wanted to give us both something and this was it."

"Why couldn't she have given us something smaller, like a cabin?" Eppie understood Madeline's motivation a bit better, but that didn't mean she had to like it.

Micah chuckled. "It's what she had to give. Believe me, Madeline is worth millions. Giving away this house isn't going to bankrupt her."

Eppie'd had no idea what her new friend was worth, and just the word millions boggled her mind a bit. She couldn't even imagine how much money that was, much less count it and keep it straight.

"So we need to go to the bank and sign the papers?" Eppie wasn't happy about it, but she knew when to retreat.

Micah smiled. "Yes, and I promise we'll go together, all four of us. No one will dare mess with Teague. He'll scowl them to death."

Eppie chuckled at the thought, but in her heart she was scared. Matilda Webster and her cronies had already come by once and treated her as if she were dirt beneath their feet. She wondered how other people in town would treat her when they found out she owned half a mansion.

Maybe it's what she needed to get some confidence back, to feel more in control of where her life was going. Even though her instincts were telling her to run in the other direction, she decided to go anyway.

"Okay, I'll go." Her stomach quivered, yet she didn't change her mind.

It took them an hour to get ready for their little outing. Eppie spent time fixing her hair so it didn't stick up every which way. Then she put on in a light yellow dress with some delicate lace around the collar. It was too big, as was everything hanging in her room, but it was clean and, in her opinion, somewhat elegant. She stared at her reflection and decided she was as ready as she'd ever be to face the people of Plum Creek.

When she walked downstairs, she found Miracle jumping around as if she were getting a special treat. Her little face was alight with joy as she danced in circles in the downstairs hallway. The sight of her twirling with her hair flying behind her like banners in the wind made Eppie smile. The child was truly blessed with an abundance of life.

"Miracle, you can't go with us, sweetheart." Micah's words fell like the clapper on a bell on a quiet Sunday morning.

"I go." She nodded and looked up at him with hurt in her gaze.

"No, we're going to the big people bank and there's nothing for you to do there. Miss Candice is already in the kitchen waiting for you to make cookies."

Miracle glanced toward the kitchen, the lure of cookies apparently strong, but then she turned back to her father.

"I go."

"No, you can't go today. I promise later we'll take Daisy for a walk down to the river." He patted her head and walked away.

He didn't see her little chin wobble or the betrayal in her eyes. Eppie did and she felt it herself. Somewhere, somehow, Eppie had been left behind and it had hurt quite a lot. She knelt down and got herself eye to eye with Miracle.

"I know you want to come with us, but your Daddy is right, you wouldn't have any fun. Truth is, I don't want to go myself, but I have to. When we get back, I would love to have fresh cookies. It would make me feel better. Do you think you could help Candice get some made?"

Miracle sniffed and nodded. " 'Kay."

"Thank you."

Without warning, the girl hugged Eppie quickly and whispered "I love you" in her ear. Then she stuck her chin in the air and walked past her father without saying good-bye. The pointed exclusion made Madeline chuckle and Teague snort.

"Did you see that?" Micah's mouth fell open. "She deliberately ignored me."

"Serves you right. She's a person, too, even if she is small. You hurt her feelings and didn't apologize." Eppie raised her eyebrows at him. "You'll need to do some groveling, I think."

"Oh, I agree." Madeline tucked her arm into Eppie's. "Nothing like a woman who's been miffed."

"She's not a woman. She's not even three years old, for God's sake." Micah frowned as he opened the door for them.

"Damn good thing you didn't give me daughters." Teague commented as he walked out behind the women.

"Who says?" Madeline sounded as mysterious as she could be.

"Is there something you haven't told me, Maddie?" Teague ran to step next to his wife. "Are you keeping a secret?"

Madeline turned to Eppie and smiled. "I hope you're taking notes, because there is a lot to learn here."

Eppie laughed, a big gut-busting laugh all the way from her toes. She didn't remember doing it before that very moment and it felt almost as wonderful as being with Micah. But not quite.

Micah fell into step beside Eppie and offered her his arm. Madeline patted her shoulder.

"Go on, take his arm. You two deserve to have the pleasure of a walk together." She narrowed her gaze at Micah. "Walk slowly. She's still recovering."

"Yes, ma'am." Micah saluted and Teague cursed under his breath.

"Don't mind them, Eppie. Ex-soldiers will always be at odds, no matter how long it's been since the war." Madeline leaned her head on her husband's shoulder as they walked. "That doesn't mean we can't ignore them, though."

Eppie smiled and slipped her arm into Micah's. It felt comfortable, even natural, to do so. They were just the right height to walk together and they fell into a natural rhythm. Perhaps that's what happened down by the river. It was meant to happen.

At least that's what she wanted to believe. If she were honest with herself, she still couldn't believe what she'd done, had allowed Micah to do. Just thinking about it made her body heat up, and perspiration popped out all over. It would probably be better to think about walking through town and going to the bank. At least that wouldn't arouse her.

They were almost to the end of the street and Eppie's amusement at her own body's reaction to Micah ended as soon as she spotted the street corner. Petals from the flowering trees floated down around them like a rain of white. It felt as if the tree were either welcoming them or warning them.

As soon as the buildings of Plum Creek came into view, Eppie wanted to turn around and go back. The house might not be home, but it was familiar and safe. Where they were headed was anything but safe. She felt almost sick to her stomach when she saw the church steeple.

That was where the awful minister must preach his fire-and-brimstone sermons. She'd do well to avoid that man for the rest of her life. It was bad enough to think he'd visit the house, she sure as heck didn't want to go to his church. God only knows what the man would do to hold her up as an example of a sinner.

It was four in the afternoon, so the streets weren't as busy as they probably were in the morning. That was at least, a blessing. Some people stared at the two couples, while others were polite enough to say hello. Eppie cursed inwardly when she saw Matilda Webster and her two blond cohorts cross the street to intercept them.

She hoped she didn't embarrass herself or the others.

"Madeline Brewster, while I live and breathe, I'm surprised to see you back in Plum Creek." Matilda smiled prettily for Teague. "And you're here with your convict again. How nice."

"Matilda, for one thing, Teague is my husband, therefore my name is O'Neal, not Brewster. Secondly, he's not a convict. As a matter of fact, your husband is the only convict I know." She nodded to the other two women. "Virginia, Beatrice, lovely to see you."

Madeline didn't miss a step and Eppie was not only impressed, she decided she wanted to be like her new friend when she got her life in order. The looks on the faces of the three blond witches were priceless. When Matilda caught Eppie looking at her, the expression of astonishment turned to malice.

"I see you brought your slave and her lover out for fresh air. Nice how their half-breed daughter can now have two parents to keep her out of trouble." With that she turned and walked away, leaving Eppie in pieces on the wood-planked sidewalk.

Eppie stopped, her breath caught somewhere in her throat. Micah put his arm around her shoulder and leaned in.

"Don't listen to that bitch, Eppie. She's unhappy because her husband is a thief and a liar. She likes to hurt other people because she hurts all the time." He squeezed her arm. "Nothing she said is the truth."

"Am I a slave?" Eppie gasped out.

"No, darlin' and I don't think you ever were." Micah handed her a handkerchief from his pocket. "I think your mother was freed before you were born. You're a beautiful, wonderful, amazing woman who came into my life four years ago. I thank God every day for it and I'm proud to be your lover."

Eppie felt so overwhelmed by the last two minutes, she allowed him to lead her down the street. Madeline and Teague had gotten quite a ways ahead but weren't walking quickly so they kept pace with them. The outing to the bank was turning out as badly as Eppie had anticipated, unfortunately.

Micah kept his grip tight as they walked and she, for once, was glad to have him there beside her. She thought him weak and dependent, but he just proved he wasn't either of those things. Perhaps all he needed was to be challenged. When

Matilda and her friends had come calling two days earlier, she hadn't allowed them to see Micah. Maybe she should have and they likely wouldn't come back.

Candice had warned her about Mrs. Webster, but Eppie honestly hadn't expected such cruel viciousness from someone. It appeared her short time awake hadn't given her enough experience with the depths to which human beings could sink. Matilda just showed her the bottom of the barrel and Eppie hoped there wasn't another level down.

"Are you okay?" Micah asked after a few minutes.

"I don't know. My heart tells me to turn around and go back to the house, but my head is telling me to keep walking and straighten my shoulders." She sucked in a shaky breath. "Life so far has been a circus with crazy folks popping up left and right. I only hope that nasty minister keeps to his church today."

Micah stopped her. "What nasty minister?"

Too late Eppie realized the things she hadn't told him were ones she probably should have. "He came by to visit the day you, well, took a bath in whiskey. I was outside getting fresh air and he appeared out of nowhere. He's the kind of man of the cloth I plan on avoiding."

"Good, because he's a small-minded bigot with as much mercy and compassion as a rock," Micah nearly snarled. "He's stirred up the town to think of me as the drunk who lives off Madeline's charity. I won't even go into what he's said about Miracle or the fact that he thinks she needs to live with a real family."

It didn't surprise Eppie that the minister had taken it upon himself to judge others, but the fact he'd picked on little Miracle made her furious. The minister would have an earful from her the next time he dared darken their doorstep. If he ever came near Miracle, she didn't know what she'd do, but he'd regret any intervention he proposed.

The anger helped push aside the hurt and the confusion,

allowing Eppie to get control of her emotions before she and Micah got to the bank.

Her first glimpse of the hub of Plum Creek was that of a small town with well-kept buildings and well-swept side-walks. The bank sat at the center, its shiny clean windows gleaming in the late afternoon sun. The name FIRST BANK OF PLUM CREEK was in gold on the windows. Eppie realized she could read the letters and inwardly did a jig of joy.

Teague held the door open and they filed in. The building looked almost as fancy on the inside as the mansion. There was only one customer in the bank at a teller station. The men and women working there were all dressed in white shirts and navy trousers or skirts.

Every one of them stopped what they were doing to stare at the newcomers. Eppie was getting used to being stared at, but it surprised her to have it happen at Madeline's bank.

It still felt odd to call it Madeline's bank. Eppie didn't know the woman owned half of the town, and was still as down-to-earth and friendly as she could be. Most rich people were more selective in their friends and certainly didn't give away mansions to others without expecting something in return.

Obviously Eppie was much more cynical than she realized.

Madeline stepped up to the first teller's window. "Good afternoon, David. It's nice to see you again."

"Miss Brew—I mean Mrs. O'Neal. I didn't know you were in town." He was a young man, probably no older than Eppie, with jet-black hair and friendly eyes.

"Yes, I arrived a week ago. I'm here to sign the deed over to Mr. Spalding and Miss Archer." She pointed to the closed door in the corner. "Is Mr. Long in there?"

"Yes, ma'am. He's been working on balancing the week's ledgers." David turned to look at the rest of them, and when his gaze landed on Eppie, he gaped at her. "Miss Eppie? Is that you?"

Damn, another person she was supposed to know. "Yes, it's me." She didn't know how long she could pretend to recognize folks before someone found out her secret.

His exclamation caught the attention of the other tellers and they stepped over, along with the gray-haired man who was there as a customer. Exclamations and genuine friendliness replaced the suspicion and malice she'd encountered from other citizens of Plum Creek.

As near as she could tell, three of the tellers remembered her, the lady teller had heard about her from the others, and the older man had known her since she'd come to town.

"The Lord surely did send his blessings down on you, Miss Eppie. Madeline and her kin have kept you safe so you could heal." The man patted her hand. "It's a miracle, just like that little girl. I've kept you in my prayers."

Madeline smiled at him. "Horace Brindle, you are so kind. I know Eppie appreciates your prayers."

Eppie nodded. "Yes, I certainly do appreciate your prayers. Thank you so much, Mr. Brindle."

Strange looks and raised eyebrows told Eppie these folks had noticed she sounded different, too. There was no way she could stop that. She didn't know how she was supposed to sound; she could only speak as she knew how.

Madeline took the situation in hand, again. "Thank you all for your good wishes." She herded Teague, Micah and Eppie toward the office.

The tellers all walked back to their positions and Eppie breathed a sigh of relief. She was glad to find someone in town who thought well of her, but it was still a bit too much to absorb all at once.

Madeline opened the door and stepped in. A tall man with spectacles and a balding head stood and smiled.

"Madeline, there you are." He held out his hand and shook hers. "I have everything ready." He glanced at everyone else. "Micah, Teague, good to see you. Eppie, I'm sorry we haven't met, but I've heard a great deal about you."

His friendliness was genuine as far as Eppie could tell. The bank, which should be the most serious place in town, was turning out to be the warmest and most welcoming.

"Thank you, Mr. Long."

"Why don't you all sit and we'll get these papers signed." There were only two chairs in front of the desk.

"Eppie, sit down with me. Let's get your half of the deed signed." Madeline smiled as she sat down.

As she sat down, Eppie's agreement to come to the bank suddenly seemed like a bad idea when she caught sight of the pen and inkwell waiting for her. What if she didn't know how to write? She obviously knew how to read, but could she write? Her mouth turned cotton dry and her face felt very hot.

She glanced at Micah and he frowned at her. Likely her face reflected the sheer panic racing through her. The bank manager was laying out the papers on the desk and Eppie's breath caught in her throat.

"Mr. Long, could you step outside for two minutes please?" Micah smiled tightly. "I need to ask Madeline a couple of questions."

"Of course." Mr. Long exited the office without question, closing the door behind him.

Micah squatted down beside Eppie. "What's wrong?"

Madeline swiveled around and turned a concerned gaze on Eppie.

"I don't know if I can write." She hated how scared her voice sounded or the fact that she hadn't even considered whether or not she could sign the papers. Micah had convinced her to come, or rather, she had convinced herself. Now it could be a disaster, an embarrassing, stupid disaster.

"Oh, honey, I didn't think of that." Madeline took Eppie's

cold hand in hers. "You did know how to write before the accident. Many nights we read books to each other."

Eppie wanted to believe her, but until she tested her abilities, she couldn't. "Let me try before Mr. Long comes back in."

Madeline pointed at the corner of the desk. "Micah, get a piece of paper so she can practice her signature."

Micah stood and set a blank piece of paper on the desk in front of Eppie. She was surprised to see his hand tremble as he handed her the pen and popped the inkwell open. Eppie took a deep breath and accepted the pen.

She knew they had to move quickly as the minutes were ticking by, but she was afraid.

"It's okay, Eppie, if you can't. We'll leave and come back when you can." Micah smiled and she remembered just how dangerous he was to her equilibrium.

She closed her eyes and thought about how her signature should look. *Elizabeth Archer.* When she opened her eyes, she dipped the pen in the ink and tapped off the excess ink. With a deep breath, she gave her mind permission to write.

Nothing happened.

She thought about the letters in her name, thrilled to realize she knew what letters were in the name. That meant she could read, but could she write?

Again, she put the pen on the paper and told herself to sign it.

Nothing happened.

Eppie wanted to cry and scream at the same time. It was so frustrating to have half a memory. Micah rubbed her back and kept silent while Madeline put her hand over Eppie's. None of it helped her feel better.

"You're trying too hard. Just relax and don't think about what you're doing. Just do it."

Eppie would try one more time and then give up. Another

day, another time would have to work. When the nib touched the paper, she let her mind go blank and suddenly her hand started moving, and so did the pen.

It was shaky, but readable. Eppie had signed her name.

Strange how something so simple could make her feel so joyous. It was as if she'd won a prize for something extraordinary. Madeline clapped her hands and Micah kissed her cheek. Even Teague grunted.

"You did it." Madeline let out a big sigh. "I knew you could. Teague, please ask Mr. Long to come back in."

When he came back in there was a flurry of papers put in front of her and Eppie realized she could read very well. Even though this house was a gift, she read through each of the papers before signing them. By the time they were done, the sun had sunk low on the horizon and the rest of the tellers had left the bank.

Eppie was in a bit of a daze as she walked through the empty lobby. She owned half a house, *her*, a blank nobody without a past or a memory, was now a house owner. It was unreal to her although Madeline talked with Micah as if nothing amazing had just happened, as if Elizabeth Archer had not just been born.

She stopped in her tracks, stunned by the notion. By signing her name she'd become a real person, someone with property, a woman named Elizabeth Archer.

"I don't want to be Eppie anymore." Her pronouncement made everyone stop at the door.

Micah looked confused while Madeline looked shocked. It shocked her, too—she'd been floundering in a sea of uncertainty and confusion about who she was and in an instant, the confusion cleared.

"Elizabeth. Please call me Elizabeth." She smiled and a great weight lifted from her shoulders.

"Are you sure? You once told me that name made you

cringe whenever you heard it." Madeline walked toward her with a frown. "We'll do whatever you feel comfortable with."

"That's what I want. It's who I want to be."

"Elizabeth's a nice name," Teague nodded. "I had an aunt named Elizabeth and she was a right fine lady."

Micah cocked his head and stared at her, a hundred emotions fluttering in his gaze. He held out his hand.

"Let's go home, Elizabeth."

Pure joy flooded her heart at his immediate acceptance and she took his hand, then stepped out into the late-day light, a new person, a real person.

Micah lay in bed, staring at the ceiling and wondering who it was he was in love with. She looked like Eppie, but she spoke and acted like Elizabeth, whoever that was. He understood to some extent why she needed to grab hold of her life and proclaim who she was, but she was so different. It confused him and made his already damaged soul even more adrift. Even his damn chest hurt when he thought about how she could walk out the door and leave them behind without a backward glance. After all, she didn't know him, or Miracle. They were strangers to her, even if he'd held her in his arms again.

He loved her. That, fortunately, hadn't changed, and God willing, it wouldn't. She was fated to be his and that was that. He wouldn't accept a different outcome.

Elizabeth was Eppie and Eppie was Elizabeth. He just didn't know which one would agree to marry him. He'd been waiting for years to make her his wife, hoping and waiting and even praying. A significant feat for him since he'd given up on God long ago.

Things were simpler when Eppie had been in the coma. He had a routine and things went along the same every day. Boring but predictable. However much he'd hoped, wished and wanted her to awaken, the last thing he wanted was to lose what he had.

Yet that's exactly what happened.

The door to his room opened slowly and he waited for Miracle to appear. She would frequently jump into bed with him when she had a bad dream. Ever since Eppie woke up, Miracle had snuck into his bed at least half a dozen times.

He propped himself up on an elbow when the door opened wider. However, the little moppet didn't appear.

Eppie did.

His heart kicked into a gallop and a flush spread from the top of his head to his feet. He lay down, regretting the fact he slept nude. He didn't want to scare her, but she was entering his room uninvited, and his body reacted.

She never needed an invitation. She could sleep there every night and he'd never complain.

He wasn't sure if he should play possum and see what she did, or be honest and let her know he was awake. She stopped in the doorway and waited, the only sounds the small sigh from her mouth and Micah's blood rushing past his ears. He thought for a moment she'd step into the room, but when she started to turn, Micah made his decision.

"Wait."

She jumped a bit, but she didn't leave.

"Please, don't go."

He saw her hand tighten on the knob in the shadows. Micah took the proverbial leap off the cliff and opened his arms. If he didn't, he might never see her come through the bedroom door again. He couldn't stand the thought of that possibility.

"I know you don't remember me or anything about what happened before you went into the coma. I'm not going to force you into anything you don't want to do, but I just want you to know that I will wait for you." He held out one shaking hand. "I only ask that you give us a chance. You found joy in my arms once already, let's start again." His heart ached with the knowledge if she walked away, there was likely no chance he'd ever get Eppie in his arms again.

Time stopped for a moment and then she closed the door. Micah could have done a jig; instead he pulled the covers back and climbed out of bed. His body tightened with arousal, hope, and downright disbelief as he approached her. She didn't move, just stood by the door, but he could hear her panting. Her scent washed over him, and the moment was so sweet, he never wanted it to end.

When he held out his hand, even in the shadows, he saw it trembling. Eppie might have been hesitant when she came into the room, but she put her hand in his immediately. He let out a sigh of relief and threaded his fingers with hers—they fit together perfectly. Micah didn't want to push her too fast, too soon, even if he felt as though he'd explode with waiting, wanting. He led her to the bed and sat down, controlling his breathing and his rampant erection with monumental effort.

"Please sit."

He could sense her hesitation, but she sat next to him. The warmth from her body reached out to his and the chill he'd felt for weeks suddenly disappeared. She was there, right there at his side. That was something to celebrate.

His voice was low enough that only she could hear him. "I've missed you."

She blew out a breath. "I couldn't stop myself from coming here. I told myself to stay in bed, but I had a dream."

"Was I in your dream?"

"Yes, and it wasn't the first time." She let out a painful chuckle. "I think my body remembers you."

Micah's heart slammed into his ribs. Her body remembered him? "I can't tell you how glad I am." An understatement, to be sure. "Will you let me touch you, Elizabeth?"

He stroked the back of her hand with his thumb and felt a tremble race across her skin.

"Yes." Her whisper was so soft he barely heard it, but it echoed through his heart loud and clear.

He leaned in and pressed his nose to her neck, breathing in her unique scent. She sat unmoving, but goosebumps raced down her skin. Smiling, he kissed her neck and collarbone, running his tongue along the little niche. She tasted of woman, of love, of pure sensuality.

His hand ran down her thigh and back, nudging her knees open. Each pass brought the nightdress higher and higher until he brushed the soft curls protecting her core. She started in surprise, but didn't pull away.

"Mmmm, you taste good." He lapped at her small ear, nibbling on the delicate shell and blowing softly.

"You feel good." She leaned forward and before Micah knew what she was doing, she'd removed her nightdress and sat just as naked as he.

His dick yowled in triumph, practically dancing in pain as it caught wind of the woman who excited him like no other. He felt amost primal as if he would throw her down and fuck her until her eyes crossed. However, he knew that wasn't the best idea. He'd seduced her, shown her the pleasures between a man and a woman, down by the river.

This time, he wanted her to participate.

"Touch me." He took her hand and placed it on his throbbing erection.

As if she still remembered what he liked, her hand closed around him and tugged. When her thumb landed on the head, she flicked the tender spot as she'd always done. Micah sucked in a much-needed breath and focused on not coming on her hand.

"Feels good?"

He let out a pained chuckle. "Any better and we'd be done already."

Her husky laugh made every small hair on his body stand up. "You're beautiful to touch."

Micah hissed through his teeth as she added another hand to the fun and cupped his balls. So good his eyes crossed in rapture, pulses of arousal radiating from his dick. "Your touch is pretty amazing."

"So is yours."

He'd forgotten about her pleasure momentarily. An unacceptable situation—Micah could still claim to be a gentleman. He cupped her breasts, the nipples begging for attention. She leaned into his touch, and he obliged by teasing, pinching and caressing until she moaned, although he was having trouble concentrating because of her talented hands.

"I must taste," he managed to get out. "They are gifts from the gods."

She chuckled. "You've been reading too many books."

He laid her back on the bed with trembling hands, eager as a schoolboy with his first woman. Yet, she was the last woman he would be with, the only woman in his heart.

His mouth closed around one pert nipple even as her hand continued to pleasure his dick. He licked, nibbled and sucked at her glorious breasts, punctuating each swipe of his tongue with a pinch on the opposite nipple.

"Micah, I need more." Eppie didn't ask, she demanded. It was a small window into the woman who used to be in his arms.

"Happy to oblige you my lady."

He nudged her legs open, finding her cunt wet and hot enough to make his breath catch. She was so perfect, so ready for him. Micah almost forgot his own name when his staff slid against her moist folds.

"Ah, God, yes." She breathed. "That's what I need."

If he had a thought in his head, he would have been overjoyed to hear Eppie needed his touch. However, he focused instead on pleasuring both of them.

Slowly he entered her, inch by glorious inch, until he was firmly embedded deep within. Bolts of pure ecstasy rippled through him and he had to pause before moving, or risk losing control completely. His heart thudded so hard, no doubt the neighbors half a mile away heard it.

"Move."

He managed a strangled chuckle at her command. Yet he obeyed. His stroke was long and intense, pulling all the way out of her before thrusting back in again. He latched on to her breast again, even as his hand settled between them to heighten her gratification.

It was a symphony of flesh, conducted for the sole purpose of mutual satisfaction. Micah knew a moment where the world around them stopped, the experience so exquisite, even time had to cease. Sweet, delicious and insatiable, he could feel her velvet walls clench around him.

Micah held onto his sanity by a slim thread as his balls tightened. When he bit her nipple, she bucked beneath him, her breath coming in gasps. Her heated core became one with his staff, catapulting him into the most intense orgasm of his life. Wave after wave of rapture crashed over him as he thrust into her. Her name sprang from his lips as their bodies fused in a melting heap of sexual energy.

Micah had no idea how long he was lost in the throes of passion. When a final shudder of contentment left him, he rolled to his side, pulling her close. Her breath puffed against his chest as their hearts thudded against each other, the ribs absorbing the rhythm of an ancient dance.

"To think I dreamed of this. It was definitely not the same." She squeezed his arm.

"I'm glad to know I can surpass your imaginings." Micah kissed the top of her head, amazed to have her still in his arms. The dark night had proven to be the light in his life.

She sighed and he sensed she was going to say something

he didn't want to hear. "Micah, what happens between us in the dark shouldn't happen again."

"Why not?"

"Because we aren't married and we haven't even begun to sort out our relationship." Eppie sat up, leaving him cold and alone on the sheets as a crack appeared in his heart.

"That's not true, and you know it. We're sorting it out right here." He couldn't lose her, not after that experience.

"That's not what I mean. There has always been a physical tie between us." She looked down at him, the moon turning her into a blue goddess. "I can't think when I'm in your arms."

"And I can't survive without being in yours."

He knew it was the wrong thing to say when she jumped out of bed. She pulled the nightdress back on, then stood for a moment, seeming to catch her breath.

"I can't be who you want me to be." She leaned forward and kissed him quick. "You're in love with a ghost."

Before he could answer, she left the room, leaving him to his self-pity. He pressed a fist to his aching heart, wishing he had the power to make her memory return, knowing she was right.

He was in love with a ghost.

Chapter Seven

For the next week, Micah and Eppie tiptoed around each other. Their morning breakfast time had been filled with uncomfortable silence. Micah wanted their easy camaraderie back, but Eppie seemed to be farther away than ever.

He watched her over the coffee cup.

"Stop staring at me." She nibbled on the biscuit with jam. "It makes me feel odd."

"Sorry, I don't mean to stare." He swirled the coffee in his cup. "I miss you."

She let out a long sigh. "I'm sitting right in front of you."

"You know what I mean. Ever since you came to my room—"

She shushed him. "There are little ears and big ears in this house."

He lowered his voice to a whisper. "Ever since you came to my room and we made love, you've been hiding from me."

Eppie opened her mouth, then closed it. She seemed to deflate in front of his eyes. "You're right."

"I am? You've been hiding from me?" He had suspected it was true, but to hear her admit it made it slam into his heart like a horse kick.

"Yes, I have." She met his gaze. "You scare me, Micah. I

want to find out who I am before I make a decision about who I want to be with for the rest of my life."

"I'm not forcing you into anything." He sounded petulant, but couldn't seem to stop himself. "You came to me and dare I say, you enjoyed it immensely."

"Dammit, Micah, that's not what I meant and you know it." She whispered harshly. "You're a forceful personality, whether or not you admit it. I can't think when I'm around you."

"You're afraid." His accusation made her eyes widen.

"Probably true, but you make me afraid. You're too much." She pinched the bridge of her nose.

Micah felt her slipping through his fingers and he panicked. He rose to his feet and watched as he threw away the relationship he'd built with her over the last few weeks.

"Then I should leave you alone for good." He threw the coffee cup into the sink, splashing coffee all over the window like brown streaks of blood. "I apologize for my rude behavior, Miss Archer. I won't bother you anymore."

Before Eppie could answer, Micah left the kitchen. He needed to go somewhere and lick his wounds. He obviously had trouble being patient and recognizing how much others were suffering. Selfish bastard that he was, Micah wanted Eppie back in his arms every day, not once in a while when she wanted to.

If the situation grew any worse, he might have to leave for a while, and give her all the time she needed without him. Perhaps he should have done that three years ago and he wouldn't have a broken heart again.

Micah headed for the parlor, ignoring anything and everything. It was time to quench his thirst.

Eppie went looking for him just before supper. She hadn't looked for him all day because of his behavior earlier. Micah had been sarcastic and mean, hurting her as he apparently was hurting. It angered her, and she'd been avoiding him all day.

Yet when Miracle came to her and asked where Daddy was, Eppie grew concerned. He wasn't the type of father to leave his daughter alone and she was scared for him.

Eppie had a feeling she knew where he'd be, and unfortunately, she was right. The parlor stank of whiskey, sweat and man, making her nose wrinkle. From what she was told by Madeline, he used to drink all the time, losing himself in a bottle more than not. However, she'd only seen him drunk once since she'd awakened from the coma.

Until now.

He was sprawled on the settee, arms and legs splayed every which way. A soft snore told her he was asleep. Eppie didn't want to feel for him, but she did. He'd come to mean something to her, as a friend and as someone who obviously cared a great deal for her.

Even if he did know how to make her angry.

Either way, he was done for the day and she wasn't about to even attempt to move him. With a sigh, she took the afghan from the wingback chair and covered him with it. He shifted in his sleep and curled into the back of the cushions.

"Eppie," he breathed.

She knew he was asleep, that he couldn't know she was standing there, yet her name on his lips sent a chill up her spine. Earlier she'd been honest with him when she said he was too much. He was so intense most of the time, Eppie didn't know how to react. Apparently he was dreaming of her in his drunken state.

She didn't know whether to be flattered or scared.

Instead, she did what she'd gotten good at. She fled the room, leaving him alone, lost in a whiskey cloud.

It had been a few days since the fight in the kitchen, since Micah had gotten drunk and woken up with the taste of old

THE REDEMPTION OF MICAH   125

shoe in his mouth and Eppie on his mind. Since then she'd been polite but so distant and cold, he could feel the ice coming off her. He'd hurt her and he owed her an apology. However, before he could find her, Micah watched as a carriage pulled up to the house with a dapper man inside. Doctor Carmichael walked out to greet him and the two shook hands vigorously. He couldn't hear what they discussed, but the stranger gestured to the bright blue sky.

Micah couldn't put his finger on it, but he knew something was different about the man. He was tall and broad-shouldered with a bowler hat perched on his head. His hair was dark and cut quite short and, although Micah certainly wasn't a man who noticed men's looks, strikingly handsome. It appeared the world descended on the house and Micah had a feeling in his gut he wasn't going to like it.

They walked up to the house together, heads bowed as they talked. Micah's stomach clenched like a fist the closer they got to the house. Whoever the stranger was, Micah knew deep down, he wasn't going to like him. More than likely, he was a Yankee like Teague.

While Teague had his good qualities, like loving Madeline the way he did, this man had all the marks of a rich city man come west.

"Who is that?" Madeline appeared beside him and he jumped a country mile.

"Jesus, did you have to scare me?" he snapped.

Her eyes widened. "My apologies, Micah, I didn't know I needed to announce myself to walk in the room. It isn't as if I tiptoe, for pity's sake."

Micah blew out a breath. "Please forgive me, Madeline. I don't have to tell you how strained things are right now."

She squeezed his shoulder. "I know, and I hope you also know that you can talk to me anytime. I will always be there for you."

Micah nodded, his throat tight with the love he had for his friend. "Thank you."

"She's very angry with you."

He sighed. "I know that. I also know I need to apologize, and I intend to, as soon as I can find her."

"Good, you two need to make peace. I can see your hearts are meant to be together." Her eyes looked glossy with tears as she wiped them away. "Enough of that now, let's get back to the stranger. Who is he?" She looked out the parlor window again, but the two men were gone.

"I don't know. Let's go find out." He turned to leave with Madeline on his heels.

They found the men in the front hallway talking to Eppie. Her face was lit with excitement and a broad smile. It was the first time in quite a while he'd seen her smile and it knocked the wind out of him. Particularly since it was directed at the tall, handsome stranger.

"It's wonderful to meet you, Doctor Lawson." She held out her hand and his almost swallowed her smaller one. "Welcome to Plum Creek."

Doctor Lawson?

"Brian surprised me by coming all the way out here from New York, but I can say I'm pleased to have him here." Doctor Carmichael's head bobbed on his thin neck. "He's the best in his field, someone whom I've consulted with on numerous occasions."

Micah watched, a stranger in his own home, as they talked and ignored him completely. Not even Eppie acknowledged his presence, and a red haze descended over him. She had obviously finished with him and found another man to take his place in her bed.

It had been hard enough to have her, yet allow her the freedom to leave him. Now it seemed his worst fears were coming to fruition. Panic threaded through him, but before he could open his mouth, Madeline put her arm through his as he shook with the fury of his situation.

"Gentlemen." Her commanding tone got their attention quickly.

Both men swiveled their gazes to Madeline.

"Good morning, Madeline. This is my colleague from New York, Doctor Brian Lawson." Dr. Carmichael introduced them with a smile on his face. "I had wired him for a consultation, but he surprised me by coming out here."

Dr. Lawson's smile was anything but shy. "I'm pleased to meet the famous Mrs. O'Neal. I've heard amazing things about you, madam." His clipped speech confirmed Micah's suspicion that the man was definitely a Yankee through and through.

Micah's gut roiled with instant dislike and hostility. There wasn't a specific reason, it was just the way Lawson spoke, looked and the way he stood too close to Eppie. Envy, anger, and hatred argued with each other to see which one would win. He'd been right, the man was there to replace him. An irrational, yet totally logical conclusion to his foolish mind.

"This is my good friend Micah Spalding." Madeline turned to him and pulled him closer.

"Mr. Spalding." Dr. Lawson inclined his head with nary a hair out of place. "How do you do?"

Micah sought Eppie's gaze and she looked away, which is when anger won the battle within him.

"I did much better before you got here, Yankee." His voice had sunk down to a growl, and the anger felt good; more than good—it felt great. "Forgive me if I don't jump up and down with joy to see another doctor here to tell us she can't remember anything."

Madeline released his arm and turned to frown fiercely at him. "Micah, Dr. Lawson is a guest in this house."

"I don't care if he's the fucking president, I didn't ask him to come here and I sure as hell don't want him here." Once the anger was set loose, Micah felt a black wave hovering, ready to consume him in a self-destructive whirlpool.

Eppie's expression hardened and disappointment was clear in her eyes. "Micah, Dr. Lawson came to help and he's traveled a great distance."

"I can't listen anymore. Ever since you woke up, the world got turned on its head and every damn day, you get farther and farther away from me. Now you have someone to turn to." He threw up his hands, tasting bitter freedom on his tongue. "I'm done fighting. I think it's time I thought about me for the first time in four years."

He pushed passed them, giving Dr. Lawson the Perfect a good shove as he stormed toward the door. The silence behind him was louder than the sound of his heart slamming against his chest. He wanted to shout, cry, and rail at the heavens, but he kept walking. Damn it all, he needed to find a place where he belonged, because it sure as hell wasn't in that mansion.

Fortunately or not, Teague wasn't in the carriage house, so Micah was able to saddle one of the horses and ride out without speaking to anyone. He had no clothes, no food, not even a hat, but he turned toward the mountain, toward his cabin.

It felt freeing to leave it all behind for once, to not think about anything but survival. Two hours later, when his cabin in the mountains came into view, he realized there was one person he left behind that he shouldn't have.

Miracle.

"Where's Daddy?" The child's chocolate eyes looked up at Eppie with bewilderment.

"He had to go away for a little while." She certainly didn't like lying to the little girl, but since she had no idea where Micah was or when he'd be back, she didn't know what else to do.

"Back soon?" Miracle was pulling on her white nightgown and her words were muffled in the cotton.

Eppie wished she knew the answer to that question. For the entire day Miracle had peppered everyone with questions about her father. If Micah were there, Eppie would have no qualms about kicking his ass from one end of Colorado to the other. The way he'd treated Doctor Lawson appalled her. Even if he'd been jealous or confused, there was no excuse for the hostility.

Madeline had tried to smooth things over and was the perfect hostess, while Eppie fumed about Micah's behavior. Other than telling her she was healthy, but thin and suffering from muscle loss and the other ills from lying in bed for nearly three years, every test that Dr. Carmichael had run had been inconclusive in determining the cause of her memory loss. She was glad to see Dr. Lawson, since her own doctor had been telling her about him for the last four days.

He was a wunderkind in New York, the most sought-after physician in the medical community. Brilliant, handsome, and gifted, Dr. Lawson could have any patient or client he wanted and he'd chosen to make the two-thousand-mile journey to Colorado to see her.

She had been excited until Micah threw a tantrum, then the rest of the day had a pall over it she couldn't shake. Even the delicious supper Candice prepared with apple pie had tasted like sawdust to Eppie. She couldn't decide exactly what she was feeling. Underneath the insane reaction to Dr. Lawson, she'd sensed Micah was hurting. It had been there in his gaze, and she'd turned away from it, unwilling to be brought into his anger. It was unfair of him to put her in that position and he knew it. This wasn't about him, this was about her getting well and trying to get her memory back.

Micah had turned it into a selfish contest. She'd felt a simmering anger toward him since he'd stormed off, yet she was also worried about him. He'd been gone half the day and she had no idea where he was. Madeline wasn't talking, other than to say to give him time to calm down. Teague frowned and threatened to find him and teach him a lesson in manners.

Eppie just wanted him back in the house, to make sure he was okay. Regardless of what she'd forgotten about their relationship, she certainly remembered every moment since she'd awoken. They'd been intimate together twice and every second of those moments replayed themselves over and over in her dreams.

He was kind, gentle, and awkward, and from what she'd seen, a devoted father. His daughter, *their* daughter, blinked up at her like a baby owl, confused and alone. Eppie's heart turned over and something inside her opened up wide, embracing the idea of being a mother.

She squatted down and scooped the girl into her arms. "How about I tuck you into bed."

Miracle snuggled her head into the crook of Eppie's neck as if she'd done it a thousand times. " 'Kay."

Trusting and sweet, Miracle was so easy to love that Eppie knew her heart had already been captured by the precocious moppet. Miracle's small body was warm against her, a natural weight she could get used to. Eppie breathed in the smell of soap and little girl. Being around a child was a new experience, of that she was certain; however, it was fast becoming very familiar.

As she stepped into Miracle's room and walked toward the small canopied bed, Eppie had a flash of another room, another time with a blue bedspread and sunshine. She lost her balance as the floor moved beneath her feet. Miracle grabbed hold of her neck and hung on like a burr.

Eppie steadied herself by grabbing the bedpost, but she kept a firm grip on the girl. Had it been a memory of another place she'd lived? Or perhaps she had another life somewhere and didn't remember. Her stomach flip-flopped and she felt the supper she'd forced herself to eat threaten to return for an encore.

"Mama?" No matter what she'd been told, Miracle still called Eppie Mama. This time it was exactly what she needed to chase away the dizziness and plant her feet firmly on the ground.

"Sorry about that. I lost my balance." She tried to sound silly, as if it was a nonsense moment, but it was anything but.

As Miracle fussed with her covers and her yarn-haired doll, Eppie tried to recall what she'd remembered in detail. It wasn't an easy task because it had only been a split second. She knew for certain it wasn't in this house because the room had been much smaller and there had been a window with a golden field behind it, not the bright greenery that surrounded Plum Creek.

She was anxious to talk about it with someone and the first person that came to mind was Micah. Strange that with two physicians in the house ready and willing to assist her with whatever she was suffering from, she wanted the crazy, sad-eyed man who'd found his way into her heart.

Miracle was watching her, for how long Eppie didn't know. "I ready."

Eppie leaned over and kissed her soft, plump cheek. "Good night, Miracle."

" 'Night, Mama." She planted a small wet kiss on Eppie's cheek. "Love you."

It was the first time Eppie had put Miracle to bed, tucked her in, and made sure she was safe. Although she hadn't realized the magnitude of the occasion, when she looked down at the toddler who trusted her, Eppie's eyes prickled with tears. She had been given a gift in this child and she fully intended to hold on to that gift with both hands.

She now understood why Micah had chosen her name. Miracle was truly a miracle.

* * *

Micah found the last few years had turned his cabin into a haven for critters of all varieties. There were so many different kinds of shit, he could barely count them. His impulsive flight from the house had put him up on the mountain for at least the night, so he had to make it livable.

After chasing out the raccoons, mice, and squirrels, he used a broom to get out the worst of the dirt and muck. Bugs, of course, were another matter. They scattered and ran into every corner. At least the furniture was still solid, just dusty and musty.

He'd built the cabin into the side of a hill beneath the wide arms of the evergreens that populated the Colorado mountains. If someone didn't know the cabin was there, they likely wouldn't see it. The trees had grown some, so things looked different but the same. Micah had no trouble finding it, however. It was the only thing in the world, besides Miracle, that truly belonged to him.

The two small windows were caked with grime and the sink had apparently been used as an outhouse for the woodland creatures, because the piss had eaten away the wood. After using his pitiful corn broom to take the first layer of dirt off the floor, he'd made enough progress to stay the night. Now he had to figure out what he was going to eat and how he was going to sleep on the bed that was just a frame strung with a wood rope lattice half-eaten by critters.

He had removed all his clothing from the cabin when he'd moved to Plum Creek, but there had been a blanket or two left in the trunk he'd brought west with him. It must've been a well-built trunk, because the mice hadn't gotten in to ruin the contents. Finding the blankets, although they were dirty, made him whoop with glee.

"Aha! I guess I did something right." He pulled the blankets out and opened them up by the open windows to air them. They smelled like a mountain man's socks.

He refused to think about Eppie or Miracle for at least the

next twelve hours. The former had made her choice in trying to find a way to live her life without him, and the latter had been caught in the crossfire. If he allowed himself to wallow in what he'd left behind, Micah knew he'd spend the night killing himself to ride down the mountain.

Instead he stepped outside and pulled at the door until he finally got it closed by kicking a chunk of moss out of the doorjamb. The sounds of the woods surrounded him, soothed him, reminded him why he'd chosen that spot to build his cabin. A peace settled over him that allowed him to simply focus on breathing in and out, ignoring the clamor in his mind and heart.

As he walked down the overgrown path, he remembered there were raspberry bushes down by the creek, or at least there had been three years earlier. At this time of year, they should be loaded with berries, provided the damn birds hadn't eaten all of them.

He took a deep breath, the taste of pine coating his tongue. It was familiar enough to soothe his tension somewhat. When he'd headed for the mountain, it had been blind anger and jealousy driving him. Now that he was there on the hill that had been his home for more than five years, he came to the conclusion it was more than anger. It was instinct to return to that which comforted him.

Ever since he'd lived in the Brewster mansion, Micah had felt as if he didn't belong. Even though Madeline had given it to him, it wasn't his home. He lived there as a permanent guest, he supposed. He'd never said anything to Madeline about his feelings, but nevertheless, he felt more comfortable in a shit-infested cabin than he did in opulent luxury.

Memories of his childhood in Virginia flooded his mind— the fancy parties, the overabundance of wealth and gluttony. His parents had owned a cotton plantation outside Richmond. Life had been full of servants, pressed clothes, too much of anything and everything.

Jesus, his father had even brought a prostitute to the house to take his virginity when he'd been sixteen. At eighteen, he had been full of ideas about his invincibility and his God-given right to be as arrogant as he possibly could.

Then the war began and life as he knew it ceased to exist. However, the hell he'd gone through fighting senseless battles had come to a fiery, bloody end when he'd made it back to Virginia. He'd been half a man and what he discovered took away whatever had been left of his soul.

Micah stopped and leaned against a tree to catch his breath as sweat poured down his face. Why the hell had he started thinking about the war and Virginia? It brought him nothing but agony. In fact he had to bend over to stop himself from vomiting as bile rushed up to his throat.

"Bastard," he spat. "Why the hell people worship You is beyond me."

It was as if coming back to the mountain had made him revert to old habits—cursing at God, brooding over the past, and generally being a miserable hermit. Micah felt himself slipping back into the black hole he'd lived in before meeting Madeline, before falling in love with Eppie.

Eppie.

The thought of the beautiful, strong woman who showed him what it meant to be human made his spiral of self-pity grind to a halt. She'd given him the gift of her love and nearly her life. He'd taken care of her for three years and now that she'd awoken, she left him behind.

Micah pressed a fist to his chest as pain roared through him. He'd lost her, it was that simple. She'd made the choice to move past him and face the future alone. The question was, was he man enough to let her go?

Chapter Eight

Eppie woke with a start, her dreams full of monsters and shadows she didn't know. Her first instinct was to find Micah and talk to him about it, which surprised her. He was never far from her thoughts, and try as she might to ignore it, she was worried about him. She lay in her bed and stared out the window at the crescent moon in the black velvet sky. Micah had been gone less than a day, and she missed him. The ache deep in her chest had been a constant since he left. It surprised her, too.

Her feelings became apparent when she was getting Miracle ready for bed and she saw how much of Micah was in the girl, and not just his wavy brown hair. She had some of his mannerisms and his quirky expressions, and even his words seemed to tumble from the girl's mouth.

Micah had been overwhelming at first, frightening her with the way he hovered and watched her. She'd come to realize he had taken care of her for so long that shifting his focus wasn't going to be an immediate change for him. He had lost himself somewhere along the way, and latching on to her had given him a purpose.

Now that she'd woken from the coma, he'd lost that purpose and didn't know what to do. He'd become more jittery and unpredictable, not that she could predict anything that man was going to do. The way he reacted to Dr. Lawson had not only surprised but confused her. No doubt he was more confused than she was. Maybe that's why he ran.

With a sigh, she climbed out of bed, knowing she wasn't going to sleep any longer. It was hours before dawn and she had nothing to do but think. That could be a dangerous proposition, so she decided to go to the kitchen and have some warm milk. Perhaps a little bit of help could get her to sleep at least a few more hours.

The last person she expected to see in the kitchen was Dr. Lawson. He'd shed his suit jacket, vest and tie, looking more relaxed and casual than she imagined he would. His chocolate brown hair was mussed as if he'd been running his fingers through the waves. A shadow of whiskers peppered his face, which currently wore a surprised look at her appearance.

He had a half-eaten piece of bread in his hand and a glass of milk on the table. A self-deprecating grin crossed his face as he rose to greet her.

"Elizabeth! I didn't expect anyone to be up." He set the bread down on the plate in front of him. "I've been travelling so much I'm afraid eating regularly has been a challenge, and well, I got hungry."

Eppie realized Dr. Lawson was more than a physician, he was a handsome, sexy man. And she noticed it at the same time she realized perhaps Micah had been right to be jealous. While her body rejoiced in joining with Micah, her heart still did not belong to his, and her head told her to keep all options open.

"Understandable. I don't think I've ever experienced a time change like that, but I can imagine it makes your stomach confused." She gestured to the food. "Help yourself. You are a guest and welcome to anything you'd like."

"Anything?" He raised his eyebrows.

Eppie wanted to fall on her behind in shock. Was he flirting with her?

"Within reason, of course." She felt her cheeks heat and her body react to him, just as she had for Micah. Was it just a physical reaction or something more?

"Were you hungry, too?"

She felt upside down and sideways all at once, and very flustered. "I couldn't sleep and thought some warm milk might help."

Then she remembered why she couldn't sleep and knew she shouldn't be there in the dark with a stranger, even if he was a physician. She'd pledged her body to Micah's and owed him more than a passing thought.

"Please let me heat some up for you." Dr. Lawson turned toward the stove, which is when she saw the pan already on the burner and realized he was already drinking warm milk.

"There's no need, Dr. Lawson. The walk downstairs has already tired me out." She felt a meal would be too intimate, and a mistake, which perhaps might lead to even bigger mistakes.

"Brian, please. Call me Brian."

Eppie shifted from foot to foot. "Thank you, but no, I'm going to back to bed."

The mention of bed reminded her of just whose bed she'd been in and whose arms had cradled her. As much as the good-looking doctor tempted her to explore things she hadn't, Eppie backed out of the room. If she had nothing of her memory, she still had honor and integrity.

And she intended to keep it.

"Are you sure?" He smiled then, a slow, lazy smile that likely had made many a woman's pulse flutter.

"I'm very sure."

As she turned to leave the kitchen, he touched her arm. The heat from his skin felt as warm as the fire in the stove.

When she looked up into his face, she realized just how tall the doctor was, and the patch of skin exposed by his unbuttoned shirt made her wonder exactly what he looked like without the shirt entirely. And she stood there in nothing more than a too-large nightdress. Then wanted to kick her own fanny for thinking about it.

"You are a very unique and beautiful woman. I'm excited to be here to help you and I'd like you to think of me as your friend." Those blue eyes of his were soft and honest.

"Thank you. Good night, Dr. Lawson," she answered, before she succumbed to the appeal of the shadows and the man. Not that she didn't trust herself, but she didn't know herself.

"Good night, Elizabeth."

This time when Eppie went upstairs, she didn't bother climbing into bed. Instead she curled up in the chair by her bed and stared out the window until God painted the horizon with pinks and oranges. That's when she'd made the decision to find Micah.

The good thing about being a hermit was there were no people around talking to him.

The bad thing about being a hermit was Micah only had himself for company.

When he woke in the morning, after a nearly sleepless night spent trying to find a remotely comfortable spot on the wool blankets spread on the floor, Micah grumbled to himself for an hour. It was barely dawn and he was already in a foul mood.

His back screamed for mercy when he rose to his feet. Served him right for running off without anything but his pride in his hands. It didn't make him feel better to know it was his fault that he was stuck in the cabin with nothing but dust, scat, two smelly blankets and, of course, his regrets.

His first impulse was to get back on the horse and ride back to Plum Creek, although he'd look like a fool for leaving and returning so quickly.

"You are a fool."

He snorted at his own stupidity and set off to get fresh water to wash up. The smell of the pines was again comforting, but the absence of the two people he loved was glaringly obvious. He missed Eppie and Miracle enough to make his heart ache. He rubbed at his chest to chase away the pain, but it didn't help. Micah's special talent was to run away when things became too much to bear. He'd done it so many times, he'd lost count. This time it might cost him his daughter and the love of his life.

Feeling sorry for himself wasn't going to make the day get any easier, so he tried his best to clear his mind and focus on putting one foot in front of the other. The sky was gray off to the west, which told him a storm was coming in. Since it was two hours down the mountain, it would be a bad idea to leave until the weather had passed.

"Punishing me again, eh?" he snarled at the sky. "You know I will just wait it out."

If the summer storm was strong enough, it might keep him in the cabin until the next day. He needed to get more food than raspberries to last him. Too bad he didn't have anything to shoot a rabbit with, dammit. He had to do everything the hard way.

With a dramatic sigh that would have embarrassed him had anyone heard it, Micah started looking for sticks to build a snare.

"You're not going up there." Teague crossed his arms over his chest and scowled. "I won't allow it."

Eppie didn't want to disrespect her friend's husband, but there was no way she'd accept his pronouncement. "You don't have to allow me to do anything. I've got a brain and a will and therefore, I am going to Micah's cabin whether you like it or not." She crossed her arms and mimicked his stance.

Madeline burst out laughing and it took all of Eppie's concentration not to crack a smile. Teague's eyebrows seemed to draw closer together the harder Madeline laughed.

"It's not funny, Maddie," he snapped.

"Oh, yes it is." Madeline clutched her stomach and wiped at her eyes. "You try to be so forceful and sh-she's so small."

Eppie turned to shake her head at her friend. "I'm not *that* small."

"And I'm not forceful, I'm being practical. She's barely out of a coma three weeks ago and she wants to go gallivanting up the mountain to find that stubborn ass." Teague shook his head. "It's a stupid idea."

"It's not a stupid idea." Madeline stopped laughing. "She wants to talk to him, even if he is a stubborn ass."

"I don't *want* to talk to him, I *need* to talk to him." Eppie had so much she wanted to say, it couldn't wait.

"May I speak?" Dr. Lawson had stood by watching their exchange, his gaze straying to Eppie's every few moments.

"Only if you're going to agree with me." Teague offered.

"Actually I am going to agree with you. I'm sure Dr. Carmichael would as well if he wasn't in town." Dr. Lawson offered her his charming smile, sending a shiver down her spine.

Eppie wasn't about to budge from her original intent to find Micah. "It doesn't matter what any of you think. I'm an adult and I make my own decisions."

"That's true, Elizabeth, but you have to think of your health. You're recovering from trauma and a coma. I firmly believe you should stay here." He put his hand on her shoulder. "At least wait a few more days to give him time to return."

He honestly looked concerned, which made Eppie hesitate for a moment. She didn't know whether to listen to him because he was a doctor or because he was worried about her. People weren't always what they appeared to be, yet she wanted to trust her instincts, which told her Dr. Lawson was genuine.

However, Eppie knew her decision had been the right one. She needed to talk to Micah, the sooner the better. The longer he brewed on what he thought was happening, the harder it would be to convince him he was wrong. Men were stubborn, that much she knew, and it was important to follow her heart.

Her heart was telling her Micah was the right man for her, and she had to find out if her heart was right.

"I appreciate your concern, all of you, but I am not changing my mind." Eppie turned to head for the kitchen and the carriage house out back. "I'm going whether or not you help me."

"Teague, take her there. You remember where it is." Madeline wasn't laughing anymore—her tone brooked no argument.

"Fine, but I'm not happy about it."

Eppie smiled and turned to her friends. "Thank you."

"She'll have to ride, you know." Teague sounded as if he was happy about that.

"Riding?" Eppie's stomach did a flip-flop. She hadn't thought about riding. "You mean we can't take the carriage?"

Teague snorted so loud, she thought he might hurt himself. "Eppie, girl, it's a mountain, there isn't a road. There's a trail and trees, that's about it."

She hadn't realized there would be a horse involved. Could she ride? "Can I ride a horse?"

Madeline's eyes widened. "I don't know. You haven't since you lived here, and to be honest, you've always shied away from horses." She turned her gaze to Teague. "Can you ride double?"

"Those nags can barely hold my weight. Even if she's no

bigger than a minute, there's no way the carriage horses can carry both of us." He gave Eppie a grim smile. "I guess that means you're not going."

Eppie wasn't about to let something like not being able to ride stop her. Micah told her she was stubborn and sassy. Well, it was about time to find those two qualities and use them.

"Then you'd better teach me really fast." She tugged on his arm. "I want to be on our way in an hour."

Teague looked at Madeline. "Is she joking?"

Madeline hugged her quickly. "I understand what it means to love."

Eppie opened her mouth to protest, but knew it was useless to argue. She might love Micah, but she wasn't ready to admit to it yet.

"You'll need to wear something more appropriate for riding. I think we've got something in your things that will do." As Madeline walked toward the stairs, Teague sputtered and protested all the way. "Give us ten minutes and we'll meet you in the carriage house."

Madeline ran up the stairs ahead of her and Eppie followed, so amazed she had such a giving best friend. Within a few minutes, Madeline had found a split skirt buried in the armoire in her room. A needle and thread flew and before Eppie knew it, she was heading out to the carriage house with a smile on her face and a split riding skirt swinging on her legs. Madeline walked arm in arm with her across the backyard.

Teague had saddled a gray mare with an ancient-looking saddle. The expression on his face hadn't changed; if anything, he looked more unhappy. "Maddie, what are you doing? You can't let her go."

"I have to let her go." She leaned in and whispered in her husband's ear. When she finished, Teague nodded tightly.

"Fine then, let's get started."

Eppie stared up at the horse. One large brown eye stared back at her. The mare looked gentle enough, but she was a horse and therefore, made Eppie's hands shake. She had no idea if she knew how to ride, but there was only one way to find out. She didn't start off well because she couldn't even get her foot up to the stirrup.

"Get her the mounting step." Maddie sent Teague in to get a block of wood from the carriage house.

Eppie was able to get much closer to the saddle, yet she still eyed the horse with more than a little trepidation.

"Now what?"

"Put your left foot in the stirrup and swing your right leg up over the saddle." For all his blustering, Teague gently helped her get herself perched up on the saddle. Way, way up.

"The ground is really far away." She swallowed hard and held onto the saddle horn with a death grip.

Teague handed her the reins. "Tug on the left one to turn left, the right one to turn right. To stop, pull back on both of them. Squeeze your knees just a bit when you want to start or stop."

Eppie held the leather in her hands and wondered if she had truly lost her mind. Then the thought of finding Micah bolstered her courage. She squeezed her knees together as instructed and jiggled the reins.

"Go."

Teague laughed and Madeline smacked his shoulder. "She's trying. Now help her."

"Fine, but I still think this is a really bad idea."

"Duly noted, now teach her, Mr. O'Neal." Madeline sounded as proper as any society lady.

"Anything for you, Mrs. O'Neal." He kissed her hard and quick, putting a flush onto her cheeks. Madeline's eyes sparkled and Eppie knew a moment of envy. The yearning for Micah and the need to find him overwhelmed her. The original im-

pulse she'd had was to make him understand that she'd finally started listening to her heart, and it was whispering his
name.

Seeing Madeline with Teague and the love pulsing so
strong between them, made Eppie realize what she was feeling was love. Even if her mind didn't know, her heart did. She
had to find him.

Teague spent the next twenty minutes patiently teaching
her to ride the horse this way and that, until she felt steadier
on the horse's back. She felt more confident and offered
Teague a huge smile.

"Thank you."

He sighed. "I don't think it's a good idea for you to go, but
at least you should be able to sit up on that horse without
falling on your head. Maddie would kill me if anything happened to you."

"You bet I would, and where would that leave your sons?"
Madeline laughed and turned to Eppie. "Are you ready?"

Her heart leapt at the thought of seeing Micah soon.
"More ready than I can possibly tell you. Can we leave?"
Eppie looked toward the mountains. "How far is it?"

"You shouldn't be up on that horse, Elizabeth." Dr. Lawson squinted up at her on the horse.

"I'm doing fine, Dr. Lawson. Just refreshing my knowledge of horseback riding." She wasn't about to allow him to
deter her from the course she'd decided on. He might be a
handsome, smart, sexy man, but he wasn't the man she
wanted.

"Don't worry, Teague will guide her up the mountain.
She'll be fine." Madeline patted the mare's neck. "Hilda is a
good horse, sturdy and strong."

"I still must protest the entire activity. Elizabeth is not
ready for this. If anything should happen to her out there in
the woods . . ." He shook his head. "She could do irreparable
harm to herself."

Eppie decided she was tired of hearing what was best for her, even if it came from a well-respected physician. She knew what was best for herself, no matter what anybody else said. While she appreciated the concern, she was done listening.

"So what?"

"Excuse me?" Dr. Lawson's perfect eyebrows rose toward his hairline.

"I said, so what? If I get hurt, then so be it. I've spent the last four weeks finding out who I was supposed to be, what I was supposed to do, and how other people thought I should act." Her voice grew stronger with each word. "I'm going up the mountain to find Micah and there's nothing anyone can say or do to change my mind."

Madeline clapped and Teague shook his head while Dr. Lawson's jaw tightened. "I thought you'd want to wish her well. She's a special woman."

"She's a fool."

Teague growled low in his throat while Madeline gasped.

"You're entitled to think what you'd like." Eppie wanted to kick him, but she resisted the urge, barely. "I am finally doing what I want to do."

"I believe I need to pack my belongings." Dr. Lawson started to turn away when Madeline touched his arm.

"You don't need to leave. Dr. Carmichael and you are welcome to stay here." She was always polite and diplomatic, something Eppie would probably never be. "Everything you've done is most appreciated, but please realize that Elizabeth is entitled to make her own choices."

Dr. Lawson nodded tightly. "I understand and I thank you for your words."

He didn't say he'd stay, but rather continued into the house, leaving Eppie wondering if she should have curbed her words more. Dr. Lawson was more than just a physician. She realized he represented the rest of the world that was trying to tell her who to be, how to be, and what to be. He was the unfortunate recipient of her personal declaration of independence. Later, after she found Micah and felt more control over her emotions, she'd talk to Dr. Lawson.

"Mama, whatcha doin'?" Miracle's little voice startled Eppie.

She smiled down at her daughter and with a little less grace than a cow, dismounted from Hilda the horse. Eppie knelt and opened her arms. Miracle came flying into them and hugged her tight. The infusion of her daughter's love and strength was exactly what Eppie needed.

"I'm going to go find Daddy, okay? You need to stay here with Miss Madeline and be a good girl." Eppie kissed both of Miracle's cheeks, then her forehead.

" 'Kay." Miracle frowned, as if she wanted to say something more, but didn't.

"I'll be safe, sweetheart. Mr. Teague is going to help me." Eppie gave her one last squeeze. "I'll be back as soon as I can, okay?"

Miracle nodded, then leaned forward to kiss Eppie gently on the cheek. "Careful, Mama."

Eppie's throat clogged with emotion yet again. Her daughter was wiser beyond any child her own age. She stood and walked Miracle over to her friend. Without hesitation, Madeline took the girl by the hand. Eppie felt better knowing Miracle was safe with such an amazing woman. She gave Madeline a quick hug, then led the horse to the mounting block. As the others watched, Eppie managed to get herself onto Hilda's back.

"Teague, please take care of her." Madeline took her husband's hand in hers, then kissed it. "She's still recovering." Regardless of what her friend had told the doctor, she obviously agreed with him, but supported Eppie. That was what true friendship was all about.

"Thank you, Madeline. I can't, well, I don't know how to say this." Eppie struggled against the tightness in her throat.

She had to let Madeline know how much she had changed
her short life for the better.

"It's okay, I understand. Go find your man and when you
get back, we'll go to the sitting room and have a good talk."
Madeline walked over and patted Eppie's knee, Miracle in
tow. "Listen to your daughter and be careful."

"She won't even get a splinter, I swear." Teague didn't
sound happy about it, but he was obviously forging ahead
with Eppie's crazy plan. "Let's go."

"Ready when you are." Eppie was anything but ready,
judging by the butterflies dancing in her stomach, the pounding in her head, and the ache in her heart. However, she
started out after Teague, on the gray mare, full of hope and
determination.

Her life had finally begun in earnest.

Micah gathered up all the nuts, berries, and wood he could
find. Rabbits, however, seemed to be in hiding. He had no
meat, no sustenance to keep him going. The sad fact was, he
hadn't eaten anything before he'd stormed off, and had eaten
only berries the last twenty-four hours. A little lightheaded
and weak, he realized there were two choices.

Leave the mountain or go out farther to find game.

He squinted up at the sky and gauged the storm would be
hitting within the hour. His horse was surefooted, but heavy
rain usually left the trail a muddy mess even the most agile
creature would have trouble navigating.

"To hell with this. I'm going home to grovel for forgive-
ness."

Within five minutes, he saddled the horse and stuffed the
meager food in his pockets. As he mounted, the first raindrop
hit his cheek. He had to hurry. Summer thunderstorms on the
mountain could be deadly.

*   *   *

Eppie had no idea how everything had gone so horribly wrong. They hadn't expected rain, much less a wall of water, but that's exactly what hit them an hour into the ride up the mountain. She could hardly see the back end of Teague's horse, but the mare was smart enough to follow the gelding without much guidance from Eppie.

Then they found the mud.

Teague was a big man and the carriage horse wasn't used to carrying his weight. The first time its hoof sunk into the mud, he was able to pull it out. The second time, Teague jumped off the horse's back and yanked the gelding out.

"We're going to have to turn back," he yelled over the rain. "This is suicide."

"I'm not turning back. We've come too far. It's got to be close." She couldn't, wouldn't stop now. She could almost feel Micah nearby.

"It's at least twenty more minutes and in this rain, it's more like forty. C'mon, Curmudgeon, we've got to turn back." He looked up at her from under the brim of his brown hat with true concern in his gaze.

Eppie, however, wasn't about to let rain stop her. "I can't." She couldn't explain why it was so important, but it was vital that she find Micah as soon as possible. "Please."

"I don't think this nag is going to make it much farther. He's going to break a foreleg if we continue." Teague tugged on the gelding's reins. "There's no choice. We've got to turn back." He led the horse around hers and started down the path toward Plum Creek.

Disappointment washed over her and she knew it wasn't just rain on her cheeks. She'd been adamant about finding Micah, about talking to him and she couldn't believe rain was going to stand in her way. Teague was at least twenty feet ahead of her when Eppie made a decision she knew would change her life.

She started up the trail alone.

"Eppie, what the hell are you doing?" she heard Teague shout. "Get back here!"

She didn't turn around or acknowledge him. Eppie kept going, her horse nimble in the mud with only Eppie's light weight on her back. She knew the cabin was only twenty minutes up the trail, he'd as much as told her where it sat. With any luck, she'd find Micah in half an hour and be out of the rain, and in his arms.

Micah realized his normal trail was a river of mud, so he took the side trail down as the rain got heavier and heavier. The sky was laden with silver-gray clouds, making the forest floor as gloomy as any moonless night. Fortunately, he'd had the same horse for ten years and the gelding knew the terrain well.

By the time Micah got through the steepest part of the climb down, he was soaked to the skin and shivering. Summer storms were the worst; usually he got sick within a week of being out in one. He hoped it wouldn't happen again this time, but he asked for it since he'd chosen to be out in the weather.

"The fucking horse can't make it! I can walk up there, Maddie, but it's going to take me about five hours in that mud and rain." Teague's voice echoed around him. The fear and anger in the other man's voice made the hairs on the back of Micah's neck stand up.

He couldn't hear the response, but knew Madeline must be nearby. Within minutes he'd made it to the backyard of the house only to find the two of them in the carriage house. Teague was covered in mud while Madeline was wringing her hands. When Micah appeared, all color drained from her face.

"Where is she?" her voice was hoarse with emotion.

His stomach flipped. "Where is who?"

"Eppie! Dammit, Micah, where is she?" Madeline stepped

out into the rain and grabbed his leg. "She's supposed to be with you."

He couldn't seem to absorb her words. Eppie was supposed to be with him? He'd gone up the mountain alone yesterday and came down alone.

"What do you mean, she's supposed to be with me? I left her here with those goddamn doctors." Micah's heart took up residence in his throat. "What's going on?"

Teague's eyebrows slammed together. "She got it in her head to go up the mountain to find you. Made me teach her how to ride and took off on her own when my horse got stuck in the mud. Damn stubborn little shit wouldn't listen to a word I said." Beneath the anger, Micah sensed real fear in his tone.

That scared the absolute hell out of Micah and made his blood run cold. Teague wasn't one to be afraid of much, ever.

Without another word, Micah turned around and headed back toward the mountain trail, with the sounds of Madeline crying and Teague cursing in his ears. His only thought was to find Eppie before anything happened to her. She couldn't have survived so much only to be lost in the mud and rain of a summer storm. God couldn't be that cruel.

Chapter Nine

Eppie didn't remember ever being so afraid, or miserable, or angry at herself. Considering she didn't remember life before a month ago, it shouldn't mean that much. But oh, how it did anyway.

She blundered on blindly in the pouring rain, hoping she hadn't just resigned herself to drown on top of a horse. The straw hat on her head had long since fallen apart, along with her courage. Twenty minutes must have passed by three times at least. The trees all looked the same, the leaves all looked the same, even the damn squirrels hiding in the leaves all looked the same.

Water came down the mountain in small rivers around her. She had no idea how the horse was still plodding along. Obviously, she was a much better mare than Teague had given her credit for. Eppie could only thank the fates for giving her such a horse.

The normal sounds of the forest were gone. The only noise left was the deafening rain all around her. Eppie knew she was lost, but refused to accept it. If she was lost, then she wouldn't find Micah, and more than likely, she'd end up exactly how Dr. Lawson predicted she would. Sad ending for such a short life, such as it was. She should have listened to Teague, to Dr. Lawson, to her common sense. How could she . . .

Up ahead she saw the boughs of a pair of evergreens hugging what appeared to be the cabin. She said a quick prayer and headed toward what she thought was Micah's home. The horse must've sensed shelter, because she got a spring in her step and brought Eppie to the opening in the trees more quickly than she thought possible.

The outline of the bottom of the door was visible and Eppie couldn't contain the whoop of excitement. She'd found it! It seemed the heavens were smiling down on her.

"Come on, girl, let's get out of this rain." She had no idea if the horse could hear her or not, but it felt good to say it anyway.

Eppie arrived at the door and glanced down at the ground— way, way down. At the house, there'd been a mounting block, but here in the wilds, there was nothing but leaves, moss, and rocks. It could've been a hundred feet or ten, it seemed an eternity stood between her and getting off the horse.

There was no other choice but to dismount as best she could, which wasn't saying much. She hung onto the pommel and swung her right leg around, keeping her left foot in the stirrup. Hanging on in midair, she hoped like hell her hands didn't slip off the soaked saddle. Slowly, and painfully, she lowered herself, supporting her weight with her left leg. Her muscles screamed from the effort as she stretched herself farther than she thought possible as her knee practically touched her nose. Finally, her toes touched something solid and she made contact with the spongy ground.

"Thank God." She pressed her forehead into the mare's flank and took a deep breath as her body trembled like the leaves on the trees. The shaking must've been from riding the horse when she wasn't used to it. She hoped it wasn't from overexerting herself, which would be the worst situation. She didn't, however, have time to think about why she was trembling—she had to get out of the rain.

Eppie kept the reins tight in her hand as she approached

the door. Someone had definitely been there recently because all the vegetation had been broken or cut away from the door. A chunk of moss was missing from the rock near the base.

Micah.

Her heart sang with gladness as she prepared to finally speak to him about all that was in her heart and her head. She knew he loved her, but it was important to let him know how she felt and what she thought.

"Give me a minute, girl, and I'll get you out of the rain."

There must be some kind of shelter for the horse nearby, but for now, all Eppie wanted to do was open the door and see Micah. She couldn't help the smile that stretched across her face or the rapid tattoo of her heart as she pushed the door open.

And found the cabin dark and empty.

Micah rode like a madman, pushing himself and his horse way past their limits. Eppie didn't know how to ride a horse; she'd never wanted to learn, either, telling him they were spawns of Satan meant to kick and bite humans. The fact that she'd made Teague teach her how to ride, then went off on her own in a humdinger of a storm to find him, made Micah's throat close up with emotion.

What did it mean?

He didn't know for certain, but he hoped it meant she was ready to talk to him, to tell him she loved him. Fanciful notions to be certain, but he could hope. Faith and hope were the only two constant companions the four years since he met Eppie. He wasn't about to let go of either one of them.

The rain continued to fall as an unending deluge. It ran off the brim of his hat like a curtain opening on a stage, blowing back as he tried desperately to get up the mountain, to find Eppie, or Elizabeth, or whatever she wanted to be called. She was out in the woods, alone, in unfamiliar territory with no one to help her.

His stomach cramped every time he thought about all the terrible things that could happen to her. From animals, to mud slides, to falling off the horse and killing herself, there were a million things that could go wrong. Each and every one of them danced around in his brain, cackling madly.

He forced the worry aside and made himself focus on the terrain in front of him so he didn't end up knocking himself unconscious instead of trying to rescue Eppie. Failing to find her and make sure she was safe couldn't enter his mind or he might fall apart. Micah had been struggling with what he needed and wanted, as well as all the personal demons who had taken up permanent residence in his heart ten years earlier.

The ground was saturated which made his horse's hooves sink into the pine needles and leaves covering the ground. He slipped occasionally but kept plodding along in the rain, proving Micah's choice of mount was the right one. He'd never felt so scared in his life, and he fought to keep the fear down since he would be no good for Eppie if he panicked.

It was only noon, but the storm kept the woods as gloomy as midnight. Micah hit the steepest part of the trail and realized there was at least six inches of mud to get through. This is where Teague must've had to turn around. There was no way any horse could carry his weight and get through the thick mud. Micah was forced to get off the horse and walk as far to the right as he could without entering the thick woods.

It was slow going and his shoes continually stuck and slipped as he climbed. He slipped and fell, sliding down at least fifty feet. The reins slipped from his fingers while his horse watched. Micah started to lose his breath and his hold on panic as he grabbed a small pine tree to stop his slide. The bark scratched his arms and his cheek, but he held on as the water and mud slid beneath him.

Micah took a few breaths before he attempted to get to his knees. It took him two tries, but he finally found his footing.

His horse stood there and watched, blinking against the pounding rain. Micah laughed and used the trees to pull himself back up the hill to his horse. It took longer than he wanted, because he kept losing his footing and had to hang onto the trees or lose the ground he'd made up. By the time he made it to the horse, he was breathing as if he were the equine. Micah grabbed the reins and pressed his face into the horse's neck.

"At least you stayed put, boy." He pushed himself into a standing position and this time took more care in climbing the hill. Micah had to resist the urge to rush, considering it had already cost him at least fifteen minutes. Hurrying again would be the worst possible thing he could do.

It had been at least two hours since Eppie had gone up the hill. Perhaps it wasn't as bad when she rode up. He could only hope she made it to the top of the steep incline without being hurt. His gaze constantly scanned the ground and the trees around him for a sign she'd been there, or possibly was still there.

"Eppie!"

His voice fell flat against the dense trees and the pouring rain.

"Elizabeth!"

It might make a difference if he used her given name, but he wasn't above trying anything to find her. As he climbed the mountain, he called her name every few seconds until his throat was scratchy and hoarse. None of it mattered, however, because if he didn't find her, he might as well let himself fall down the mountain.

When he got within ten feet of his cabin, he spotted a hoofprint. His heart leapt into his throat and his eyes stung with tears. She'd made it this far, he was sure of it.

"Eppie! Elizabeth! Whoever you are, please tell me you're here!"

Micah dropped the reins and ran toward the cabin, heedless of the bushes and branches scratching and slapping him.

He nearly tripped on a tree root but caught himself in time and kept running. He listened for a response, anything that told him she was nearby. As he neared the door, he noticed a few broken branches by the door and realized she must have made it all the way and found the cabin. He shouldn't have doubted her ability to survive, based on how she'd done with everything life had thrown in her path.

He was almost to the door, when his right foot landed on a patch of moss and suddenly he was looking at the sky as his head came down hard on the rock tucked beneath the leaves. Blackness roared through on the heels of pain.

Eppie had managed to start a fire in the potbellied stove and light the lantern, which was still warm, letting her know Micah had been there recently. At least she hoped it was Micah, or she was in a stranger's cabin making herself at home. Her instincts told her this was his, though aside from that, she could smell his scent, and her body recognized it, raising goosebumps on her arms.

In fact, when she first lit the lantern, a memory of a blue bedspread, of that very bed, bubbled up in her mind. It wasn't her childhood bed she had remembered back at the house, it was Micah's. She'd been there before, with him. Her mind had been trying to tell her what her heart refused to her—Micah was part of her.

She pushed away the lingering fear from her wild ride up the mountain. The horse had followed her in the door, which was a near disaster since the animal had to squeeze herself in. She stood by the fire, with steam rising from her coat. Eppie knew Micah likely wouldn't be happy to see a horse in his cabin, but she couldn't leave the poor thing out in that terrible storm.

As she stood beside the horse, rubbing her hands together and trying to dry off, she heard something above the rain. Her heart slammed against her ribs when she realized it sounded like a shout. When she heard it again, she pushed past the horse and ran for the door. She flung it open and stared out into the storm and saw Micah running toward the cabin, with her name on his lips.

She'd finally found him. After two days of waiting and needing to see him, there he was right in front of her. He looked as wet as she was, but with his hat down, she couldn't quite see his face. Eppie clasped her hands together and thanked whatever forces had been looking out for them, bringing them to the point where they were together.

He almost fell but kept on running toward the cabin. He was only a short distance away when his feet slipped out from under him and he landed on the ground with a thump and a splash of water. Eppie waited for him to get up, but he didn't.

Worry raced through her as she stepped back out into the pouring rain to his inert form. She hoped he'd simply knocked himself out, because anything else would be completely unacceptable. As she knelt on the ground beside him, water soaked through her new riding skirt. Her hand trembled as she reached out to touch him. His skin was clammy and wet, but beneath his wet clothing, she felt the steady thump of his heart.

Eppie blew out a shaky breath of relief. Then it dawned on her that she had to get him out of the rain before he drowned. She stood and gauged the distance to the cabin to be about ten feet. Micah wasn't a big man like Teague, but he was a man, tall and muscular. When she tugged on his arm, he felt like a felled tree, way too heavy for her to move alone.

There wasn't anyone else around to help, however, so she had to think of something else. She glanced around but didn't see Micah's horse, which left the mare. Likely the nearly dry horse wouldn't want to go back out in the rain, but there wasn't a choice. Eppie needed her help to get Micah in the cabin.

She made her way back to the cabin and began looking for

rope. There wasn't any to be found except in the poorly strung bed. The only other usable items were wool blankets, which they'd need when they came in out of the storm.

Eppie found a rusty knife in the kitchen and cut the rope from the bed, then tied it together to make something resembling a loop. It didn't have to be pretty, just functional. She led the horse back to the door, and thankfully the mare didn't shy away. The rain soaked them again and she silently apologized to the sturdy animal.

Micah lay where she left him, still unconscious and unmoving. Eppie looped the rope around his shoulders and pulled him sideways with as much strength as she could muster until his head was facing the cabin. She sucked in a much needed breath and ignored the screaming muscles in her back and shoulders. After tying the rope to the reins, she leaned into the horse to speak in her ear.

"I know it's been a long day, girl, but I need you one more time. Help me save him, because I don't think I'm going to want to ride back down the mountain without him." She could swear she received an equine nod in acknowledgment and gave the horse a quick hug. "Okay, let's get this done."

It seemed as though the ground wanted to keep hold of Micah. The rope creaked as the horse plodded forward, unused to a man's weight behind her. Eppie grabbed the rope with her hands and put what little strength she had toward helping the animal. With excruciating slowness, the ground finally gave up its hold on Micah's inert body. The horse kept her footing in the mossy area in front of the cabin.

Eppie thought her arms were going to come out of their sockets. It might as well have been a mile to the cabin instead of ten feet. She slipped and landed on her side, but the horse kept going. Likely she thought the warmth of the cabin waited for her and she was a pretty smart horse.

Thankful for the horse's assistance even if she was looking to get warm, Eppie got to her knees. The cool water on the ground felt good on her rope-chafed hands. Finally able to get to her feet, she caught up to the horse as she reached the door.

"Hang on girl, we need to get him in safely." Eppie guided the mare through the door, realizing too late the reins were pulling to the right and Micah was stuck outside the door. "Dammit! Stop, stop." The horse was almost completely in the cabin and Eppie had to crawl through the horse's legs, not the safest place to be, to get outside and help Micah.

He was on his side; fortunately, his face was not in the water. Eppie rolled him on his back and gave him a quick, hard kiss on his cold lips.

"Almost there." She took his left arm and pulled him until he was straightened enough to get through the door.

Later on she'd probably wonder how she did what she was doing, but right then, all she could think of was getting them both inside the cabin. She crawled back under the horse's legs into the cabin, picking up a few splinters along the way. The horse stood with her head down, water dripping onto the dusty wooden floor.

"Almost there, girl, almost there." Eppie pulled the horse forward slowly, pulling Micah into the cabin. It was a good thing he'd built the ceiling high enough to accommodate the mare or Eppie would never have been able to get him inside by herself. "Whoa, whoa." She stopped the horse just as she reached the fire, apparently her ultimate goal.

Eppie shut the door to keep out any more of the rain. She couldn't untie the rope from the reins, so she just took the loop out from underneath Micah's shoulders. Later on, when the rope dried, she would untie the wet, tight knots.

She looked down at Micah and shook her head. They were both as wet as they could be. Thank God she hadn't used the blankets because they'd need them to keep warm. Eppie focused on getting Micah's wet clothes off, which wasn't an easy task because they seemed to be glued to him.

When he was only in his drawers, she finally stopped and glanced down, then gasped. She hadn't seen him in full light, hadn't know how many scars lay beneath the clothing. He'd endured quite a lot, including burns, what appeared to be bullet marks as well as long, whitened zippers made by a knife or sword. She assumed the same types of scars lay on his soul. No wonder he drank—she'd likely drink, too, if she'd been so grievously injured.

"Don't worry. I'll take care of you this time." Eppie took off her outer layer of clothing, leaving on only her chemise and drawers. The chill in the air belied the late summer heat that should be instead. She took one of the blankets and rolled him onto it, then tugged him until he was closer to the fire.

She tried not to look at his face or his scarred body, afraid she might lose her nerve. He'd been such a staunch presence by her side since she'd woken up, and he hadn't asked for anything but a chance. Eppie knew she'd done him wrong by doubting him, by accusing him of nefarious things, and by allowing them to come together without giving him her heart first.

The truth was, he already owned her heart. She knew that now, and not only that, she accepted it. Perhaps getting out of the house and into the world outside Plum Creek had given her the impetus to make that leap of faith.

With infinite tenderness, she used the other blanket to dry him off until color returned to his skin. Still he slept on, and she hoped he wasn't suffering the same malady that had stolen three years of her life. She checked his head and found a large goose egg at the back where he must've struck it. It was a big lump, but there was no blood, so she came to the conclusion he'd simply been knocked out by the force of the fall.

The rain had stopped, giving Eppie the opportunity to put Hilda back outside where she could eat and be more com-

fortable. The horse must've been tired of the small cabin because she went outside without hesitation.

"You were great, girl, now let us have some time alone."

After tying the mare's reins to a sturdy tree, Eppie went
back inside to her man. The scent of horse still permeated the
small cabin, but it had definitely gotten better with the mare
outside.

She shed the rest of her clothes, then lay down next to him
and covered them both with the blanket. Soon the heat from
their bodies combined with the heat from the fire, and for the
first time in hours, Eppie felt warm. She closed her eyes and
gently placed her arm across Micah's chest.

Chapter Ten

Micah came into consciousness in stages. He was first aware of feeling warm and safe, which was a different sensation for him. Normally he felt adrift and found himself searching for warmth and security. Next thing he realized was he wasn't alone. There was a woman beside him with soft, smooth skin whose breath blew gently on his chest.

Eppie.

As her scent washed over him, his heart jumped to life when his nose confirmed what his body knew. It was definitely Eppie and she was in his arms.

He nuzzled her hair and pulled her closer. She sighed and put her leg over his. Micah floated between asleep and awake, reveling in the sensation of having the woman he loved sleeping beside him.

The third stage of wakefulness rolled over him slowly, when he recognized the other scent in the room as horse. That's when it hit him that he was on a hard floor in his cabin.

"Holy shit." He sat up abruptly, rolling into Eppie.

The entire wild ride up the mountain raced through his head, his desperation to find Eppie, the realization she had made it to the cabin, then everything had gone black.

"What's going on?" Eppie blinked and rubbed the back of her head.

"How did I get here?" he croaked.

When he turned to look at Eppie, all thoughts of confusion and annoyance flew out of his head. She was nude. Deliciously, wonderfully nude. Her cocoa skin glowed golden in the firelight, and her sleepy gaze locked with his. A pulse snapped between them, turning the moment into one of arousal.

"Eppie." He breathed her name with reverence, unsure if he was dreaming or awake. "Are you really here?"

She smiled then, a smile many men over history had been subjected to, and fallen under the spell of. Micah was no exception.

"Yes, I'm here." She reached up and cupped his cheek. "Does your head hurt?"

"At this moment, my leg could fall off and I probably wouldn't notice." He was immediately and painfully hard, his dick pushing at his drawers with a force he hadn't felt in quite some time.

She chuckled and ran her hand down his chest, toward the throbbing member aching for release. "I guess so."

When her hand brushed against him, a jolt of tingles spread through him from the contact. He had to hold back from losing control before he even touched her, as if he was a young boy of fifteen and not an old man over thirty.

"Later on, you can tell me why you risked your life to come to my cabin. But for now, may I touch you?" He shook with need, but he didn't want to overstep any boundaries she'd thrown up while he'd been passed out. Yet her being nude either meant they were both soaking wet, a likely event, or she expected to wake up in his arms and make love. The latter, of course, was his preferred reason.

"I was hoping you would," she said almost shyly. "Micah,

I know I've made mistakes, but there are some things I need to tell you."

He pressed his fingers to her lips. "Not now. Please let's find pleasure in each other, then we can talk."

She nodded, but her eyes promised many secrets were still hiding behind their dark depths. "Then touch me."

He needed no further invitation. It was as if a bountiful buffet had been laid out for him and he was a starving man. He wanted to make it perfect for her. She'd come to him before but had been almost hesitant, as if she was testing what she wanted. This moment, however, went far beyond that night in the gloom of his room.

He ignored all the twinges of pain making themselves known and focused on the woman in his arms. Taking her hand in his, he kissed each long finger, sucking gently on the tip. A shudder rippled through her, and her nipples hardened as he watched. The temptation was too much; he had to taste them.

He lowered his head, keeping himself at a pace to let their pleasure last. There was no need to hurry. The rain still pounded on the roof and they were together again, at last.

Micah nuzzled her breast, licking the underside and working his way up to the turgid peak. He circled around and around, avoiding that which called him and, he was sure, where she wanted him to land.

He smiled when she huffed out an impatient sigh.

"You are torturing me."

"No, just making sure you feel good." He reached out his tongue and barely skimmed a nipple.

She started and moaned softly. "Hm, it feels good."

"Then I'm doing my job." He couldn't resist any longer and he gave in to the temptation. As his mouth closed around the amazingly hard nipple, a bolt of arousal slammed through him, right down to his dick. It jumped against her thigh, and she chuckled.

Until, of course, he sucked hard, drawing her deeper into his mouth. He used his tongue, teeth and lips to pleasure her while his hand tweaked and pinched the other nipple. Eppie leaned toward him, her skin beginning to shine in the firelight.

He swirled the nipple around, tugging on it until she gasped. The he switched sides, willing to give each beautiful breast equal attention. They were, after all, equally tempting.

Desire coursed through him as the smell of her arousal tickled his nose. He breathed in deep, eager to be one with her again. She reached down and grabbed him, her small fist much stronger than expected.

Micah forgot everything but the sensation of her fingers gliding up and down his staff. She must've remembered what to do, because damn, she did it well. Sweet, heavenly strokes from her hand had him harder than he thought possible within minutes.

He let her nipple loose with a pop and breathed on the peak, enjoying the sound of her kittenish moan even as a primal one exploded from his throat.

"I think I need you inside me." She sounded whispery, as if she could hardly catch her breath.

Micah shucked his drawers in an instant. He knew how she felt, that was for certain. When he'd come to the cabin he never expected to have Eppie in his arms again, yet she was there. Her hand wrapped tightly around his cock, pulling him closer and closer to an orgasm.

"I think I need to be inside you." He slid up and captured her mouth in a kiss. As their tongues dueled and danced with each other, he nudged open her legs and positioned himself at her opening. The damp curls embraced him, welcomed him.

Micah stared down into her eyes, the pupils dilated with desire, sparkling in the meager light. She was the one who'd been in his heart for so long, he'd forgotten every other woman but her. Eppie had been the one to show him what love was, and now he had to return the favor and show her how much he loved her.

As he slid into her, time seemed to stand still. The sounds, smells and sights disappeared except for her, for Eppie. She clenched around him, bringing him deeper into her body until he was fully encased in her heat.

Utter bliss.

He pressed his forehead against hers as they breathed in each other's air. Truly one heart, one life, one soul.

Eppie wriggled beneath him and he began to move. The slow, deliberate strokes were designed to make her arousal grow steadily. He pushed against her, making sure to tease her nubbin of pleasure with each thrust. She gasped when he bit her right nipple and strengthened his stroke.

"Oh my," she whispered. "Do that again."

"As you wish." He'd oblige the lady for as long as he could.

This time when he bit her nipple, he licked and sucked it first, making the bite sting a bit. Her muscles rippled around his dick, nearly pushing him over the edge. He had no idea how much she liked a bit of pleasure and pain together.

"Again."

Micah switched to the other nipple, licking it until it was wet, harder than a diamond, then he bit, thrusting home with a grunt. Her back arched and she pushed up against him.

With a quick flip, he was beneath her and she straddled him. Her confusion quickly turned to pleasure as he lifted her by the waist and brought her back down to impale herself on his staff.

"Ride me, sweet Eppie."

"Mm, I like this." She placed her hands on his chest and rose, slowly lowering herself onto him. Within moments, she had a rhythm going, taking control of both of them.

Micah gladly handed it over to the woman who owned him. Her breasts bounced with each thrust, tempting him to pleasure them again. Her nipples were so sensitive, he had to have at them again, so he reached up and squeezed. She gasped and slammed down so hard, he nearly came again.

"Goddamn woman, that felt good."

"Again." Eppie was a woman of few words, but he understood them well enough.

He pulled her down toward him until he could reach her, then he could pleasure her as she pleasured him. He cupped her ass, helping her move up and down even as he bit, licked and sucked at her nipples. His balls tightened up, he knew he was close, really close.

Micah could hardly form a coherent thought, but he wanted to be sure she found her joy along with him. One hand pleasured her nipple while his mouth had the other, with his other hand, he reached between them and flicked her clit.

The magic combination found, Eppie screamed his name as she came, his dick caught in the throes of her ultimate pleasure. The muscles pulled him in until he touched her womb, then his body exploded, bucking and thrusting into her.

He captured her lips, kissing her as they sealed their union with their bodies. Micah rode the most intense orgasm of his life as he pumped into the woman he loved. She kissed him back just as fiercely as she ground her cunt into him, pulsing with her own little death.

They dozed after the incredible moments they shared as one. Micah felt the aches and pains of his run through the woods, not to mention the rock that had said hello to his head. Eppie must've been just as exhausted, not to mention how the hell she got him into the cabin alone. He had a feeling the horse had something to do with it, but he was too tired to ask.

With the woman of his dreams finally in his arms, Micah drifted off into a contented sleep.

Eppie lay awake, watching Micah. The rain had stopped and the woods outside returned to its normal symphony of sounds. As a bird sang to its mate high in the trees, she stared at Micah's chest as it rose and fell with each breath. He had shown her, without words, how much he loved her. This time she listened.

The relationship had entered a new area, one she was unfamiliar with, no matter how much he'd told her about what had happened before. She'd accepted the fact her memory would likely never return. Sometime during the time she'd been bleeding and injured, death had stolen that part of her, one she was glad to give up if it meant keeping her life.

Yet, with it, she'd lost what she had with Micah. However, deep in their souls, what they had still remained, but hidden behind secrets. Micah had so many, she could hardly imagine what they were, but she did know they ate away at him. After so long, there was a chance he may never be whole again, but Eppie was willing to try.

Eppie rose from their makeshift bed on the floor and slipped on her clothes. It made her feel a bit stronger to be clothed, more ready to face what was coming. She opened the cabin door and confirmed the rain had stopped. The woods looked as if a raging tornado had torn through them. The sun peeked through the evergreens, spreading its healing warmth on the wounded.

Eppie went outside to check on Hilda. The horse was contentedly munching on the thick grass that grew on the mountain. Eppie patted the horse's neck, surprised when Hilda lifted her head and neighed.

An answering neigh sounded from the dense trees. Eppie hoped no one had come to the cabin, because she needed this time alone with Micah. However, it was his horse that appeared, riderless and alone. Relief washed through her that the horse was okay, as well as that she and Micah were still alone at the cabin.

When the gelding stepped up, the mare nuzzled his snout, clearly glad to see another equine companion. Eppie petted the gelding's nose, absurdly glad to have both horses safely make it through the storm.

"Good boy. I'm sure Micah will be glad to see you. Now the two of you stay here." She secured the other horse's reins to another tree and went back into the cabin.

It was time to talk to Micah.

The fire burned as embers, bathing Micah in an orange glow. She thought he was still asleep, but his eyes were wide open, watching her. The silver glittered in the meager light filtering through the two windows.

"Your horse just arrived."

He smiled. "He's a tough old man, just like his owner. Is he okay?"

"Seems to be. I tied him up with the mare." She walked toward him, very cognizant of his nudity beneath the blanket. It was hard not to think about the fact they'd been intimate only an hour before. She pushed it aside, with effort, and sat on what was left of the bed frame.

"You look very serious." Micah sat up, tucking the blanket around his hips.

Eppie took a deep breath. "I am. There are so many thoughts in my head, I don't know which one to pay attention to first."

"Start with the first one," he said simply. "Nothing you can do will be wrong."

"If only that were true." She searched for the right words. "When I first woke up from the coma, I was so frightened, I felt as if I'd been adrift in an ocean and could hardly swim. You scared me more than anything."

He looked shocked and hurt. "I scared you?"

"Maybe scared is the wrong word. I knew you but I didn't. Your voice was familiar, and so were you, but there was this blackness I couldn't see through. I pushed you away because I didn't know what to do." She took a deep breath and willed away the shaking in her belly. "I felt as if I were no one, with no past, no future, nothing but that room."

"Oh, honey, I'm so—"

"Please just let me talk. I don't think I'm going to get it out right if you interrupt me."

He nodded and locked his gaze with hers.

"There was too much to absorb, to accept and to understand. You hovered over me so much I pulled farther away. And then, something magical happened." She managed a small smile, even as her courage grew stronger. "I went to the river and discovered our spot. My body and heart recognized you even as my head kept saying no. Eventually I allowed my heart to override my head, and before I could tell you, you were gone."

"I'm sorry." His quiet apology made her pause.

"I think I know why you left, but it was so important to me that I find you. I forced Teague and Madeline to help me, so please don't be angry with them." Eppie took his hand in hers. "I am Elizabeth Archer, but in my heart I'm Eppie, and I'm in love with you."

He closed his eyes for a moment, and when he opened them, they shone with moisture. His throat worked even as he opened and closed his mouth. It was important they were completely honest with each other.

"Whatever happens, I wanted you to know that. I think I offended Dr. Lawson, and likely will never remember my life before the coma. I'm a bit stubborn, headstrong and forgetful." She chuckled at her own attempt at levity. "I have fallen in love with Miracle and I want to build a life with both of you."

Micah held up one hand and Eppie waited for him to catch his breath. In a few moments, he blew out a breath and met her gaze.

"I've spent the last few years hoping I'd see you open your eyes again, and when you did, I reminded myself to be happy even if you didn't remember me. Then when you came into my arms—God, I couldn't believe how amazing it was. I could only pray you would be there again. And you were." His smile was so bright it made her smile in return. "I waited so long to tell you I love you, I can hardly believe it's finally now."

Eppie's heart leapt with joy. "It's now, with the help of some guardian angels looking out for us."

He rubbed a hand down his face. "I feel like I'm dreaming, darlin', and I hope like hell I'm not going to wake up soon." What sounded like a sob burst from his throat. "Irony is something I never expected to come full circle. I don't deserve this, but that doesn't mean I won't grab on to it with both hands."

Eppie slid down to the floor and knelt beside him, more than concerned about Micah. "Everyone deserves love, a chance at happiness."

His laugh sent a chill up her spine and a coil of dread settled in her belly. "I am the last person on earth who deserves love or happiness. I've done so many things to put my ass straight in hell, I deserve nothing but misery and eternal damnation."

The most frightening thing about his speech was she could see in his eyes that he meant every word of it. Micah firmly believed that not only was he damned but there was no force that could change his fate. Eppie vowed to prove him wrong, come hell or high water. She almost laughed at the image, considering it was the high water that had brought them to the cabin in the first place.

"Tell me," she commanded softly.

"I can't. You see, if I let them out, I might not get them back in." Ancient dark shadows lurked behind his gaze, so sharp and deadly, Eppie wanted to move away.

But she didn't. Instead she took his cold hands in hers and settled at his side.

"Tell me." This time she was more forceful, determined to ferret out what haunted the man she had come to love.

He blew out a long sigh. "I wouldn't know where to begin."

"Start where you grew up. If you told me any stories, I've forgotten them." She smiled. "I'm like a sieve that way."

Her silly joke made the corner of his mouth kick up. "I grew up in Virginia on a big tobacco plantation. My grandfather had been a bastard who knew how to make money on the backs of others, and I gladly sat up there with him, eating, drinking and whoring from the time I was sixteen."

She wanted to say something about a sixteen-year-old whoring, but kept quiet, silently urging him to continue.

"I had four good friends from similar backgrounds, and we spent our time doing whatever we felt like. I never worked a day in my life those wonder years, never had to even lift a finger to dress myself." He shook his head. "Shallow, empty-headed son of a bitch. If you had known me back then, you would have hated me."

The self-hate was evident in everything from his posture to his tone, but Eppie didn't succumb to it. She squeezed his hand, giving him the encouragement of her love.

"When the war began, I was just twenty-one, so stupid and foolish, I assumed I'd be given a command and be home within a month, perhaps two. It gave us an excuse to go to Maryland and find new whores to play with." He clenched her hands so hard, the bones smashed up against each other. "I didn't *know*, you see, how wrong I was about everything, about life and how much I deserved. I was put in an infantry unit beside gap-toothed morons who likely were born from years of careful inbreeding."

In that moment, Eppie heard the spoiled Virginia plantation owner, the man who Micah hated, but who also lurked beneath the surface of the twisted soul he'd become.

"I was muddy, cold, tired and miserable every second of every day. I complained mercilessly until the captain threatened to hang me if I didn't shut up. He whipped me in front of the squad, in front of the regiment's major. My friends turned their backs and pretended not to know me." His body heated as he spoke, and Eppie felt perspiration gathering on his skin. "From then on I was a ruthless soldier, killing without thought or remorse, anything to release the rage and frustration at where I was. My bloodletting caught the attention of a lieutenant in the regiment and he promoted me to sergeant and gave me my own squad to command." His smile set off the warning bells in her head to run.

Eppie stayed put and swallowed the fear. This was who Micah was, and she had to love all of him, even his secrets.

"My squad became known as the Red Grays because of all the kills we claimed during raids and battles. I remember one boy who was so afraid he shit his pants right before he killed his first man. From then on, he had the same bloodlust I did. That boy died a week before the war ended by his own hand." He looked up into Eppie's eyes and the ghosts of the war were clearly writhing in his memories. "I was left without a squad, without a friend, and without even a goddamn pair of shoes. After four years of killing, I didn't remember much else. They sent me home and when I got there"—he swallowed so hard she heard the gulp—"I wanted to go back to the war."

He stood up so fast, Eppie fell forward, narrowly missing the bed frame. Micah paced the cabin like a mountain lion, naked and glistening with sweat. He was a great beast, caged by his memories.

"My father was dead, as was my eldest sister. My mother and younger sister were still alive, and they'd turned themselves into whores. I found my b-best friend Edward fucking my mother for fifty cents a toss, on what was left of her marriage bed. He'd been the first to turn his back on me, yet there he was getting his dick serviced by my goddamn mother." He finally stopped and leaned his hands against the wall, pressing his forehead into the rough-hewn boards. "I don't remember much except blood, and my sister Sarah screaming and pulling me away."

The silence in the cabin crackled louder than the dying fire. Eppie wanted to ask what happened, but knew if she spoke, the moment would shatter into a thousand pieces, and perhaps Micah with it.

"I killed Edward, cut off his head and his dick. My mother was covered in blood and naked when she picked up the sword and sliced my face open."

Eppie couldn't contain the gasp that flew from her mouth. His mother had been the one to give him the terrible scar. The war had completely destroyed who Micah had been, everything he had, and his future. She couldn't imagine a worse fate than going from having everything to having less than nothing.

"I might have killed her if it hadn't been for Sarah. She stopped me, but not before I'd punched my mother into unconsciousness. Sarah sewed me up with a needle and thread from the kitchen and left the house. For nearly six months I wandered west, surviving sometimes on air and self-pity for days on end." He patted the wall in front of him. "I built this cabin with all the fear, the anger, and the misery I'd been carrying around for almost five years. Even then there was so much more left inside me."

He turned to look at her and she could see him trembling. "I never thought I'd find love, that I'd find you, Eppie. I'm afraid now that you know who I am, I've lost you." Micah slipped on his damp clothes as he spoke. "I am a monster, but I don't want to hurt you, ever. You can walk out of this cabin and you'll never be bothered again." After yanking on his boots, he walked toward the door and paused with his hand on the knob. "I love you."

As soon as the door closed behind him, Eppie wept, the tears coming from deep down inside her. She cried for Micah and for herself. He might have done terrible things, but without them, he wouldn't be the man she fell in love with. Did that make it right? She couldn't answer that question without tumbling into the blackness that swirled around him.

Micah was a different person than the spoiled boy who'd gone off to war fourteen years earlier. He'd literally lived through hell and emerged on the other side a changed man. She knew he expected her to reject him for all he'd done, but God had brought him into her life, had kept him by her side. She wasn't about to throw that away because of past sins, even if they were tearing him up inside.

Eppie had to help him overcome those memories, the dark dreams that plagued him even when he was awake. The layers were deep and thick, likely covered with thorns, but she'd battled her way up from a coma. She could defeat Micah's demons.

Micah walked around for an hour, blindly following trails he knew by rote. He passed by three rabbits and wondered where they'd been yesterday when he was hungry. Now he was numb, or rather, he was so overwhelmed by every emotion known to man, he couldn't feel anything more. The bad memories had poured forth from his mouth and she listened to every one of them. He didn't leave out one detail, much to his dismay. It was the details he was most worried about.

He fully expected her to quietly walk away from him. Any woman who wasn't loco would. Yet there was some part of him, a tiny spark of hope that refused to be extinguished, that counted on Eppie staying by his side. They had endured much together, and he hoped their bond was strong enough to overcome his sordid, bloody past. It was a most impossible situation, but it was of his own making.

He shouldn't have told her about the Red Grays and he sure as hell shouldn't have told her about Edward. Yet once the words started coming, it was as if a cork had been pulled out and he couldn't stop himself from confessing. She'd been like a man of the cloth, listening to his sins and offering him absolution. However, unlike a minister, it was up to Eppie as to whether or not she would absolve him.

The image of Edward and his mother had woken him in a cold sweat many nights. He tried in vain to remember exactly what had happened, but still he couldn't quite get all the details clear. The room had been full of shadows, yet the noises were clear as a bell since it had been two people having sex. Micah didn't know what he imagined when he returned home, to the beautiful plantation resembling heaven in his mind.

It hadn't been a home anymore. What the Yankees hadn't taken, they'd burned or broken. The fields had been ripped up and salted and looked like a battlefield rather than the lush green memories of his childhood. The house had been gutted, with only remnants of furniture remaining. Anything with value was gone, except for his mother and sister.

He remembered walking through the door, hearing his footsteps slap on the bare floor, his voice echo through the empty shell. Then he heard the grunts and the slaps. Before he could think about what he was doing, Micah had run up the stairs two at a time, to see his mother on her marriage bed with Edward. He'd gone berserk, he knew it, but he had been outside his mind and body. Truly he remembered watching what happened instead of participating.

But oh, how he'd participated. The screaming, the blood, the confusion. Sarah appeared like a small, lithe creature with the saddest eyes he'd ever seen. She was emaciated, with gaunt cheeks and dirt embedded in her skin. At first, Micah had thought she was a ghost, then she'd spoken.

Micah stopped in his tracks, awash in a memory he'd repressed for years. Sarah had followed him to the kitchen, the screams of their mother echoed through the house. Vivian Spalding had been a spoiled, shallow woman who had lost what mind she'd had during the war. She'd treated Micah as a convenient heir to the fortune and had never once hugged or kissed him his entire life. Sarah, however, was a different story.

She was six years younger than Micah more strength than any woman he'd met until Madeline and Eppie came into his life so many years later. Sarah was quiet and reserved, but so smart and clever. She'd brought life into Micah's existence. He'd ignored her most of her life, except when she pushed her way through the haze. Sarah was a constant in his tumultuous life, and there she'd been again, saving him from himself.

In the kitchen that fateful day, she was the one who stitched his face and bandaged him. She even gave him some of their precious stash of food and a pair of his father's shoes hidden in the closet wall. There was even a hat she produced from somewhere to give him. Micah didn't know what to say to her, so he'd said nothing. Sarah, however, had something to say. He was finally remembering her, and her gift to him.

"You must go now, Micah. I will take care of her. Please, keep yourself safe." She hugged him, the first of his life, then disappeared back upstairs.

Micah dropped to his knees on the wet ground as the image of his sister burned in his mind. How had he forgotten Sarah? She'd saved his life, maybe his soul when she prevented him from killing their mother. There hadn't been anyone in his life who had accepted him as he was except his sister.

A hand on his head started the tears flowing, and Eppie was there beside him, wrapping her arms around his shoulders. A storm of pain wreaked its havoc on him and the love of his life was there for him. He sobbed for the boy he was, the man he was ashamed of, and the man he wanted to be. He cried for Eppie and the lost days of her life, and for the moments he'd lost with her. Then, finally, he cried for all those souls he'd taken from the world, praying for them and for himself.

Through it all, Eppie was there, in his arms, his heart, and in his soul.

Chapter Eleven

"Tell me about Miracle."

Eppie snuggled against Micah's chest as they lay in front of the fire, exhausted from an emotional explosion. After returning to the cabin, they simply lay together, quiet and spent. She was proud of him, of his courage to face that which lurked in his memories, ate away at his soul, and kept a piece of his heart.

It had been hard to accept his sins, but since she had no idea what sins lay in her past, she had no right to judge him. She only knew Micah as he was, not as he had been. It had been easy for her to make a decision to keep him close. Only seconds after he left the cabin, she went after him. It had been a good thing his footprints had been easy to follow in the mud.

When she'd seen him kneeling on the ground, crying as if his heart were broken, Eppie knew she'd made the right choice. Giving him her heart had been the easy part; building their lives together would be the hard part. Miracle was a bond they both shared, and although she'd known her for a month, she needed to know more.

"What do you want to know?" His voice was hoarse, as if he'd been shouting, but she knew it was worn from the emotional storm he'd endured.

"Everything. Tell me about the day she was born. When is her birthday?"

Micah smiled slowly, a father's pride on his face. "Believe it or not, she was born on Christmas."

Eppie sucked in a surprised breath and thought about the implications of having a child born on such an amazing day. It would be a memory she'd never share and she wanted to find out every detail she could. "What happened?"

"You know, you're the first person to ask." He rolled over and bracketed his arm with his elbow. His gaze went to a memory, to a far, faraway place. "It was the most harrowing experience of my life."

Two beats passed by before Eppie answered. "Do I want to know how close I came to dying?"

"No, and I don't think I can let myself remember." He touched her nose with a fingertip. "It was the second time I'd almost lost you."

"Was Doctor Carmichael there?"

He nodded. "Madeline paid him to stay at the house the last two months. He's the reason both of you are still alive, and for that he has my gratitude forever. After that night, there was only one thing I could name her."

"Miracle." Goosebumps raced across her skin.

"Miracle. She howled with a pair of lungs to rival an opera singer. It was the sweetest music I'd ever heard."

Eppie pictured the baby version of Miracle, squalling and fighting her way into the world. There were many things she knew Micah wouldn't tell her about the birth of their daughter. Judging by the lingering pain in his gaze, she would never know.

"She was worried about you."

Micah's smile faded. "I owe her an apology. I owe you an apology." He sat up and took her hands into his, clutching them firmly but without hurting her. "I ran because I was afraid. I thought I'd lost you, that you'd made the choice to do what you could to regain your memory. It was cowardly, and believe me, I know what cowardly is."

She shook her head. "You're a fool, Micah. I never made such a choice. And you are no coward."

"I'm more than a fool." He chuckled without humor. "But I couldn't lose you again." The agony was clear in his voice.

Eppie knew his love would be an enormous thing. He loved her so much, it had survived death twice, and more than three years of her floating between two worlds. The strength of his love was now so clear it shone like the full moon outside the window.

"You didn't." She kissed his hand. "I'm right here."

Micah closed his eyes and pulled her close to him. His heart thumped hard against her. Eppie breathed in his scent and thanked God she'd survived to find a man who loved her enough to battle death. Life, it seemed, triumphed after all.

They spent the rest of the day sleeping, talking and making love. In the morning, it was time to return to Plum Creek and to Miracle. The sun shone brightly on the forest floor, making the greenery sparkle. Eppie hadn't felt as happy since she'd woken from the coma.

They rode the horses carefully down the mountain, with Micah showing her the side trail she would have found quite useful the day before. It took longer than the main trail, but the incline wasn't as steep and they made it down to Plum Creek in three hours. It was a comfortable silence that lay between them during the ride, making Eppie feel as though she had finally found peace.

The house looked the same, with the beautiful flowers blowing gently in the breeze. Eppie looked for Miracle or Daisy to pop up or to come around the corner, yet nothing moved but the petals and the porch swing.

The good mood began to fade as a feeling of dread crawled up her skin. The hairs on the back of her neck stood up and she turned to look at Micah. His smile had faded to a frown; he was apparently feeling as apprehensive as she was.

"Something's wrong."

"Maybe they're just worried about us." Eppie shifted on the saddle. "We did both disappear up the mountain."

Micah's nostrils flared as he gazed around the yard. "No, that's not it. Something's wrong. There hasn't been a sunny day all summer that Miracle hasn't been outside with that dog."

"Madeline is keeping her inside so she doesn't go look for us." Eppie wasn't ready to believe her own excuse, but it was a reasonable one.

As they made it to the carriage house, the eerie sound of the wind whistled through the open door. Micah dismounted and came around to assist Eppie. His strong hands felt warm on her waist, but it didn't chase the chill away.

Eppie swallowed, but just barely, past the lump in her throat. She walked slowly toward the back door, unwilling to speculate as to why she felt so uncomfortable.

When the door burst open, she jumped a foot in the air in fright. Teague stood there, his face a mask of fury and distress.

"Thank God. Get in here now." He didn't wait for them to respond. He turned around and disappeared into the house.

Eppie was glad for the split skirt as she ran for the house, terrified of what they'd find. So many scenes ran through her mind, from Miracle falling down a well to being bitten by an animal to her running away. She imagined so many awful things that tears were already falling from her eyes by the time she made it into the kitchen.

Madeline sat at the table with red-rimmed eyes, a cup of coffee in her hands. Teague stood behind her, arms crossed, the ever-present deep frown creasing his forehead.

Miracle was nowhere to be seen.

"Where is she?" Micah voiced the words stuck in Eppie's throat.

Eppie's terror over what had happened to their daughter knew no bounds. She had finally found where she belonged, had accepted the love Micah was willing to give, and had even fallen in love with the little girl who called her Mama. Now, it appeared, God was ready to shatter that happiness.

"Mathias took her." Madeline's voice was hoarse with emotion.

"Fucking son of a bitch." Micah punched the wall. "He had no right to touch her. I told him that."

"Who's Mathias and why did he take Miracle?" Eppie felt helpless in the face of a stranger taking her daughter.

"The good reverend." Micah spat. "Where did he take her?"

"I don't know." Madeline shook her head as tears streamed down her cheeks. "I'm sorry I failed to protect your daughter. She was outside playing and I came in to get my hat. When I went back out, she was gone." Her voice caught on the last word.

"I scoured the house and the property for her." Teague finally spoke. "That's when I found the letter stuck in the door."

Eppie finally noticed the paper lying on the table, curled onto itself like a dead spider. Bile crawled up her throat as the claws of terror sank into her. She reached out and picked up the letter with her fingertips, unwilling to touch it more than necessary.

Mr. Spalding,
   I warned you that your daughter needed two competent parents. Now it appears you've left her under the care of an accused embezzler and her convict husband. I cannot let that situation continue in good conscience. I've taken Miracle to a family with two parents of her kind who can take care of her properly.

   Reverend Elmer Mathias

Eppie read the letter out loud, her fear shifting into rage. By the time she was done, she was ready to find a gun and shoot the pompous, self-righteous son of a bitch.

"He'd threatened this before?" she asked Micah.

Micah clenched his hands into fists. "Yes, he did, but I was always here to stop him. I never thought he was watching the goddamn house waiting for us to leave at the same time."

"It appears that's exactly what he was doing." Madeline wiped her eyes. "I sent Teague down to send a wire to our attorney in Denver for help."

"Attorney? Do you think this will become a legal fight?" Eppie was still learning about the world around her. The fact that a court could be involved hadn't entered her mind yet.

"Absolutely. He's kidnapped her, forced her to leave her home. You can be damn sure he won't get away with it." Madeline rose, her tears giving way to the same iron resolution Eppie felt. "Let's go talk to the sheriff."

"What the hell is he going to do? The boy can't be more than twenty." Micah scoffed. "He barely shaves."

"I believe he's twenty-five, and he's honest, for one thing. He has a good heart. He can help us." Madeline put her cup in the sink and turned to Eppie. "I'm so sorry, Elizabeth."

Eppie swallowed the tears back, knowing if she let them out again, she'd have trouble getting them back in. Instead she hugged her friend quickly, then stepped back.

" You have nothing to be sorry for. Let's go find her."

The four of them left the house together, ready to mount the search for the missing child.

Micah wanted a drink. The need was so strong, he had to keep swallowing the saliva that gathered in his mouth. Whiskey was a powerful draw and he barely resisted the urge to run into the house and bring a bottle of it with him.

Two things prevented him from falling back into the bottle.

Miracle and Eppie.

Miracle needed her daddy and he hadn't been there to protect her. For that he might never forgive himself. Someone had taken her away from her family and he intended to make the reverend pay for his crime. First, however, he needed to find his little curly-haired moppet and bring her to safety.

Eppie was the heart beating in his chest. She'd seen him in the throes of drunkenness before and no doubt she hadn't forgotten it. The details were hazy for him, unfortunately, and he was embarrassed that he'd even succumbed to the lure of liquor. Yet the love he had for Eppie was stronger than any need for whiskey.

Teague hooked up the carriage horses and drove the women into town while Micah rode beside them on his buckskin. The faithful equine must've sensed his master's anger, because he danced a bit when Micah mounted him. Micah had to remind himself that anger could and would cloud his judgment, to keep control over his emotions.

But oh, it was so hard. He kept imagining Miracle alone, crying and asking for her Daddy. Or worse, being beaten or punished for not listening to her "new" parents. The thought of anyone hurting his daughter made him want to howl in rage and frustration.

Eppie seemed to be having the same problem. Her jaw was clenched so tight as she rode in the carriage, he swore he heard her teeth grinding from ten feet away. Her normally vibrant skin was pale and washed out. She had been telling the truth when she said she'd fallen in love with their daughter. Obviously her feelings were as strong as his.

They had to find her or Micah didn't think he could live with himself or his failures. Eppie and Miracle were the glue that held him together. Without them, he'd be a shell of a man, adrift in a sea of misery.

The sheriff had been on the job since the prior sheriff, the infamous Jackson Webster, had been jailed for his crimes.

The young man had moved to town from a nearby rural area, eager to serve the citizens of Plum Creek. Daniel Morton had been faithful in that regard, earning the respect and loyalty of the town.

However, Micah had distrusted the law almost as long as Daniel had been alive. Just because the new sheriff was friendly and didn't rob people blind, Micah wasn't ready to throw away his hard-earned skepticism.

When they arrived at the sheriff's office, Eppie climbed out of the carriage before Micah had even stopped his horse. She marched to the door and walked in, leaving Micah to follow.

By the time he entered the sheriff's office, Eppie was introducing herself to Daniel. She'd never met the man, considering she'd been in a coma when he started the job.

"I've been hearing folks talk about you for the last month. It's a pleasure to finally meet you, Miss Archer." Daniel was pleasantly bland, as usual.

"It's a pleasure to meet you, Sheriff Morton." She glanced at Micah, controlled fear and anger in her gaze.

Daniel was a blond with bright blue eyes. He was fresh-faced and looked as though he hadn't had one thing go wrong in his life. Perhaps that was one of the reasons Micah didn't like him, if he were honest with himself.

In any case, the sheriff rarely had a harsh word for anyone and somehow managed to keep order in the small town without making enemies or putting in a hard day's work. As far as Micah was concerned, if a man didn't sweat, it wasn't a hard day's work.

"Mornin', Micah." Daniel nodded from his perch on the corner of his desk.

"Daniel." He stood next to Eppie, marking his territory.

"Mr. Spalding and I have a problem and we need your help." She took Micah's hand into her cold one. "It appears Reverend Mathias has kidnapped our daughter."

Daniel's eyes widened. Two beats passed by. "Pardon me? He did what?"

Eppie pulled the letter from her pocket. "While Micah and I were out of the house, the reverend took it upon himself to kidnap our daughter." Her hand shook as she held the paper out for the sheriff, yet her spine remained ramrod straight. "He needs to be found, arrested and charged."

To Daniel's credit, he only blinked once before he took the paper. Micah had expected him to scoff at their story and chuckle about how children tend to disappear for a bit, then come home when they're hungry. Cynicism certainly had its roots deeply woven within Micah's mind.

"Where were the two of you when he took her?" Gone was the silly, blank-faced boy and suddenly in his place was an alert man. Micah couldn't have been more surprised.

"We were up at my cabin. Had some things to take care of." Micah wasn't about to reveal exactly what things they took care of.

Daniel nodded. "I've seen your cabin. I'd say you had more than a few things to do. Did anyone see Mathias?"

Madeline appeared in the doorway. "No one saw him. I had gone inside for two minutes to fetch my hat. Mathias must have been watching the house."

The fact that the reverend had obviously waited until the girl was out of sight and alone made Micah's fury surge anew. That sick bastard had warned him, as much as told him he'd take her away, yet Micah had been too stupid to listen.

His stomach churned to think of Miracle in the reverend's filthy hands. She was barely a little girl, and so special, whatever the man had in mind for her couldn't be any worse than what Micah imagined.

"You sure about that?"

"He's come by the house lots of times telling me Miracle needed a proper set of parents. I always told him to leave."

Micah regretted that now. He should have already told Daniel what had been happening. "I was obviously a complete idiot."

"He also came by when I was alone shortly after I woke up from the coma." Eppie visibly shuddered. "Told me God had been punishing me for having a child outside the bonds of matrimony."

Daniel frowned and glanced at the paper again. "He's well respected in town."

"Only by people like the evil blond triplets." Micah mumbled under his breath.

"What was that?" Daniel looked at him questioningly.

"Nothing. I can't imagine his fire and brimstone sermons actually endear townsfolks to him. They tolerate him because he's an old man who wears a minister's collar." Micah remembered the one Sunday he'd ventured to Plum Creek's church. Even he'd been shocked by the ferocity of the reverend's hell and damnation speech.

"While I don't get to church much, it's true what you say. He definitely can tell a hair-raising tale." The sheriff rose and walked around to the chair behind his desk. "Let's start from the beginning."

Micah wanted to mount a search immediately. In fact, he had trouble restraining himself from insisting on it. Yet, Daniel showed common sense, and Micah recognized the younger man had a better plan than his. He always did have trouble with controlling his impulses.

Madeline proceeded to tell the story of her adversarial relationship with Reverend Mathias. He'd come to town when she'd been ten, a formidable man who bullied his way into the church when the elderly minister had passed away.

"He'd always spend his time judging other people, trying to force them to be what he expected them to be instead of who they were." Madeline's tone reflected an old hurt and anger. "My father tolerated him in the house because of his influence on the rest of the town. I've never trusted him. A spiritual leader should never judge, belittle or frighten any member of his flock."

"I have to agree with you there." Daniel took notes on a scrap of paper as she spoke.

"It only got worse when Teague and I, um, found each other. If Mathias had had his way, I would've stayed a spinster for the rest of my life. In his opinion, Teague isn't good enough to be my husband or the father of my boys. He tried his damndest, pardon my language, to ruin our relationship." Madeline had gained momentum and showed her anger instead of pain. "Reverend Mathias is a bigot, a bully, and apparently also a kidnapper."

Eppie's face had grown paler as Madeline spoke. "I didn't know," she barely whispered.

"I'm sorry." Madeline put her hand on Eppie's shoulder. "It never crossed my mind that he was bothering Micah or that he'd go so far as to kidnap Miracle."

Eppie visibly swallowed. "He sounds like a monster."

"He is." Micah slapped his hand on the desk. "We need to stop talking and start walking."

"If we don't get all the facts before we begin investigating, then we might miss something. I know you're anxious to find your daughter. I can only imagine what you're feeling, but please let me do my job." Daniel kept a steady gaze locked on Micah.

Eppie swayed, and Micah took hold of her arm. "This is too much for you." He was concerned about how she was reacting to Miracle's disappearance.

"No, I'm not going home. There's absolutely no way I will step foot in that house without Miracle in my arms." Her voice was a lot stronger than her body. For that, Micah was proud of her, yet that didn't make him any less concerned.

Daniel tapped his pencil on the desk. "Then we'd better

get all the information we need. Micah, tell me about the reverend and his threats."

Micah took a deep breath, swallowing the panic along with the bile that had risen up his throat. "He started coming round the house a few months after Madeline and Teague moved to Denver. Eppie, I mean Elizabeth, had recovered from the gunshot wound, but was still in the coma."

He took a step back in time, remembering the first time he'd had occasion to meet the not-so-good Reverend Mathias. "It was a Saturday afternoon and I was outside working on the fence. Orion was still alive then. He lived with me in the house, puttering around doing small repairs and tending to the garden."

"Who's Orion?" Daniel paused, pencil in midair.

"He was the former sheriff's servant, who became my friend and houseguest after Jackson Webster went to jail as he deserved." Madeline's vehemence surprised even Micah. Teague put his arm around her shoulders.

"If it were up to Mathias, I'd have been strung up." Teague said quietly. "He as much told me that once."

"I didn't know that." Madeline looked up at him with regret in her eyes. "You never told me."

The corner of Teague's mouth lifted. "I'm a big boy, Maddie. I can take care of myself."

"I thought the same thing, big boy. Now look what happened." Micah was starting to lose control of his emotions again. "He came by every month for the next two years. Every time, he kept after me about Miracle and a proper home. Goddammit, why didn't I pay attention?"

Micah wanted to punch, kick, kill something. He felt a haze of red drop over his eyes and he lost track of where he was. Eppie's voice pulled him back from the edge of insanity. He found himself on the floor being held down by Teague and Daniel.

Blood dripped down into one eye and his hands hurt like hell.

"Micah, please, stop." Eppie was cupping his face, looking down at him, eyes wide with fear.

"What happened?" he croaked.

"You beat the shit out of the wall with your face and hands." Teague punctuated the statement by pressing down on his shoulder. "Thought I was going to have to knock you into next week."

"Let him up." Eppie pushed at the two men, as if she wasn't half their weight.

"Only if he promises to stop picking fights with the jail." Daniel's words were light, but his tone wasn't.

Micah shook with the knowledge he'd lost control of himself completely. The last two minutes didn't even exist in his memory. Obviously he could do it at any time, any place without warning. God, he could hurt those he loved instead of just himself.

Teague finally released the pressure on his shoulder and Daniel helped Micah to his feet. His head swam for a moment and he was almost grateful for Teague's big presence. After he wiped the blood from his eyes, he finally saw his hands. The knuckles were not only bloodied but filled with splinters and pieces of glass.

What had he done?

"I'd blame it on the whiskey, but I know you haven't had any." Teague walked him over to the chair in front of the sheriff's desk. "Now sit down and let your woman tend to those wounds."

Micah more or less fell into the chair and waited for Eppie to yell at him. Jesus, he wanted to yell at himself. He had lost the control he'd fought so long to maintain. It was as if he was back on the battlefield again, full of bloodlust and fury.

"I'm sorry." He whispered to her as she kneeled in front of him. "I didn't mean to make things more difficult."

She pulled a handkerchief from her sleeve. "It's okay. I wish I could do the same thing, but my body doesn't have the strength." She tended to his hands as Teague and Daniel spoke quietly in the corner.

Micah forced himself to look at the wall and window, shocked by the amount of damage he'd inflicted in only two minutes. At least half a dozen boards were broken, many with fist-sized holes in them. The window frame was bent and the entire lower pane shattered. Blood peppered the shards sticking up. His stomach did a flip at the sight.

"What have I done?"

Eppie wrapped the handkerchief around his hand and met his gaze. The fear was gone; in its place were determination and strength.

"She's a part of both of us. Anger is natural. Fear is, too. Let's fight to find her instead of fighting the feelings." The old Eppie would have yelled at him and likely smacked him upside the head. The new Eppie used logic and was calmer than a pond on a cloudless day.

He was proud of her.

"You shame me. I wish I had half the mind you do." He managed a tremulous smile.

"You've got twice the mind I do. Now let's focus on Miracle so we can find her."

Micah nodded, too overwhelmed to speak. He took another handkerchief from a very concerned and disapproving Maddie. After wiping the blood from his eye, he nodded his thanks to her.

"You'd best get yourself in order, Micah Spalding. Your daughter won't appreciate her father being a mess." Madeline was nothing if not honest.

Eppie rose and turned to the sheriff. "I think we've given you enough evidence to launch a search for Miracle. With the letter and all the testimony there is no reason not to believe us."

"I do believe you, Miss Archer. I'm trying to determine where he might have taken her." Daniel glanced at his notes on the desk. "Did he mention any families in particular when he was talking about it?"

Micah thought back to all the times the man had visited the house. "No, none that I can think of."

"That would've made things a bit easier, but we can do this step by step and find her." Daniel met Micah's gaze. "I don't want to have to arrest you for killing the man."

Micah knew what the sheriff was letting him know, without actually telling him—control himself. The truth was, Micah could have easily used his wartime skills to kill Mathias, but that would leave Eppie without a husband-to-be and Miracle without a father. He wasn't about to risk everything he held dear because of one bastard who thought he was better suited to determine the course of other people's lives.

"I don't expect you'll have to. I plan on bringing him to justice, the lawful kind." Micah knew the sheriff didn't entirely believe him, but it didn't really matter too much. It only mattered that the man help them.

"I'm glad to hear that. Now let's see if we can get some folks to help us."

Micah nearly choked himself on a snort. "You expect people in town to help us search? That's nigh on impossible, Daniel."

"No I don't think so. Believe it or not, most folks in Plum Creek are friendly and like to help their neighbor." While Daniel was convinced of what he said, Madeline looked as distrustful as Micah felt.

"I suppose it can't hurt anything to ask." Eppie kept her expression neutral, but there were doubts dancing in her eyes.

"Let's start with Candice. We know at least she will help us." Madeline started out the door with Teague on her heels.

Eppie looked between Daniel and Micah. "I'm counting

on the two of you to bring my daughter home safely, or my heart will most assuredly break." Her voice was low and hoarse, filled with a hundred emotions, not the least of which was guilt.

Micah felt the same measure of guilt. He'd spent so much time worrying about how he felt, he ignored the one person who deserved much more than he gave her.

"My heart's already broken." He kissed her on the forehead. "I promise you, I will bring Miracle home or die trying."

That was one promise he intended to keep.

Chapter Twelve

Eppie kept pinching the back of her hand to focus. Her heart ached so much, the pain was nearly unbearable. The selfish needs of the adults in her life had left Miracle alone and unprotected. If Eppie kept imagining what was happening to her daughter, she might simply lose whatever mind she had left.

They walked together as a group to Candice's store. It was getting close to dinnertime, so there were more folks out and about, on their way to wherever the meal place was for them. Daniel, bless his heart, spoke to each one of them as they passed, recruiting volunteers.

"Good morning, Hiram."

The older man with the wispy white hair stopped and nodded to everyone. "Mornin' Daniel. Miz O'Neal." For Madeline, he smiled, apparently smitten with the tall dark-haired banker.

"Things are going well on your farm?" Madeline asked politely.

"Yes, ma'am, they surely are. Thanks to you and that extension you gave me. The missus and me are mighty grateful for it."

"I'm glad to hear that. We need your help now, Hiram." Madeline tended to take control of situations, and Eppie was glad of it. She didn't think she could explain everything coherently. She was having trouble not falling into a pile of anger and pain, as Micah had done in the sheriff's office. It had scared the hell out of her, but deep down, she understood his struggle for control. He'd traveled to hell and back in his lifetime and carried many ghosts on his back.

"Little Miracle Spalding was taken this morning by Reverend Mathias. He apparently intends on giving her to a family to adopt." She gestured to Eppie and Micah. "Without her parents' permission, of course. Will you help us look for them?"

Hiram looked horrified. "He done took a child? What was he thinking? A'course I'll help. Let me tell the missus and I'll be back in a jiffy." He tipped his hat to Eppie. "I'm right sorry about your daughter, ma'am."

With that, he shuffled off down the street at a pretty brisk pace for an older man. It appeared they had one more person to help with the search, a blessing to be sure. However, Eppie wasn't certain many more people would help, given the way she'd been treated in town.

However, Eppie was glad to be proven wrong. By the time they'd made it to Candice's store, they had five more men willing to help in the search. Every one of them expressed the same sentiment to Eppie as Hiram had. And each time they did, Eppie felt stronger, more hopeful.

Until they ran into Matilda Webster.

The former sheriff's wife and her two constant companions, Beatrice and Virginia, walked down the sidewalk toward the general store. When Matilda caught sight of them, she smiled. However, there was no joy in that smile.

"Well, what do we have here? Madeline, I'm surprised to see you in town." She flicked her gaze across the group. "Is there a fire somewhere? You all seem to be in a hurry."

Madeline had more diplomatic skills than Eppie could muster. "Hello, Matilda, yes I'm in town for a visit. And yes, we are in a hurry. If you'll excuse us?"

They tried to move around her, but she stepped in their

way. Eppie's anger surged through her. She didn't have time for this woman's petty games. It was time Eppie stood up to Mrs. Webster.

"I'm not sure how much misery one person can heap upon a town, but it seems you're trying to find out." Eppie approached the woman, until they were nearly nose to nose. "I am tired of your malicious petty ways and you are hereby on notice that I won't accept it any longer."

She pushed at Matilda's shoulder and the blonde stumbled backwards.

"How dare you touch me?" Matilda hissed.

"Oh, I'll do more than that if you don't get out of my way." Eppie had built up a good head of anger and Matilda would be the recipient, lucky girl. She glanced at the two women currently backing away from the confrontation. "Your friends obviously realize you've gone too far, Mrs. Webster. I suggest you leave with them."

Matilda glanced at her friends and sneered. "How can you possibly be afraid of this scarecrow?"

Eppie hung on to her temper by a slim thread. "Get out of my way, Matilda. I am trying to find my daughter and every second I spend talking to you is time wasted."

"Your daughter?" Matilda smiled. "You mean you've lost her? Well, perhaps it's for the best. Mongrels don't fit in well in the world."

That, as they say, was the straw that broke the camel's back. Eppie didn't even remember making a fist, but she surely remembered punching Matilda, who flew backwards, landing on her perfect behind on the dusty wood-planked sidewalk.

"Oh, thank God. I've wanted to do that for years." Madeline tucked her arm into Eppie's, and they walked away.

Eppie shook with anger, enough to make her stomach roil. Micah put his hand on the small of her back, leaning down to whisper in her ear.

"I'm proud of you."

That was what she needed. Eppie nodded, sniffing away the tears, and continued on to Candice's store. She had to put Matilda and her small-minded bigotry out of her mind. Miracle needed her mother.

Eppie hadn't expected the townspeople's help, but was grateful for it, more than she could express. Candice's reaction, however, was shocking. Instead of squaring her shoulders and running out the door to look for Miracle, she fell to pieces, sobbing in Madeline's arms.

"I'm sorry, oh God, I'm so sorry." Candice's words were almost incomprehensible.

"It's not your fault, Candice." Madeline patted the redhead's back. "There's no need to blame yourself. Help us find her."

Candice pulled back, swiping at her eyes with a handkerchief. "Oh yes, I am to blame. That man scared me, and I did my best to stay away from him. Only I saw him talking to Miracle and I didn't stop him."

The world came to a stop as Eppie absorbed what Candice said. "What do you mean, you saw him?"

Candice turned her red-rimmed gaze Eppie. "Twice in the last month, since you woke up, he's talked to Miracle when she was outside with Daisy. I s-saw them through the window. I knew he was likely filling her head with nonsense, b-but I did nothing."

Eppie absorbed what Candice said and had to swallow the lump of anger that rose in her throat. The older woman wasn't responsible for the minister's actions, but oh, how Eppie wished she'd have mentioned what she saw. It might have prevented the kidnapping, or at least put everyone on guard. They'd had no idea he had been alone with Miracle.

Micah, however, wasn't as forgiving.

"Dammit, Candice, why the hell didn't you say something?" He stalked the perimeter of the store like a panther, shouting from the dry goods aisle. "I would have kept her inside."

"I'm sorry, Micah." Candice sobbed anew. "I was a coward."

"Why?" Eppie finally spoke. "Why were you so afraid of him?"

Candice visibly shuddered. "After my brother passed away, Reverend Mathias came to me and tried to convince me to sell the store. When that didn't work, he pressured me. When that didn't work, he threatened me."

"He threatened you?" Micah stopped in his tracks and walked back toward the group.

"How did he threaten you?" Daniel now had his pencil and paper ready, blond brows furrowed in concentration.

"One night at the store, I had just turned the sign to CLOSED when he came in. Each time he'd visited, he'd gotten more and more, let's say, forceful in his campaign to get me to sell the store." Candice glanced at Madeline.

"I didn't know. I'm sorry." Madeline took her friend's hand.

"You were the one person who believed in me, and so I'd kept refusing even though I was terrified of being on my own. You were an inspiration to me, a businesswoman who had taken control of her money and made a place for herself." Candice squeezed Madeline's hands. "You have nothing to be sorry for."

"What did the reverend say to you?" Daniel interjected. "Or do to you?"

Eppie hadn't realized the man would stoop to physical intimidation, but Candice's reaction to the sheriff's question made it clear that's what had happened.

She stiffened and inched closer to Madeline. "I told him the store was closed, and he gave me that toothy smile and said he wasn't there to purchase anything. I-I thanked him for stopping by, but I had a supper engagement. He didn't listen and followed me into the back."

Eppie could tell Candice was struggling with her story as she began to shake even harder. "I asked him to leave, but he kept going on about how a woman alone was open season for any predators of the two-legged kind. He p-pinned me against the desk and . . . and made sure I wouldn't tell anyone what he'd done."

She turned her face away, shame written on every square inch of it. Eppie went to her and pulled her into a fierce hug, aching for what the kind woman had endured.

"I'm sorry for what he did." Eppie had underestimated the shopkeeper's strength. She didn't know if she could survive being raped and go on every day seeing the man who'd done it.

"I'm sorry for not telling anyone until now. Miracle might still be safe if I had spoken up."

Suddenly the fact that Miracle was in the reverend's hands, the man who had raped Candice, made every hair on Eppie's body stand up at attention. She released Candice and turned to look at Micah, who appeared as frightened as she was at the possibilities of what might have already occurred.

"Jesus Christ, we have to find her. *Now*." Micah clenched his hands into fists and held her gaze. "Daniel, I've changed my mind. If he's done anything to harm my child, I will kill him."

The cold detachment in his voice told Eppie he would do exactly that, without question or hesitation. She was afraid she agreed with him; a vengeful mother inhabited her soul.

"Candice, later on we will charge him with the crimes he inflicted on you." Daniel was proving himself to be a capable, smart sheriff. Eppie was eternally grateful Micah had been wrong about him. "For now, I need you to wire neighboring towns, including Denver, with a description of Miracle and Mathias. Alert the lawmen that he might try to give her to a family. Can you do that?"

Candice straightened and swiped at the tears on her face with the backs of her hands. "I can and I will. Then I'll help you look for him. I am done hiding behind my fear. I want that man in jail."

"As soon as we can find him, he will be." Daniel handed her a piece of paper. "Here's the wire. We'll be canvassing the town starting now."

Daniel outlined his plan, including the pattern to search, using the store as the center point and working outward in a widening, circular pattern. "Stay together so one can come back here if any information comes up."

Micah nodded. "It's a good plan, a military one if I may say."

Daniel tucked the paper and pencil in his pocket. "You're not the only former soldier here, Micah."

That was a surprise to everyone, judging by the looks on their faces. Eppie didn't care one way or the other who had fought for whom, she just wanted to start searching.

"Let's get started. Remember to come back here and let Candice know what you found or didn't find. She'll be the center of the search." Daniel touched the brim of his hat. "I appreciate your help, Miss Merriweather."

Candice had already started walking toward the telegraph machine in the corner. "I'll be here until we find her, no matter what."

The conviction in Candice's tone let Eppie know the panic and guilt had been overtaken by logic and determination. This was good news for everyone, especially Candice. They needed someone to be at the center and she was the perfect, and obvious, choice.

The five of them filed out of the store and met up with the men who'd volunteered to help. Daniel quickly explained the plan and the men, including Daniel, split off in groups, leaving the four of them alone on the sidewalk.

Eppie couldn't help the tears that pricked her eyes. "I'm ready." She took Micah's hand. "Let's find her."

"No, you and Madeline will stay together and search in town. Teague and I can cover more ground without you." He had apparently already made up his mind. With a quick, hard kiss, he turned to leave the two women alone. When he turned back, agony flashed in his eyes for a brief moment. "I love you, Elizabeth Archer."

She managed a smile. "I love you, Micah Spalding. Find our daughter, please."

"Yes, ma'am." He didn't wait for Teague and started off at a run toward the church.

Teague grunted and kissed Madeline on the cheek before he followed Micah. "I'll try not to kill him," he called over his shoulder.

Madeline took Eppie's arm in hers. "Let's find your Miracle."

Together, they walked from house to house in a circle, recruiting four more people to help. Within thirty minutes, there were at least fifteen people searching for Miracle. Each moment that passed made the ball in Eppie's stomach grow tighter and larger.

She tried not to think about what Mathias had done to Candice, or what could happen to a girl barely out of diapers. She wasn't even three, for God's sake. Even if Miracle was stronger than any child her age, she was still a little girl, unable to fight against an adult man.

Eppie couldn't help but wonder how Micah and Teague were faring, if they'd found any information. That led her to think about whether or not Candice had received any response to her wire. Where was Miracle and why hadn't anyone seen anything?

"Stop it." Madeline stopped in the middle of the sidewalk.

Eppie turned to look at her. "Stop what? Let's keep walking. We need to find her."

"Stop brooding and thinking so hard about what could happen. Miracle is an amazing child, with more courage than most grown people I know. She's fine, but I'm sure she misses her family." Madeline wagged her finger at Eppie. "Her mother wallowing in panic and self-pity isn't helping at all."

Eppie opened her mouth to say she wasn't wallowing but closed it without speaking. Madeline was right. Eppie had allowed herself to sink into a hole of dark thoughts, and it wasn't helping Miracle one bit.

She nodded instead, duly chastised for her selfish, maudlin behavior. The last thing Miracle needed was for her mother to lose sight of finding her, no matter what.

As soon as Eppie took a deep breath, her head felt clearer and her thoughts much more focused. For the next fifteen minutes, they continued in their assigned circle and ended up back in front of the store with no information and no leads whatsoever. Eppie was disappointed until a sudden thought struck her.

"Has anyone checked the church?"

Madeline glanced toward the white building just off the main street. "I don't know. I would have thought Teague and Micah did, but I don't remember the sheriff assigning it."

"Then we're going to check it." Eppie marched down the street, determined to be the one to find Mathias. She heard Madeline behind her as they rushed to the church. Eppie was glad for the split skirt, which allowed her to almost run.

When she got to the church, a light shone beneath the door. Her heart leapt into her throat as she ran up the steps. Madeline shouted behind her as Eppie slammed the door open.

Micah's head snapped up when he heard a woman's shout. It sounded like Madeline and it wasn't a happy sound by any stretch. He tried to figure out which direction the shout had come from, but with the clear sky and the trees scattered throughout town, sound bounced around quite a bit.

They were at the school, searching the grounds and inside to see if Mathias had been there. Teague poked his head out the door.

"Did you hear something?"

Micah walked around to the front. "I did. It was a woman, but I couldn't tell what direction it was from." Dread became a companion to the fear, guilt, and fury that surged through him. He heard Eppie's voice whip through his head.

Give me my daughter.

Something was definitely not right.

"It's Eppie. I think she's found him."

Give me my daughter.

Teague joined him outside and they started walking back toward the center of town. By the time they'd walked fifty yards, Micah started running. Teague's strides were longer, but he kept pace with Micah, without asking questions or speaking. Micah wasn't sure where he was going, but he followed Eppie's voice. It was in his heart and his head, louder than the frantic sound of his blood rushing through his body.

You bastard, give me my daughter.

Within ten minutes, Micah brought them to the church. His heart skipped a beat at the sight of the door wide open. He thought he heard a muffled voice coming from within, which only made him run faster. Even Teague didn't catch up, but Micah didn't care. He heard Eppie screaming, and this time it wasn't in his head.

He flew up the steps into the church, his feet barely touching the wood. Micah burst into the building, momentarily blinded by the dimness of the interior after being in the sunlight for so long. He saw someone struggling near the altar and realized there were three people.

Micah reached the altar and was flabbergasted to find Eppie and Madeline holding Mathias down. His woman's face was a mask of hatred and anger, her lips pulled back into a snarl. "Give me my daughter."

One foot pressed his wrist into the floor while the other stood on the minister's neck. Madeline kneeled on his chest and other arm. Micah couldn't have imagined a more shocking scene.

"What the hell is happening?" Teague boomed from behind him.

"We found him sneaking around in here and he won't,"— Eppie pushed down on Mathias' wrist, making him screech— "tell me where Miracle is."

"So you decided to hold him down and beat him until he gave you the information you wanted?" Micah wouldn't have thought Eppie or Madeline would or could have the backbone to do such a thing.

"Yes." Eppie looked up at Micah, the fierce expression of a mama lion on her face.

"Have you checked the church to see if she's here?" Micah glanced around at the pews askew, bibles scattered on the floor. "Is there a root cellar?"

"No, nothing like that," Madeline pushed her braid to her back. "The only other place to search is the rectory. It's next door."

Micah squatted down and looked into the reverend's face. What he wanted to do was join in the fun of beating the man, but he held himself back, keeping the beast chained deep inside. It howled, however, so loudly Micah could barely hear anything else. "I'm not sure why you think it was acceptable to steal my daughter, but you picked the wrong man to cross, Mathias. Tell us where she is, and I won't kill you."

Judging by the look in the minister's eyes, he believed Micah. Yet Mathias didn't say a word, or even blink his cold blue eyes.

"Teague, go search the rectory. Madeline, you help him. I'll take over guarding the prisoner." His smile was apparently as frightening as it felt because Mathias shook his head. "Too bad you don't appreciate my selection of guard, because it's not your decision."

Eppie looked at him, wisps of hair from under her hat tickling the perspiration drops on her forehead. "I'm glad you're here."

"Me, too." Micah didn't know how he'd face Miracle's disappearance without Eppie.

Madeline wanted to protest, he could tell by the expression on her face, but she allowed him to take over and left with Teague. When their footsteps had faded from the church, Micah turned back to the prone minister.

"I didn't want my friends to hear this, but believe me when I tell you that if anything has happened to my daughter, I don't care what the law does to me, you will be dead." Micah leaned in close, hatred for the man nearly overwhelming him. "Until she is safe in her mother's arms, I hold you personally responsible for everything. I plan on seeing you imprisoned for your crimes and if I had my druthers, strung up on that big oak tree at the edge of town. Do you understand me, Mathias?"

He blinked his eyes twice, then gave a slight nod.

"Good, then let's start again." He looked at Eppie, who watched him with an intense dark stare that sent a shiver up his spine. "Are you all right?"

She didn't answer Micah's question. "Make him tell us where she is."

"I will." Micah hadn't told her everything he'd done during the war, but fortunately or not, he would be able to use those skills on Mathias.

"Good." She took her foot off the minister's throat. "You don't have any more chances, Reverend. I suggest you tell us what we need to know." Eppie's body shook as she moved back another step. "I won't stop Micah."

Micah closed his eyes, thankful for the God who had seen fit to give him a woman who accepted him with all his faults, or his demons. She simply acknowledged what he could or would do without condemning him. He'd always known Eppie was strong, yet this was even more than he imagined.

He had known they were a good match when he met her

so long ago, but he hadn't known they had been made for each other. Now he knew.

"Farm." It was the first sound Mathias had made since Micah had entered the church.

"What was that?" He leaned in close to the minister, his nose wrinkling at the smell of fear emanating from the older man's body.

"Farm, ten miles east." Tears ran down from the reverend's eyes. "A colored couple couldn't have children. God gave them Miracle."

Micah took hold of the man's shirt and pulled him up off the floor. His entire body shook with rage as he barely retrained himself from strangling the bastard. "No, you son of a bitch, God gave Miracle to her real parents."

"They'll kill to keep her." The reverend managed to grin.

"What does that mean?" Micah twisted the shirt harder in his fist. "What did you tell them?"

"That God had seen fit to bless them and they must do everything they can to keep her safe, and to make sure their guns were loaded and ready." He managed a strangled chuckle. "She wanted a child so badly, she was willing to pay for it with her life and what little money they had."

Dammit, it would make getting Miracle back in their arms that much harder, and would require weapons. He glanced at Eppie and knew she had come to the same conclusion. Micah didn't know why Mathias would do such a thing. Perhaps he was one of those miserable people who liked to make others miserable, too.

It didn't matter, because Micah was determined. "I'm going to drag you to the jail and make sure you are behind bars, then I'm going to go find my daughter. If she isn't on a farm ten miles east of Plum Creek, I will be back and then you and I will have our reckoning."

Teague and Madeline reappeared in the doorway of the church. Madeline looked relieved to find the minister still alive. Micah wanted to be angry with her for it, but he couldn't. He'd promised the sheriff he'd let the law take care of Reverend Mathias, but it was a hard promise to keep.

"He's told us where she is."

"Thank God." Madeline took Eppie's arm. "What's next?"

"We bring him to Daniel, then we go get Miracle. She's with a couple that apparently were warned to protect her, by force if necessary." Micah glanced at Teague. "She's out at a farm ten miles east of town." His stomach jittered with the knowledge he'd have his little girl back in an hour.

Eppie walked over to him and cupped his face. "I'm coming with you, Micah, and there's nothing on earth that will stop me."

Micah leaned his forehead against hers, then closed his eyes for a second. When he opened them, he managed to make his voice work, even as emotions threatened to break his self-control.

"Will you marry me?" he whispered.

Her eyes widened. "Now?"

"No, not now, but soon. Please. I want Miracle to know she has a home with a mother and a father, a family who loves her." Suddenly, making Eppie his wife was crucial. "Please."

This time, there was hope in her gaze as she nodded. "I'd be honored."

Micah breathed a sigh of relief.

When they turned to Mathias, he'd been helped to his feet by Teague. The tall, potbellied man was stooped, apparently defeated in his madness.

There were so many things Micah wanted to say to Mathias, but he wasn't what was important. He would save his questions for the minister until later. Micah took Eppie's hand and squeezed. "Let's go find our daughter."

Chapter Thirteen

They arrived at the sheriff's office in record time. It seemed Mathias kept trying to slow them down, but Teague simply dragged him along regardless of what he did. The last five minutes, Teague literally picked the minister up and threw him over his massive shoulder.

Eppie, satisfied the evil man would have no opportunity to run, ran ahead of the group. Daniel wasn't in the jail, but his keys were lying on the desk. She opened the cell and waited for the rest of the group to arrive. Fortunately she didn't have to wait long. A good thing for the floor, as she'd paced a hundred times in two minutes.

"This idiot needs a muzzle," Teague groused as he ducked to step into the jail.

Reverend Mathias was apparently giving a sermon from his perch on Teague's back. Quite loudly. Eppie didn't know what to make of the man's behavior, and if she were honest, she didn't care at that point. All she wanted was to find Miracle and leave the minister locked up until Daniel came back to take care of arresting him. Teague dropped his prisoner on the cot in the cell, exited, and slammed the door shut. Eppie had never been so glad to hear keys turning in a lock.

"I'll stay here with him." Madeline offered, earning an enormous sigh from her husband. "You go find the sheriff."

"Thank God. I might have to uh, put him to sleep if I stayed here." Teague didn't wait for a response and went back out the door in seconds.

Micah kissed Madeline on the cheek. "Thank you, my friend."

"Anything for you." Madeline's eyes were suspiciously moist. Eppie gave Madeline a quick hug, then took Micah's arm.

"We'll be back as soon as we can." Micah looked down at her. "Ready?"

"You shouldn't even have to ask."

They hurried to Candice's store to retrieve the carriage. Ten miles was too far to cover on foot and Eppie was glad to be riding instead of walking. The day had exhausted her beyond measure and if she didn't calm down, she was afraid she would collapse.

Lord knew what Micah would do if Eppie had a fit of the vapors. He'd likely tie her to the bed to keep her in one place. It was too important for her to be there when they found Miracle. The reunion would be a pivotal moment in their family's future, and now that she and Micah were to be married, it was even more important.

"Do you know where you're going?" Eppie managed to ask without wheezing.

"Not sure, but we'll ask Candice. She'll know what farm he was talking about." Micah bounded up the few steps into the store and held the door open for her.

Eppie took a deep breath and tried to pretend she wasn't on the verge of falling on her face. Candice rushed toward them with hope and worry on her face.

"Did you find her?"

"Not yet, but we did find the good reverend. He told us Miracle is at a farm about ten miles east of town. A couple who couldn't have children apparently took his word she was a child without parents." Micah's razor-sharp tone told

Eppie exactly what he thought of someone who would simply accept a child without question. There was no doubt Miracle would have told them she wanted to go home to her mama and daddy.

Not having children might turn folks selfish and Eppie could imagine turning away from what she knew was right when it came to children. Funny how she didn't even think she could ever be a mother a month ago. Now she couldn't imagine ever not being a mother.

Candice, to Eppie's relief, nodded. "Eloise and Homer Prentiss. I know them, but not well. Probably around thirty or so. They have dairy cows, chickens, goats and a highly productive vegetable garden. Bought some of her canned beans last year."

Eppie could hardly focus on Candice's appraisal of the Prentiss family. She only thought about the fact that Eloise and Homer had her daughter and she wanted her back.

"Do you think they'll be any trouble?" Micah clenched his jaw so hard Eppie heard it pop.

"I'm not sure. They were always polite, but not friendly. I know I've sold them bullets and cartridges."

"Dammit." Micah ran his hand down his face.

"What's wrong? What did he tell you?" Candice frowned at them.

"He said they would kill to keep her." Eppie felt a chill creep across her at the thought of having to fight to the death for her daughter. How did things get so upside down?

"Sweet Jesus," Candice breathed. "You're welcome to take whatever you need. Anything I can do to help."

"Thank you." Eppie gave her a quick hug.

Candice met Eppie's gaze. "Where is he?"

"Locked up under Teague's guard." The fear in her friend's eyes made Eppie's heart ache for her.

"Good. I just wanted to say thank you for listening to me. I know most womenfolk don't let on when something bad happens for fear it might happen again." The shopkeeper ducked her head, shame replacing the fear.

Eppie took her by the shoulders. "You have nothing to be ashamed of. He does. That bastard put his hands on you without permission and committed a crime. You are the victim. Do you understand me?"

Candice nodded, but Eppie had a feeling the other woman didn't believe a word she heard. It was too bad women were told to keep their mouths shut and endure.

Eppie would never allow herself to be a victim, no matter how loud she had to be in order to be heard.

"We're headed out then to the Prentiss farm." Micah glanced at the rifles hanging on the wall. "Can we borrow one of those?"

Candice's eyes widened, but she nodded. "You think it will come to shooting those folks?"

"No, but we need to be armed, to be sure we can do what we need to get her back. There's no way in hell I plan on leaving there without Miracle. I want to make sure they understand that." He picked up a big one with a brass loop behind the trigger. "You've got a new Winchester lever action."

"It came in about six months ago, but the man who ordered it never picked it up." Candice wrung her hands together. "I never liked guns. They only lead to someone being shot and killed."

"I'm sorry, Candice, but sometimes you need to go beyond simply talking to people. I will defend my daughter, no matter what I have to do." Micah's hand was steady as a rock as he picked up a box of cartridges from the shelf beneath the rifles. Eppie knew his history and what he was capable of. She hoped he wouldn't have to show her.

Daniel arrived as they walked out of the store. He frowned when he saw the rifle. "Where you headed, Micah?"

"The Prentiss farm to get our daughter back. If you try

and stop me, I might have to knock you into next week."
Micah had never sounded so hard.

Daniel held up his hands. "Don't fight me, Spalding. I am
helping you, remember? Now let me ride along with you so
the Prentisses know you have the law on your side."

"You're right." Micah let out a breath. "I'm sorry, Daniel.
I, it's just, well, really hard."

"I know, so let's work together." Daniel mounted his horse
and waited as Eppie and Micah climbed into the carriage.

Dozens of butterflies swarmed Eppie's stomach while a
hive of bees buzzed in her head. She was nervous, frightened
and excited all at once.

When they returned to Plum Creek, they'd either have
Miracle with them, or one of them might not come back at
all.

As they drove out of town, folks who had been helping
with the search waved. Some shouted "Good luck" while
others said "Go get that little girl." Eppie had thought Plum
Creek was full of selfish, mean citizens who treated her as if
she had the plague. Now she realized it was only a few bad
apples, that many of them were worthy of more respect than
she had been giving them.

There was no doubt people like Matilda Webster and her
entourage of hatred would always be around. Eppie had
hopes the good would outweigh the bad and when they got
Miracle back, they could be a family in Plum Creek.

She fidgeted in the seat, pulling at the seam on her split
skirt, biting her nails, even tapping her feet. Micah kept
glancing at her and she could tell he wanted to tell her to
relax, but judging by his posture, he surely wasn't relaxed either.

The ten miles seemed to take ten years, but in reality it was
only about an hour and a half in the carriage. They could've
taken the horses alone, but then Miracle would have had to
ride back in their laps. Truth was, Eppie was glad to take the

carriage, even if she wanted to get to the farm as fast as a bolt of lightning. Having Daniel with them was a help to her frazzled nerves, but it didn't cure them.

Finally they crested a hill and saw a small farmhouse nestled at the base of a hill. Beside the house was a barn and a small corral. Black-and-white cows dotted the lush green hillside. An idyllic looking setting, yet to Eppie it represented a prison. Miracle's prison.

Micah turned to her, his expression as tight as his grip on the reins. "What if she's not there?"

Eppie's heart stuttered at the thought. She'd blocked the idea that the minister could have been lying. Miracle *had* to be there.

"I can't think about that. She's there. I can feel it." Eppie pointed at the house. "She is there in the house with Mrs. Prentiss, waiting for us." Tears burned her eyes as she swallowed the lump of emotion. "It's been the most incredible, frightening and amazing day. I'd like it to be over."

Micah nodded, looking scared and determined. "Me, too."

He flicked the reins and the carriage headed down the hill toward the farm. The closer they got, the tighter her stomach clenched. When the carriage stopped in front of the house, Eppie thought she might vomit.

Micah, however, was the rock to which she clung. He jumped down and came around to her side. His silver gaze met hers as he picked her up out of the carriage and set her on her feet. Daniel dismounted and stayed beside them.

Without a word, they walked the five feet to the front porch. Eppie shook like a leaf in a summer storm; her teeth even clacked together.

"Let's try the front door and see if they will be reasonable," Daniel suggested.

Micah snorted. "I doubt it, but we can try. My guess is they're out working, since this is a farm."

The door was a plain wood front with an iron latch. Behind that door, Eppie was going to find her daughter. Micah knocked once and they waited an eternity.

No one answered.

Micah knocked a second time, bouncing on his heels as they waited again.

No one answered.

"Maybe they're in the barn or the corral." Eppie's mouth had dried out so much she couldn't swallow. Panic threatened to overwhelm her.

"Maybe." He looked around, but nothing moved aside from the chickens scratching the ground. "Listen."

Blood rushed around so fast all she could hear was the beat in her ears. "I can't hear anything."

"Shhh, listen." He tucked her under his arm and took off her hat. "Close your eyes and listen."

Eppie obeyed, closing her eyes when all she wanted to do was scream and stamp her feet in frustration. He held her close, his solid presence soothing and calming.

At first she heard nothing, then very faintly, a giggle. The pure, sweet sound of Miracle. A surge of the purest hope filled her heart.

"Where is she?" her voice even resonated hope.

"Somewhere toward the barn. We're going to have to be quiet. I don't know what to expect. Jesus, even knocking on the door almost made me jump out of my skin. Something is wrong here at this farm, and I don't trust these Prentiss folks. Not a whit." He met her gaze. "You should stay here with the carriage and let me and Daniel handle this."

"No. I will not stay here and wait as if I haven't been dying inside since I found out she'd been taken." Eppie wouldn't be treated like a weak woman, even if she was currently feeling weak.

"It's safer for you to stay with the carriage. Micah's right." Daniel wasn't very helpful.

"I don't want to worry about both of you." Micah scowled at her.

"That's too bad for you. I will not be left behind. She's my daughter, too."

Micah kissed her hard. "And I can't tell you how long I wanted, waited, wished to hear that. I love you."

"I love you, too." She kissed him back. "I'm still going with you."

He managed a small smile. "Stay behind us, and for God's sake, don't make any noise. We want to surprise them."

As they started down the porch, Micah stopped and went back to the carriage. Eppie wanted to stop him, but she knew he was determined. He loaded the gun and came back to her, his expression unapologetic. Daniel pulled his pistol from its holster and nodded at Micah.

"I won't take a chance with Miracle's life or yours." Micah said when he saw the expression on Eppie's face.

"I know, but I don't have to like it." Although she didn't want him to even have the rifle, much less use it, she understood the necessity. God forbid one of the Prestisses saw the rifle and started shooting. One thing Eppie did know about herself—she hated guns.

"I don't have the time or the patience to have our first argument. Just stay behind us."

"I'm going to take the right side, you take the left. Don't do anything stupid." Daniel pointed at the rifle. "Don't shoot and then ask questions, okay?"

Micah's lips tightened. "I'll try."

"I don't want to have to arrest you. Just be smart, Micah. You won't get her back unless you are." Daniel disappeared around the right side of the house.

Micah took Eppie's hand and crept around the side of the porch. "It's good, isn't it?" she whispered as they stepped into the tall grass. She stuck to his back like a burr.

"What?" his boots made a soft shuffling sound in the grass.

"She's laughing. That's good. It means she's okay." Eppie couldn't get the sound of Miracle's giggle out of her mind. Miracle was happy, if not entirely safe. At least she wasn't screaming or crying. Eppie hung on to that thought. It was the only thing she could cling to.

"I hope so." His answer was barely audible.

"Where are they?" she whispered.

He paused, closing his eyes. Eppie wanted to shake him and force him to simply find Miracle. Micah had been a soldier. No doubt he could track or find someone when needed. However, that didn't make her feel any better.

"Behind the barn, in the corral, I think," he finally answered.

They crept along with Eppie's heart residing somewhere near her throat. Their path was excruciatingly slow, much to her dismay. She'd only heard the one giggle and now the only sound she heard was a cow lowing from the barn and a hawk crying overhead.

It was a beautiful late summer day. Too bad they had to steal back their child. When they reached the barn, a thump from within told them someone was inside.

Micah's gaze met hers and he made a funny motion with his fingers she didn't understand. When she shook her head, he leaned in close and whispered fiercely in her ear.

"Stay here. I'm going to see who's in the barn."

Before she could protest, vehemently, he darted back toward the front of the barn. Eppie wanted to scream in frustration at being left behind, particularly considering she told him she refused to be. Yet he'd done it anyway.

A squeak sounded from her right and she got on her hands and knees to crawl over to the edge of the building. Her breath came in short gasps as she dared to expose her presence and peer around the corner. Her heart beat so loud, it made her ears hurt—she'd never been so afraid even after waking up in a strange house with a strange man hovering over her.

She moved a smidge at a time until she could actually see behind the barn. There was a clearing, the edge of the corral, and on top of a horse, Miracle. Eppie bit her tongue to keep from screaming in surprise and joy. A woman had the horse's reins, leading the brown and white equine in a circle. Miracle was smiling, but she had a firm grip on the saddle horn.

Eppie hadn't thought she had motherly instincts, but seeing her daughter way up on top of that beast made those instincts stand up and bellow like Vikings. How dare they put such a little girl on top of such a big horse? She could break a leg, an arm, or her neck.

Anger surged ahead of fear and apprehension and Eppie decided she needed to do something or risk losing her mind. She didn't know where Micah was, and she couldn't wait for him. Miracle could be hurt at any moment and it was up to her mother to save her.

Eppie knew enough not to spook the horse by shouting, so she decided to try the not-so-sneaky approach. She'd simply walk up and say hello.

Micah was both relieved and disappointed the noise from the barn was a milk cow. She looked at him with big brown eyes and let out a soft "moo." A hysterical laugh bubbled up in his throat, but he swallowed it back down. No need giving himself away.

He was going to go back to Eppie, but a missing board in the back caught his eye. No reason not to take a peek outside and see what he could see. It might give him a bit more information about exactly who or what was on the Prentiss farm.

When he crept up to the hole, he was careful not to disturb any of the dust accumulated on the wall. He didn't want them to discover he'd been there and then catch him by surprise. Sounds of a horse and a woman filtered through the hole, and what sounded like a faint scraping noise.

Micah put his eye down to the hole, which looked like it came from a horse kick, and looked out. He nearly swallowed his own tongue when he saw Miracle up on a horse and Eppie walking toward her.

"Jesus Christ." He backed away from the hole as quickly as possible and tiptoed out of the barn. Fortunately no one saw him, and no critters raised the alarm. Good thing, too, because his hands were so sweaty, he'd probably shoot himself if he had to use the rifle.

He had no idea what Eppie was up to but damned if she didn't listen very well. Micah had been a soldier—he knew what he could, should, and would do to survive. She had no idea, yet she just gallivanted off and put herself in danger, and her only about a hundred ten pounds soaking wet.

Micah darted around the back of the barn, keeping his ear tuned to what was happening, growing more incredulous the closer he got. *Where the hell is Daniel?*

"I am simply parched." The rich southern drawl poured out of Eppie's mouth like warm honey. "That liveryman simply has to be more responsible when he rents buggies. I could've been killed."

The drama playing out was enough to make him want to wring her neck, or kiss her for being so brilliant.

"You're welcome to as much water as you need." A woman's voice answered, soft-spoken and polite. "My daughter and I were just playing a bit."

My daughter.

Like hell.

"She looks awfully small up there on that large horse." Eppie laughed as if she didn't have a brain in her head. "I declare I don't think I've seen such a pretty girl in a dog's age. What's your name, sugar pie?"

Micah held his breath, wondering if Miracle was smart

enough to play along with Eppie's farce. If she wasn't, everything would happen fast. His hand tightened on the rifle as he waited for the girl's answer.

"Betsy." The name sounded hollow and so damn wrong coming from Miracle, it made his stomach roll over.

"Betsy is a lovely name for such a lovely girl." Eppie sounded farther away as if she'd walked a distance.

Micah crawled up to the corner and forced himself to look around the corner. Eppie was at the water pump with a dipper in her hand. She leaned against the pump head, just as casually as if she'd been going for a walk.

The woman was dressed in a plain blue dress without even lace on the collar. Her black shoes were serviceable if not military looking. She appeared to be in her mid-thirties with her hair pulled back in a tight knot at the back of her head. No doubt wondering who the crazy woman was who'd dropped in on her farm unexpectedly, Mrs. Prentiss had her hand on the reins of the horse and looked ready to bolt.

Save her, Eppie.

He put his trust, and his faith, in his woman. She was smarter than most men, and clever to boot. Micah didn't want to threaten anyone or worse, cause bloodshed, but he would without hesitation. Miracle was his daughter, his flesh, his blood. That woman was not her mother, nor would she ever be.

"Betsy was my mama's name," Mrs. Prentiss finally answered.

"A family name? That's precious." Eppie set the dipper back in the pouch hanging from the pump handle and meandered back toward Miracle. She kept her steps steady and slow, but Micah could see her trembling with whatever emotions raced through her.

"Where do you hail from, Miss?" the other woman led the horse to the corral and secured the reins to the fence. Micah hoped like hell she'd take Miracle off the saddle.

"Originally from Virginia. My parents were lucky enough to be born free, so I was, too. After the war, we moved out here to start over." Eppie fanned her face with her lace handkerchief. "Landsakes, it's hot out here today. Feels like summer doesn't want to let go."

That was the truth. Sweat slid down Micah's back like a snake in a river. If it got any hotter, he might not be able to see for the perspiration in his eyes.

"Yes, it surely does. Do you want to come in the house and sit a spell? Homer should be back in an hour or so and can drive you back to town." Mrs. Prentiss reached for Miracle's waist, and Micah had to bite his lip to keep from shouting in triumph.

"That would be very neighborly, Mrs. Prentiss. A bit of shade would work wonders for my constitution." Eppie should look into the theater, because she was playing the role better than any southern belle he'd known.

As soon as Mrs. Prentiss put Miracle on her feet, she ran over to Eppie and hugged her legs. Micah didn't know who looked more surprised, Eppie or Mrs. Prentiss.

"Why, your daughter is very affectionate." Eppie's voice sounded strangled.

"Apparently so." Mrs. Prentiss held out her hand. "Come now, child, let's go inside."

Miracle stood in front of Eppie and folded her arms, the stubborn look Micah had come to dread on her face. "No."

"You mind your mama now, Betsy, and come inside the house." Mrs. Prentiss didn't sound angry, but annoyed nonetheless. While Micah wanted to sympathize with her, he only grinned at his daughter's bravery.

"Mama's here now. I wanna go home."

Three things happened at once and Micah never had a chance to stop them.

Eppie grabbed Miracle and started running.

Mrs. Prentiss let out a holler and followed.

A gun barrel pressed into the back of Micah's head and the unmistakable sound of a trigger being cocked echoed through his ears.

They'd been caught.

Eppie hugged Miracle to her chest. Her little body trembled even as she clung on with her legs wrapped around Eppie's waist. Nothing had ever felt as sweet or as perfect as holding her daughter in her arms. She skidded to a halt as she saw Micah stand. Presumably it was Mr. Prentiss with a rifle pointed at his head. Daniel appeared from the other side of the barn in the corral, his pistol trained on Mr. Prentiss.

She closed her eyes and prayed, hoping God would take pity on the woman he'd let sleep for three years and give her back the joy in her life.

Mrs. Prentiss tried to take Miracle, but the child was good and truly attached. Eppie bared her teeth at the older woman.

"Get your hands off my daughter."

Surprise lit Mrs. Prentiss's brown eyes. "Excuse me? Betsy is my daughter. Now give her to me."

Eppie didn't think she was a courageous person, although in the last month she'd had to test that assumption a few times. Never more so than at that moment. She swallowed the knot of fear in her throat and straightened her spine.

"Ask her." Eppie shifted Miracle to her hip.

"What?" Mrs. Prentiss reared back.

"Ask her who her mother is. Ask her what her name is." Unleashed, Eppie's courage grew to limitless proportions. "I'll tell you. I am her mother and her name is Miracle Spalding." She pointed at Micah, trying to forget he had a gun at his head. "And that is her father Micah Spalding. Miracle was kidnapped from our house this morning by Reverend Mathias. We've come to take our daughter home."

"Impossible." The man behind Micah finally spoke in a deep, rich voice while his massive hands never wavered from the rifle. "The good reverend has been telling us about Betsy for months. Said she was an orphan, a good girl who needed good folks. We didn't think we was cut out to be parents, so we said no for a spell. Until last week."

While Mrs. Prentiss kept trying to pluck Miracle from her arms, Eppie dodged her and kept on talking.

"Reverend Mathias is a kidnapper. He's sitting in the Plum Creek jail right this moment. This girl is my daughter and I will die before I let anyone else take her."

They must have heard the conviction in Eppie's voice because Mrs. Prentiss stopped and her husband lowered the rifle.

"That true? He's in jail?" Homer scratched his head. "He's a nice fellow, him being a preacher and all, it still don't seem likely."

"She's right, ma'am. Reverend Mathias is under arrest for taking the girl." Daniel walked closer. His hands gripped the pistol steadily.

"If you don't believe the sheriff or us, then come back to Plum Creek so you can see for yourself," Micah suggested. "We've told you the truth."

Mrs. Prentiss looked between the two of them. "I still don't believe it. No white man is going to marry or have a child with a colored woman. It just ain't done." She folded her arms across her chest.

Eppie saw the anger pass over Micah's face, and she was sure it was echoed in her own. "That's ridiculous. Did you take a look at Miracle? She has her father's beautiful hair." Eppie stroked the curls.

"And her mother's beautiful eyes and cheekbones." Micah met Eppie's gaze across the fifteen feet that separated them. "They're both exquisite."

"I still ain't believing a word of it." Apparently Eloise was the stubborn one in the marriage.

Eppie was finally able to get Miracle to lift her head. "What's your name?"

"Miracle." The little voice barely carried on the breeze.

"Where's your daddy?"

Miracle pointed at Micah.

"Where's your mama?"

Miracle pushed her hair out of her eyes. "She waked up and found me." She kissed Eppie's cheek. "Mama."

Eppie had trouble keeping the tears from falling out of her eyes. The day had been so full of many different emotions. She'd begun the day unsure of anything but her love for Micah, now she was engaged to be married and truly, thankfully a mother with a wonderful child.

"That don't prove a thing."

"Let's go with them to Plum Creek." Homer slid the rifle out of Micah's hand. "I'll hold on to this shiny thing until we figure the situation out. The sheriff there can keep an eye on both of us."

"Yes, let's go to Plum Creek." Eppie started walking back toward the house. "I'm eager to see just how much trouble Mathias is in."

"It ain't a good idea to speak badly of a preacher." Eloise was not a happy woman, no doubt about that.

"I don't care if he rots in hell. The man deserves every second of it." Eppie's fury rushed out of her mouth. "He's caused numerous people pain and agony. It's about time some came into his life."

Eloise gasped, but didn't say another word, which was a good thing. Eppie might have punched her.

Chapter Fourteen

Micah had never been so nervous in his life. The Prentisses obviously wanted to keep Miracle, and judging by the way they reacted to Eppie's claims, they didn't believe a word she said.

The possibility these strangers might keep his daughter made him break out in a cold sweat. Homer had taken the rifle and he had no way to protect himself, except for his intelligence. Perhaps the man would be reasonable enough to listen.

"Mr. Spalding here can help me hitch up the wagon. The women folk can ride together." Homer didn't appear to be agitated or concerned.

"We have a carriage."

"You and me can fit in the wagon then while they ride in the carriage. Missus can drive a team all right. The sheriff there must have a horse. Let's get moving." Homer took Micah's arm and veered toward the corral. His long strides ate up the ground and Micah had trouble keeping up with him. The man seemed to be on a mission, even if his tone didn't convey it.

Micah glanced back at Eppie. She held on to Miracle, her chin in the air and her back straight. Her gaze met his and he read the love in their chocolate depths.

Without words, he told her how much she meant to him, that he loved her. She nodded slightly and kept walking beside the stoic, severe Eloise. Miracle kept her head buried in Eppie's neck, not raising it to even look where they were going.

Micah's fury surged anew. Miracle was afraid, really afraid for the first time in her short life. No child should ever be scared, or God forbid, suffer through being kidnapped. The Reverend Mathias was lucky he was in the jail, or Micah would have killed him with his bare hands at that moment.

He'd been thinking only of himself, and his own fear over what had happened to Miracle. He should have been thinking about how she would feel. God knew he was still trying to figure out how to be a father, another example of his own imperfections.

Homer led him to the wagon parked near the corral. The men hooked up the horses without a word while the women stood and watched. Eloise had a stare that could melt iron, and she kept it focused on Micah. She must've been waiting for him to try to take the rifle from Homer or something equally bad. However, Micah had had no plans to do so, yet. Not when Eppie and Miracle were in danger. He wouldn't risk their lives for anything.

Homer laid the reins on the wagon when they were done. "Where's the carriage?"

"Out by the road, behind the knot of pine trees." If he had been thinking, he would have hidden it closer, then perhaps they might have gotten away from the farm without being caught.

"Let's all ride up there, then. Missus, why don't you climb in the back with the woman and Betsy."

Micah was surprised to hear Eppie growl. It even scared him. She turned a razor-sharp gaze on Homer.

"Her name is Miracle, not Betsy."

Homer must've been a wise man, because he simply nodded and helped them into the back of the wagon. Micah climbed up into the seat, proud of his woman and her fierceness. Daniel stayed calm, a solid presence between the two men.

They drove out to the carriage and Homer dutifully tried to help the women down from the wagon. When he attempted to take Miracle from Eppie's arms, both of them growled.

"This child was not so disrespectful today." Eloise huffed as she climbed down on her own. "I can see why the reverend would take her away from you."

Eppie turned and went nose to nose with the woman. "You don't know us or what we've done in life to survive. Don't you even dare judge us."

It was like watching two cats hissing and scratching at each other. Homer scrambled back in the wagon and picked up the reins. Micah wanted to laugh at the uncertainty on the other man's face. He had obviously very much underestimated Eppie and her ability to protect herself.

Micah had, too.

The "new" Eppie was well spoken, polite, and didn't appear to have the spark she had before the coma. He'd been wrong about that, very wrong. Not only did she have the spark, but it was a flaming bonfire. She was still Eppie, just an improved version. Micah didn't know why he hadn't seen it before. Perhaps he'd spent so much time mourning the woman he fell in love with, he didn't realize she was right in front of him, no longer a girl, but a woman.

After everyone was settled, albeit uncomfortably close to each other, they set off for Plum Creek. Daniel kept his back straight and never took his eyes off the rifle in Homer's hands. Micah had never experienced a stranger two hours in his life. Homer spent his time fiddling with the reins while Micah watched Eppie attempt to keep as far from Eloise as possible on the carriage seat.

The excruciating ride took longer than usual due to the slow pace kept by Homer's horses. They were two old nags who likely were nearly twenty years old if they were a day. They had good hearts, although the geldings would need a day's rest once they made it into town.

Micah wanted to ask him about where he'd found the ancient nags, but didn't feel that polite conversation was in order. He had to keep reminding himself it wasn't Homer and Eloise's fault that Miracle was kidnapped. His anger should be focused on Mathias and his crimes.

By the time they saw the town in the distance, Micah was ready to tear out his hair. The hardest thing was straining to hear Miracle speak. However, she didn't make a sound the entire time. It made his worry for her even greater.

"Where is the jail? I ain't been there before." Homer sounded sincere, and Micah believed him. The man didn't appear to be the type to break the law for any reason.

"Down toward the hotel, then it's up ahead on the right." Daniel pointed although there was no way Homer could see the building clearly.

"Is it near Miss Candice's store? I know where that is." Homer slowed down even more as they lumbered into town. Micah thought he saw a turtle passing them.

"No, it's down farther than that. Just keep going." *And hurry the hell up before I explode.* Micah's patience was nearly gone.

He turned around to glance at Eppie, but she was whispering to Miracle. The picture they made forced a lump to his throat the size of an apple. He had truly hoped there would be a bond between them, but he hadn't realized how deep it would be. Somehow when he was off drinking and feeling sorry for himself, Eppie and Miracle became mother and daughter.

He turned away, unable to look at them a moment longer or he might embarrass himself by crying. God knew he'd done enough of that to last him two lifetimes.

They finally made it to the jail without any incident. Five or six folks were gathered outside and stepped out in the street when the wagon pulled to a stop. These were all men who volunteered to help look for Miracle. When they spotted Micah, they nodded. When they saw Miracle, they cheered.

Miracle finally looked up at them and frowned. Eppie said something in the girl's ear, and she nodded.

"Daddy," she called to him.

Micah didn't think he ever moved so fast. He literally vaulted off the wagon and ran to his daughter's side, plucking her off the carriage. He carried her to the cheering men as they clapped him on the back and congratulated him on a job well done. Daniel even had a small smile for them.

Miracle watched with wide eyes until the noise had faded to a dull roar.

"Say thank you?" she asked him.

"Of course you can."

"Down." She wiggled until he put her on the sidewalk. She smoothed the gray dress, an awful, hideous color, and looked up at the men.

"Thank you for help," she said to each of them in turn.

Every man took off his hat and knelt down to accept her hug of gratitude. Micah was proud of her and so immensely thankful the men had pitched in to help look for her. He'd hidden from the townspeople for so long, he had missed out on making friends.

"Afternoon, folks." Homer stepped up beside them. Micah had nearly forgotten about the Prentisses.

The men straightened up and eyed Homer. A few of them murmured a hello, while others nodded.

"This is Homer Prentiss. He and his wife Eloise live on a farm right outside town."

What Micah didn't say was they had accepted a kidnapped child as their own, or that they refused to believe she wasn't theirs to keep.

"If you'll excuse us, we need to talk to Reverend Mathias." Daniel had a way of making folks listen. As the men walked away, Micah took Miracle by the hand and opened the door to the jail. Eloise marched past him with Homer at her heels.

Eppie appeared beside him and took his other hand. Her dark eyes were full of uncertainty and determination, a strange combination on any other day.

They walked in together, finally a family united.

"Let's get to jawing with the reverend so we can get this settled. He gave us this girl to keep." Eloise sounded as unmoving as she had at the farm.

"She is their daughter and Mathias had no right to give her to you." Daniel gestured to Miracle. He'd apparently waited to speak his piece until they got back to town. A smart man, considering the Prentisses' insistence on keeping the girl for their own. "I can't let you keep her."

Eloise looked truly shocked. Micah realized she expected to be told they'd been lying about Miracle's parentage.

"These two folks here," she looked at Micah and Eppie. "That woman birthed that *white* baby?"

Eppie almost exploded. "First of all, she's a little girl who is loved by her parents. I don't think people should label others, especially children. We were warned you would do anything to keep her and I see now that means belittling others." She pulled Miracle to her side. "I know you weren't the criminal here, Mrs. Prentiss, but I think you should now accept that you will not have this child. Ever."

Eloise lost all color in her face as Eppie spoke, and Micah even felt sorry for her, a little anyway. Homer had a resigned expression. Too bad his wife didn't share his conclusion.

"I want to see Reverend Mathias." Eloise crossed her arms.

Micah almost heard internal groans from every person in the room.

"Bad man." Miracle looked up at Eloise with shadows in her brown eyes.

Micah's fists once again clenched, the nails biting into his palm to the point of pain. Micah wanted, needed to punch something. Instead he knelt down and cupped Miracle's chin.

"He'll never hurt you again, sprite, I promise."

She nodded sagely, always far too mature for a child her age. " 'Kay."

When he straightened, Daniel was beside him.

"I'm going to take Mrs. Prentiss in to see Mathias. I don't think she's going to give up until she sees him. They're both crazy as batshit as far as I'm concerned."

"He needs to go to prison for good. I'm counting on you to make sure that happens." He glanced down at Miracle. "Too many people have been hurt by that bastard."

"I know, and I'll do the best I can." Daniel turned back to Eloise. "If you follow me, Mrs. Prentiss, I'll take you to see the reverend now."

The next three minutes were quite possibly the worst in Micah's life, which was saying a great deal. He should've realized how much Mrs. Prentiss had been hurt. The stiffer she became, the more she must've been storing up her fury.

When he heard Daniel shout, Micah headed for the cell, which was tucked away in the back of the building. He hadn't made it two steps when a gunshot shattered the afternoon. His heart jumped to a gallop and he remembered Eloise was carrying a reticule.

"Jesus Christ!" Daniel shouted again. "Mrs. Prentiss—"

Sounds of a struggle came as Eloise grunted and Micah's stomach flipped upside down and bile coated the back of his throat. He turned to Eppie.

"Run."

She was a stubborn woman, and instead of running, she shoved Miracle under the desk and started toward the jail cell. Micah stepped in front of her, determined to keep her from getting shot again.

Before he could get her to leave, Eloise came around the corner. She was transformed from the mild-mannered farmer's wife she'd been before seeing the reverend. Her face was a mask of pain and age, with her lips pulled back into a snarl that reminded him of a hellhound.

Her once pristine light blue dress was splattered with blood and what Micah thought was brains. In her hand was a Colt long-nosed pistol. It too was dripping with blood. Eppie gasped and Micah knew a moment of absolute fear she would shoot Eppie and declare herself Miracle's mother.

"What did you do, Eloise?" Homer moaned from behind them. "What did you do?"

"An eye for an eye, a tooth for a tooth." Eloise met Micah's gaze. "He promised us that child, gave us his word she was ours. I won't let him or anyone else take her away."

Micah ran toward the woman, willing to sacrifice himself to save his woman and child. There was a split second when he hoped Eppie would forgive him, then he was locked in a struggle with Eloise.

He didn't think she was very strong, but she appeared to be as capable as a man. They were equally matched; her fanatical anger must have given her the power she lacked. Micah's hand slipped on her wet hand and they crashed into the wall. Eppie shouted at Homer while Micah shouted at her to run. Vaguely he heard Miracle crying from beneath the desk.

Eloise frightened him because if she got past him, she'd kill Eppie. That thought gave him a burst of energy and he slammed Eloise into the wall, nearly dislodging the gun. However, she seemed to have a death grip on the handle and likely wouldn't let go unless she was dead.

Micah had killed many men in his life. Some deserved it,

while others were victims of the same war he'd signed up for. He'd never killed a woman, though, and the very thought would have been repulsive a month ago. Now, he had no qualms about doing anything he needed to.

"She. Is. My. Daughter." Micah said through gritted teeth.

"God gave her to me!" Eloise was winning as the barrel started to turn toward Micah's head. He quickly sent "I love you" to Eppie with his heart. His muscles screamed from the effort of trying to stop Eloise. Her hot breath gushed across his face and he knew the last two moments of his life. He only wished he could see Miracle grow up.

Suddenly Eloise screamed and a blur of movement came from the right. She reared back and that's when Micah realized the struggle between the two of them had added a third person.

Eppie.

Memories flooded through him and panic sank its claws into him.

As he sprinted through the kitchen, he heard Eppie's voice. She was being her usual sassy self, a bad sign. He heard a man's voice responding in kind. Then he heard something that made his stomach drop to his feet.

The sound of a struggle.

He ran as fast as he could down the hallway toward the front door. The sun streaming in blinded him a bit, but he could see two people locked in combat in the threshold.

A split second before he reached them, the bigger one drew his arm back and hit the smaller one as hard as he could. Eppie fell to the floor, hissing and screeching.

A growl of rage burst from his throat as he jumped on the man that dared hit Eppie. Sheriff Webster looked more than surprised to have Micah at his throat. Although pretty evenly matched physically, Micah had fury on his side.

"Get out of this house!" he shouted.

"What the hell are you doing here? This isn't your house," Webster grunted through his teeth.

"Madeline is my friend, and I am watching her property for her while she's gone, you son of a bitch. Now get out!"

"I will not! I have a warrant —"

Micah snorted and pushed the sheriff back toward the door. The lawman's boots slid across the shiny wood floor. Bless Eppie for keeping it that way.

"A fake warrant from a crooked judge is not recognized in this house!"

The sheriff tried to push back, but it was no use—he was nearly out the door. Micah tasted the need for revenge in the back of his mouth for the bastard that would hit Eppie. He brought his arm back to punch the son of a bitch.

That's when Webster pulled his gun.

That's when Eppie screamed *"No!"* and threw herself into the fray. He felt her small body try to get between them.

That's when the gun went off and Eppie fell to the floor in a pool of her own blood.

Micah tried to shake off the memory of when Eppie had been shot by Jackson Webster, but it was as if he couldn't see anything but the past.

He felt Eppie's body press against his as Eloise turned her attention to the small woman who had no regard for her own life. He couldn't, wouldn't lose her again. Not again. His heart beat so fast, he felt dizzy with the blood rushing through him.

"Eppie, get out of here."

"No," she grunted as she tried to knee Eloise in the back. "I won't let her take you from me."

He wanted to cry out in rage at the unfairness of finally having all he wanted, only to have it ripped away.

"You bitch, you whore. God wouldn't give you such a miracle to keep. She's too perfect for you." Eloise elbowed Eppie in the face with a resounding crack.

The sound echoed through Micah's head and heart. She was getting hurt again because of him and he just couldn't allow that to happen. Perhaps deep down he'd been keeping himself from using deadly force against Eloise. No more.

His training as a soldier flashed through him and a burst of energy so strong followed. He whipped his arm up and in one quick move, pushed Eppie out of the way, and pulled the gun from Eloise's hand, tossing it in the corner.

She grunted as he twisted her arm around her back and forced her to the dusty ground. Dirt stuck to the blood and sweat on her face. She tried to buck him off while screaming obscenities.

Homer rocked back and forth hugging himself and mumbling, "Dear God in heaven."

"No God is looking out for her anymore. By my guess she killed two men already. You want me to kill her or would you like to stop her?" Micah was tired of the man's calm demeanor. It was time he showed some courage and backbone.

"She don't know what she's doing. They killed our children, you see, a boy and a girl who were just getting started. The men came and killed them while we was out in the fields. Eloise found them." Homer shook his head. "She ain't been right since then."

Micah felt a twinge of remorse for their dead children, Homer, and maybe even a little for Eloise, but it passed quickly. She had lost whatever respect or rights she had as a human being as far as he was concerned.

"Get over here. Now!" Micah shouted at Homer. "Before I have to kill her."

"Oh, Eloise, what have you done?" Homer appeared to be lost in some kind of haze. Perhaps the war and its aftermath had been too much for both of them. Eloise transformed into a righteous killer while Homer became a shell of a man.

"Go check on Daniel and Mathias." Micah glanced at

Eppie. A stream of blood led from the corner of her mouth. The sight of it made his throat tighten. He sucked in a deep breath and counted to three before speaking again. "If Daniel needs a doctor, we need to get Carmichael down here."

Good soldier that she was, Eppie obeyed this time and walked toward the cell. He wanted to protect her from what she'd see. Gunshot wounds, especially at close range, were messy. However, she couldn't keep Eloise contained by herself. She simply didn't weigh enough, and the other woman's strength was too great.

"Miracle, you all right?"

"I'm okay, Daddy." Her voice sounded so small.

"Good. Stay where you are until Mama or Daddy get you." He looked around for rope, but didn't see an inch of it anywhere. No doubt the meticulous Daniel kept everything in its place.

Eppie came back around the corner, her face a mask of disgust and fear. "She shot Mathias in the face. There's not much left of him to identify. Daniel was shot, too, but the bullet put a furrow in his scalp. He's bleeding but alive."

"Can you run to the house and see if you can find Doctor Carmichael?" He was concerned about her health, but she had to be the one. "Take Miracle with you. She doesn't need to see or hear any more of this."

Eppie nodded, then leaned down and kissed him so hard, he felt it all the way to his toes.

"Stay alive, you hear me?"

"Yes, ma'am." He was never more proud of her than he was at that moment. She was so full of courage, it put his cowardice to shame. Eppie was a warrior, while he had been a sneaking killer. "I love you, Elizabeth."

She tried to grin, then winced. "That's Eppie, and I love you, too."

Eloise struggled beneath him, but he waited until Eppie

and Miracle were safely out of harm's way before he released her. He heard Eppie coax Miracle out from under the desk, then with one last glance his way, they were gone.

For the first time since they'd walked into the jail, Micah was able to take a deep breath. Although Eloise was still dangerous, he could focus on keeping her contained rather than protecting his family.

"Let's get to the cell, Eloise." As he pulled her to her feet, she kicked him in the balls so hard, he almost blacked out.

Before he could recover his wits, and convince his balls to come back down from where they were hiding, she'd run out into the street. Micah knew she would go after Miracle and he had to stop her. Ignoring the excruciating pain between his legs, he limped toward the door. When he noticed the gun was missing from the floor, fear coated his tongue. She would kill Eppie, he was certain of it. Micah couldn't let that happen.

"I'm going to kill her this time," he said to Homer as he passed the nearly silent man.

"God forgives you," Homer whispered. "I hope He can forgive her."

Micah hated to leave Daniel lying on the floor, but he couldn't let Eloise get to his family. He headed out the door, running so fast his feet barely touched the ground.

Chapter Fifteen

Eppie walked hand in hand with Miracle down the street as quickly as they could. She was surprised how many people said hello or told her they were glad Miracle had been found. Others simply ignored her, but even they didn't cross the road as she expected.

Miracle was as quiet as she had been all day, very unusual for the precocious three-year-old she'd come to know. She was a chatterbox, with a never-ending stream of questions about anything and everything. Eppie wanted to rail at the people who had taken away that spark of life from her daughter.

However, the sight of Mathias with his entire face a bloody mass of flesh, blood, and bone had cured her vengeful urges. It was apparent now the stoic demeanor Eloise showed the world was a façade. She must've struggled to keep the rage hidden, like a cork in a bottle.

That cork popped in the jail, and it was as powerful as a tornado ripping through a house. Eloise would never be the same person, and neither would Eppie. It was horrific and frightening to see a person fall into a dark pit in their mind. She hadn't expected it and certainly wasn't ready for it.

When she realized Eloise had killed Mathias and shot Daniel, Eppie had to stop herself from vomiting at the sight. She hoped Daniel would recover. His heartbeat was steady,

but she hated leaving him like that. Micah had been right—
she needed to get Miracle to a safe place and get the doctor to
help the sheriff.

As they turned the corner on the road to home, Miracle's
hand tightened on hers. Eppie stopped and squatted down to
meet her daughter's gaze.

"What's wrong, honey?"

Miracle's dark eyes were wide as saucers. "She's coming."

"Who's coming?" Eppie looked around but saw nothing
but two inquisitive squirrels and a crow.

"New mama's coming." Miracle shuddered.

Eppie's heartbeat, which had finally slowed to a gallop,
kicked up again into a frantic rhythm. She looked down the
road, peering to see if she could see something. There was
nothing. During the last month, Eppie had realized her instincts were always to be trusted. This was no exception.

She picked Miracle up in her arms and ran for the house.
That's when she heard the scream.

It sounded a bit like a coyote who'd been caught in a trap
and was busy gnawing its leg off. The scream echoed through
Eppie's body, giving her an extra boost of energy to run even
faster. The hundred yards seemed more like a thousand.

Her breath came in short bursts as Miracle's tears began to
soak her dress. Eppie had never felt so scared, even when
threatened by Eloise in the sheriff's office. Then she had Miracle safely tucked under the desk. Now they were out in the
open and vulnerable to Eloise's attack.

Her shoes slapped against the hard-packed dirt. That's
when she heard the footsteps behind her, coming faster than
humanly possible. Panic and fear blended within her. Sweat
ran down her face and spine, blending with the tears which
had started falling from her eyes.

"Please God, help me," she whispered against Miracle's
neck.

The footsteps grew closer even as Eppie reached down deep inside her for a well of strength to make it to the house safely. When she heard the sound of a gun hammer cocking, a sob burst from her throat. She didn't want to die in the street like a dog cut down for running wild.

Eloise had no right to Miracle and she surely had no right to kill Eppie for being her mother. The other woman obviously needed more than any doctor could give her. Perhaps whatever happened to them, her children being murdered, had taken away whatever kept the woman sane. Now she was focused on Miracle and obsessed with making her into the dead children she'd lost.

The first shot went past her and embedded into a pine tree to her left. Eppie ducked to the right and tried to make herself as difficult a target as possible. The second shot grazed her shoulder, burning through her shirt and skin. She cried out in pain but didn't lose a step.

Hot blood trickled down her arm and Miracle cried even harder. Eppie thought for a moment she would not survive this time. After all she'd been through, how long she struggled to stay alive and find her place in the world, it seemed tremendously ironic to die by gunshot.

"Eppie!" Micah's voice came from behind them. She had never heard a sweeter sound.

"Help me, Micah!"

The next gunshot went in the other direction and Eppie realized Eloise was shooting at Micah. If she killed him, Eppie would have no qualms about returning the favor. She couldn't worry about him, though, Miracle was the most important thing right then. She kept running, the front gate almost within reach.

She found the strength and grace to jump over the two-foot-high gate and land on the walk with a painful crack in her ankle. The pain moved through her leg and up to her hip.

She knew she was going to fall and twisted around to land on her back.

The ground seemed to be as hard as steel when she thumped onto it. Her back took the brunt of the fall, stealing her breath.

"Mama?" Miracle disentangled herself from Eppie's prone body.

"Run." Eppie managed to wheeze. "Inside."

The girl seemed to understand the danger, because she got up and ran into the house. A second later, Eloise was there, climbing over the fence. Eppie found the strength to get to her knees and grab the other woman around the legs before she could follow Miracle.

The gun was pressed into Eppie's temple. "Let go of me or I will kill you."

A ball of yellow fury appeared from the left, barking and snarling.

Daisy.

The pup latched onto Eloise's leg and gnawed at her, yanking and tugging with all her canine strength. Eloise raised the gun to bash the dog in the head. Eppie couldn't let that happen, not to the brave little puppy who would help save her pint-sized master.

She pulled as hard as she could on Eloise's legs, making her lose her balance. When she hit the ground, Eppie jumped on her, straddling her waist while the other woman tried to point the gun at her head.

They struggled for life and death as Daisy continued her own assault. The gun barrel came perilously close to Eppie's face. The heat from the barrel singed her ear. Her energy began to fade from the run, the injury to her arm, and the fear.

Eppie didn't know if Micah was alive or not, but her heart told her he was. Miracle was also safe inside the house. That left her to stop the threat against her family.

"You bitch, you won't take my child again." Eloise punched Eppie in the arm where she'd been shot.

Eppie gasped at the pain, but didn't loosen her grip. "She's not your child," she growled.

Eloise must've found another well of strength because she gained the advantage again, and the gun inched toward Eppie's face. When it seemed her life would end in seconds, she heard Micah's voice again.

"Let her go." He landed on his knees beside them. His strength combined with Eppie's were too much for Eloise. Micah pulled the gun from her hand with a grunt.

Eloise, however, wasn't going to give up fighting. Her hands closed around Eppie's throat and squeezed. Eppie tried to pull her hands away, but the other woman's grip was stronger. Micah shouted and tried to peel Eloise's hands away.

"Dammit, let her go or so help me God, I'll shoot you." Micah beat at Eloise's arms, but it seemed nothing would stop her from killing Eppie.

Eloise would win, after all.

Everything started to turn black and Eppie gazed into her beloved's beautiful steel-gray eyes. She mouthed "I love you" to him, saying good-bye.

"No!" Micah's shout was full of pain and fry. He pressed the gun to Eloise's forehead and cocked the trigger. "Let her go."

Eloise was already lost to the world and appeared not to hear him. She hardly resembled the conservative woman they'd met only a few hours before.

A roaring sound filled Eppie's ears as the sound of a gunshot echoed through the summer afternoon.

Micah pulled Eppie off Eloise's prone body and laid her on the flower bed. He'd seen the light fading from Eloise's eyes and knew he had no choice. He had to kill her or she would have killed Eppie. He couldn't have allowed that to happen.

He pressed his ear to Eppie's chest and felt a steady heartbeat. Tears ran down his cheeks as relief flooded through him.

"Oh, darlin', I knew you were a fighter."

Daisy appeared beside him, her muzzle spattered with blood, tongue hanging out. He gave the mutt a scratch behind the ears.

"You, puppy, have earned yourself a permanent spot in this house. Good girl."

She woofed softly and nudged Eppie with a whine.

"She should be okay. Let's go inside and get both of you cleaned up." He picked Eppie up and carried her in the house, Daisy at his heels.

He kicked at the door with his foot. "Madeline? Teague?"

The door opened and instead of one of his friends, Miracle poked her head out.

"Daddy?"

Micah smiled at her. "Let us in, honey. I've got to put Mama in her bed and find the doctor."

She nodded and opened the door wide, peering around him to see in front of the house.

"Don't look, baby. Just shut the door." Although he could tell she wanted to argue, she did as she was bid. Although she was young, Miracle had an old soul and the gravity of the situation didn't escape her. He was incredibly proud of her.

He carried Eppie up the stairs two at a time and put her in her bed. Soon it would be a guest room when she moved into his room, but for now, she needed a place to recuperate.

"Miracle, do you know where Doctor Carmichael is?"

She stood in the door, her hands behind her back. "Don't know."

"I need to go look for him." He brought the basin over to the table beside the bed, then poured water into it. "Can you stay here with Mama and put cold water on her neck and face?"

" 'Kay." She came over to the bed and patted Eppie's face with her little hand. "Mama wake up soon?"

"I hope so. I'll be right back." When he left, Miracle was wringing a rag out and patting Eppie's face with it. With the threat of Eloise gone by his hand, there was no need to fear for them being alone. Eppie might have a headache, but God willing, she would suffer no permanent effect from the near strangling.

He ran down the hallway, finding no one in either of the doctors' rooms. Downstairs, the house was empty as well. Where were Teague and Madeline? They weren't at the sheriff's office, which meant they were probably with Candice.

Micah was torn between wanting to stay with Eppie and finding the doctor. He wasn't blessed with any medical skills and both Daniel and Eppie needed more than he could give them. With a determined grimace, he left the house.

Homer sat beside Eloise's body, holding her hand. Micah had forgotten all about him until that moment. Then a fresh wave of fear hit him. Although he'd warned the man of his intent to kill Eloise, Homer could still exact revenge if he was so inclined.

"Homer." Micah waited, fists clenched, pistol tucked into his waistband. He would do what he needed to.

"She used to be such a fine woman. Folks always commented about how nice she looked on Sunday in her church clothes. The children, too. Little Betsy was the spitting image of her mama. While Ephraim wasn't smart like his sister, he was a good boy." Homer's gaze was in the past, ten years or so, as he saw his family when they'd all been alive. Micah felt his pain, his agony over losing them.

"I'm sorry."

"Ain't nothing for you to be sorry for. It was a blessing what you did. I was too much a coward to do it. She ain't been right since they raped and killed Betsy. Left her on our bed they did, while we was out in the fields." He shook his head. "Ephraim had tried to save his sister, and they took an axe to that boy."

The horror of what he'd endured humbled Micah. He didn't know if he would be as calm if his children had been murdered so brutally. He hadn't realized the Prentisses had been through such an excruciating, violent loss.

"She was going to kill my woman."

Homer met his gaze. "I figured she would try. Your woman and that little girl of yours are beautiful. Keep them safe." He picked up his wife's body and walked through the gate, leaving Micah to stare at the bright red pool of blood on the green grass.

His stomach bubbled at the sight. Even after all the atrocities he'd committed during the war, this had been so personal, such a struggle for life and death. It affected him more than he thought possible.

He had to shake himself free of the mesmerizing sight of Eloise's blood. The doctor needed to be found as soon as possible. Micah ran back toward town until he reached the jail. He skidded inside, heart pumping, and found Doctor Carmichael tending Daniel.

"Micah, there you are." Madeline straightened from a crouch beside the sheriff. "Is Eppie all right? What happened?"

Micah sucked in a much needed breath before speaking. "I'll tell you the whole story later. Is he going to be okay?"

"He should be fine." Dr. Carmichael answered. "The bullet just grazed him, but when he fell, he slammed his head into the floor. That knocked him unconscious."

Daniel looked up with pain-filled blue eyes. "Did you get her?"

Micah nodded tightly. "She's not getting back up this time." He turned to Dr. Carmichael. "Where the hell were you? And where is Doctor Lawson?"

"Unfortunately, Dr. Lawson is gone. And I was at the store

with Candice," Carmichael snapped. "She had a fit of the vapors after you left and I had to give her something to calm her down."

Madeline raised one brow. "Eppie and Dr. Lawson had words and apparently he decided to leave Plum Creek. I'll let you ask her about it."

"Well, I didn't like the man, but dammit, I need a doctor for her." He glanced at Doctor Carmichael, and took a deep calming breath. "When you're done here, I need you to come to the house. Eppie was almost strangled."

Madeline gasped. "What?"

Ignoring his friend, Micah continued. "She's unconscious, but her heartbeat is strong and steady. I've got her lying in bed with Miracle putting cold rags on her to cool the skin down. She was probably a minute away from dying."

After he said it out loud, his heart clenched so hard, he actually saw stars. She'd been almost dead, literally dead this time. The life within her was strong enough to fight back until he could save her. Eloise had left him no choice, yet he still regretted killing her. Grief could be such a powerful force; it pushed Eloise over the edge to insanity.

"Jesus Christ. Was it the Prentiss woman?" Teague appeared from behind them, startling Micah. A man that big shouldn't be so damn stealthy.

"Of all days, you picked a hell of a time to sneak up on me," Micah snapped.

Teague held up his hands. "I was sitting in Daniel's chair when you came in like a storm."

Micah threw up his hands. "I'm trying to find a fucking doctor for Eppie."

"Easy, Reb, easy." Teague patted his shoulder. "Maddie and I will go over now and help little Miracle until the doctor is done here."

Dr. Carmichael looked up at Teague. "Try to elevate her feet and keep the cool compresses on her. We want to try to minimize the swelling. If there's a springhouse with cool water, use that instead of well water. Ice would be the best thing, but I don't think we have that luxury here."

"No, there's no ice, but there is a springhouse." Madeline snapped out of her shock and took charge. "Teague, go on ahead. I'll meet you at the house in a few minutes."

She approached Micah and gave him a back-cracking hug. "I'm sorry."

He nodded but couldn't respond. His throat had tightened up again. If the day didn't level out and get back to normal, he might have to jump over the edge of sane reason, too. Micah watched Teague leave and waited not so patiently for the doctor to finish with the injured sheriff.

"You want to tell me what happened?" Daniel winced as the doctor started stitching the furrow in his scalp.

"She came after Eppie and Miracle. Ran faster than anyone I've ever seen in my life, and that's saying something. During the war, retreating troops had wings on their feet, I swear. But her," Micah shook his head and squatted on the floor next to the sheriff. "She seemed to have the speed of hell behind her and a gun in her hand. Took a shot at Eppie and at me while she was running. By the time I got to her, she nearly had the gun in Eppie's mouth."

The image of that scene would haunt his dreams, his nightmares, for the rest of his life. He probably would have lost control completely if Eloise had succeeded in pulling the trigger. His berserk behavior in the sheriff's office in the morning would have been nothing.

"How did Eppie get wounded, then?" Daniel's voice brought Micah back.

"After I got the gun away from Mrs. Prentiss, she strangled Eppie. Her fingers were like damn steel bars and she was killing her. I didn't want to kill her, I swear I didn't." Before he knew it, he was sobbing, tears streaming from his eyes as his own grief poured from him.

Madeline took him in her arms and held him while he cried like a newborn babe. He wept for Eppie and Miracle, for his sister Sarah, for every boy he'd killed in the war, for Eloise, and lastly, for himself. He had spent so much time causing hurt, this time he finally came to the point where he couldn't deny the pain anymore. It surrounded him, filled him, left him a shell of a man.

Micah didn't know how much time had passed since he lost control of his emotions. When he was able to form a complete thought again, Madeline was rocking him and holding on tight.

"It's okay, it's okay. Let it go, Micah." She crooned to him. "Let it go."

For a rich boy turned assassin turned hermit, Micah was likely the luckiest man on Earth. He deserved to be strung up from the big oak tree at the end of the main street. Instead he'd been given gifts of friends, of a wife he loved, and a daughter who was more precious than life.

When he met Madeline's gaze, she handed him a handkerchief and he gratefully wiped his eyes and nose. He was a bit embarrassed but didn't have time for such petty things.

"Thank you," he whispered, his voice hoarse with emotions.

Madeline smiled. "That's what friends are for. You know I'd do anything for you, Micah. Love is what life is all about."

He nodded, moved by the depth of love he had for his friend. She was an amazing woman.

"Let's go make sure Eppie is okay." She rose and held out his hand.

Micah was surprised to find the sheriff and the doctor gone. He hadn't even heard them leave the room. Likely they were polite enough to leave him some dignity, and he truly appreciated it.

He rose to his feet a bit unsteadily, then ran his hands down his face. "I'm ready."

Life had given him gifts and he intended on treasuring them. He put his arm in Madeline's and allowed her to steady him. The last twelve hours had sapped his strength, and the emotional storm had taken its toll. His legs were unsteady and his head was swimming.

Madeline steadied him, her strong grip keeping him upright. "Do you need a drink of water?"

He nodded and wiped one shaking hand across his brow. Madeline fetched a glass from the pitcher behind the sheriff's desk. The water wasn't cool, but it was wet, and it helped him get his bearings back.

Micah smiled sheepishly at Madeline. "I guess I'm not invincible, am I?"

"No, but you are amazing. Come on, let's get you back to your family."

As she helped him out the door, into the fading sunlight, he smiled. Yes, his family was waiting and Micah was nearly there with them. Thank God they'd all survived. The future awaited them, together.

Chapter Sixteen

She had come into awareness slowly over a period of time. The smells and sounds around her familiar enough to tantalize her into consciousness. A small hand held hers, and Eppie realized Miracle was at her side.

Her eyes seemed to weigh a hundred pounds and her throat felt as if it was on fire. She tried to swallow but couldn't.

Eppie must have made a sound, because a little voice whispered in her ear. "Mama?"

She groaned and squeezed the little hand.

"Mama's wake!" Miracle went screaming out of the room.

Eppie wanted to smile, to laugh, but she could barely move. A cool hand touched her forehead.

"Hey there, Eppie."

Micah.

She forced her eyes open and looked up at him. His face was drawn, cheeks sunken, with bags under his eyes. His red-rimmed eyes were smiling along with his whisker-covered mouth.

"Don't try to talk. You were almost strangled. The doctor says you're going to be okay, no bones broken. You have a lot of bruising, though."

She managed to nod and looked at the glass on the table.

"Oh, I'm an idiot. Of course you're thirsty." He poured a

glass with shaking hands. With an apologetic smile, he cupped the back of her neck then brought the glass to her lips. Cool water coated her mouth and tongue, sliding down her throat and helping to dull the fire within.

Eppie mouthed "thank you" and sank back into the pillow.

He caressed her cheek. "I almost lost you again. It seems there are plenty of things that want to keep us apart. I'm sorry I didn't get to you in time."

She shook her head. "You did." Those two words felt like sandpaper in her throat.

"If I had, you wouldn't be lying there recovering from almost being strangled." Micah was always hardest on himself, finding fault with everything he did or didn't do. "I'm just glad she wasn't able to finish it."

"Me, too." Whispering was better than trying to speak. It at least allowed her to continue with Micah, and it seemed extremely important to finish the conversation.

"It was the second worst day of my life, and yet it was one of the best days of my life." He gave her a bit more water.

"Survived." She reached up and cupped his cheek. "Love you."

Micah closed his eyes and when he opened them, they were bright with unshed tears. "I love you, too, Elizabeth Archer."

She smiled. "Eppie."

"Eppie." He tried to smile, but he couldn't quite do it. "I am so sorry for everything. I expect you to light into me as soon as you get your voice back."

"No." She shook her head, unwilling to accept any more of his self-flagellation. "No more. Forgive."

"You forgive me? Thank God." He blew out a breath and sat back, wiping his brow.

"Forgive yourself." Her whispered command made him jump off the bed.

"What do you mean?" He paced back and forth to the door. "I don't know what you're talking about."

She struggled to a sitting position, even as her head swam. Eppie looked around and spotted a pencil and paper on the bureau. She pointed at it.

"You want to write something?" He fetched the pencil and paper and handed it to her.

Eppie thought for a moment about what she wanted to say to him, and decided the straight truth was required. Micah was a grown man and he needed to find a way to put the past where it belonged. She put pencil to paper and wrote a love letter to him.

Micah watched her write and wanted to snatch it from her hands. He had a feeling he didn't want to read what she wrote. What if she told him to leave? That she didn't want to be with him anymore?

His cabin was at least clean and ready for him to return to. Although if she left him, he would probably lie there and do nothing until the critters came to gnaw on his bones.

What a pitiful shell of a person he was. Why the hell couldn't he just be a normal person?

After ten minutes, she finished writing, wiped her eyes and handed him the paper. He took it with shaking hands and read, his heart lodged somewhere near his throat.

> Dearest Micah,
>   The world is a harsh place and you have been through so many terrible things. Life wasn't kind to you and you have not been kind to yourself.
>   We all do things we regret, things that we never dreamed we would do. You were a boy forced to become a man, to commit acts of survival.
>   God has forgiven you.

Please, forgive yourself. Life is waiting for you to shed the sins you carry on your back.
Please, forgive yourself and begin the rest of your life with me and Miracle.

All my love,
Eppie

He tried to swallow but couldn't. The truth was laid out in front of him in Eppie's neat handwriting. He had a choice to make and if he made the wrong one, she and Miracle were lost to him.

Micah fell to his knees, pressing the letter to his chest, feeling the love coming from each word as he absorbed all she had given him. Before he realized what she'd done, Eppie was beside him on the floor, a smile on her face and tears in her eyes.

"I love you so much," she whispered.

He nodded and carefully set the letter on the floor. "I love you right back."

This time when she came into his arms, it was the purest moment he could imagine, full of love and life and the promise of the future.

Miracle was as chatty as ever the next morning. Micah had made her eggs with a biscuit and she sat at the table, legs swinging, and spoke of nothing and everything.

Eppie had insisted on coming downstairs to take the meal with them. She sipped tea and watched both of them with her chocolate-brown eyes.

"Mama 'kay now?"

Eppie smiled. "Almost," she whispered, then pointed to her throat, liberally decorated with bruises. "Ow."

Miracle nodded. "Bad lady hurt you. Daddy hurt her."

Micah's stomach cramped when he realized his daughter

had seen everything. The choking, the fighting, the killing, *everything*. She wasn't even three years old and she'd seen people at the basest level.

God knows what that would do to her and how she saw the world.

He squatted down beside her and tried to think of a way to explain to the little girl what she'd seen. "Mrs. Prentiss had an owie in her head and her heart. She lost her little girl and boy a long time ago. She was going to hurt Mama because she hurt so much on the inside." He put a fist to his chest. "Now she's in heaven with her son and daughter and we're safe. Do you understand?"

Miracle, who constantly surprised him, didn't fail him this time. "Daddy saved Mama. Daddy saved bad lady."

He didn't think of what he'd done as saving Eloise, but perhaps he had. The fact was, she had been stuck in hell on earth, unable to continue living normally after what she'd been through. Maybe the eyes of a three-year-old saw what he couldn't.

"You're right, honey. Now it's all over, and we can live here like a family."

Miracle nodded and pointed at the half-eaten breakfast. "Can I play with Daisy?"

"Yes, you can play with Daisy. Go ahead."

She scrambled from the chair and hugged him so hard, his bones nearly bent. "Love you, Daddy."

When she got to Eppie, she gave her mother a gentle hug, mindful of all the wounds peppering her body. "Love you, Mama."

With that, the girl who was aptly named skipped out of the kitchen and left her parents alone. Micah met Eppie's gaze and the love he saw shining from their depths humbled him.

"Upstairs?" She pointed at the ceiling and waggled her eyebrows.

"Are you sure? I mean, you were almost strangled and,

well are you sure?" He wanted nothing more than to make love to her, but not at the expense of her health.

She nodded and stood. Micah wasn't going to let the opportunity pass by. He scooped her up and she let out a little squeak, grabbing onto his neck.

"Hold on. We're going on a ride."

This time Eppie laughed and kissed his ear. "Ready."

Micah could hardly contain his excitement and his cock certainly knew it. The damn thing had already grown too large for his pants by the time he made it to the top of the stairs. He headed straight for his bedroom.

Eppie was nervous, more nervous than she'd been when she rode up to the cabin in a torrential storm to find Micah. This was their first night as a soon-to-be-married couple.

Madeline had surprised her with a gift earlier in the day and she couldn't wait to show it to Micah. She felt his body heat seep into hers and knew he was anticipating their joining as much as she was. This was the moment they truly formed their union, an everlasting bond of mind, body and soul.

He set her down gently in front of the master bedroom, his room, and wiped his palms on his trousers as if he was nervous. "Is this okay?"

She nodded and stood on tiptoe to kiss him. What she didn't expect was for him to grab her by the waist and kiss her back like a man dying of thirst who'd found an oasis.

Micah planted sweet, slow kisses, one right after the other, not even giving her a chance to recover before he plundered her mouth again. His lips were soft but insistent, traveling across hers with little nips as he went. She gladly threw herself into the sensations he elicited with only his mouth.

His tongue tickled her lips and she smiled, allowing him to slip into the cavern within. His tongue skimmed along her teeth, teasing hers until they finally came together, dueling in a dance older than time itself. Eppie sighed into his mouth, so happy she could burst.

He pulled back after one more spine-tingling kiss. When he gazed into her eyes, she was so grateful to see peace shining from him. It had been a lifetime for him since he'd known what peace felt like, and finally he'd accepted it back into his heart. She was proud of him, and oh so grateful.

"What are you smiling about?"

"You. I'm a lucky girl." She nipped at his full lower lip, then licked at the spot.

A shudder ran through him and she felt his hard staff pressing into her belly. Micah was obviously ready and she couldn't wait to pleasure him this time.

"I'm the lucky one. Now are you ready to cross the threshold, my future wife?" This time he waggled his eyebrows and she laughed.

"Yes, but then you'll need to give me a few minutes to get ready." She hoped she gave him a mysterious look. "I've got a surprise for you."

Eppie actually felt his heart kick against her chest, and her smile widened.

"What surprise?"

"Oh, you're not going to find out that easily. Now carry me through the door so we can get started." She laughed at the forlorn expression on his face.

"I don't know about you, but I've already started."

She almost choked on the snort that threatened to explode. "I felt that already."

He swatted at her behind. "Vixen."

"Hm, maybe, now get a move on, Mr. Spalding."

"Now that sounded like the Eppie I know and love." He picked her up as gently as he'd put her down and carried her into the bedroom.

The morning sunshine streamed in through the white sheer curtains. Tears pricked Eppie's eyes as she realized she'd be waking up in this room, in Micah's arms, for the rest of her life. It seemed God had seen fit to finally bless her, bless both of them, with happiness.

"Now shoo before you see something before I'm ready to show you." She made a sweeping motion with her hands and he backed toward the door.

"For how long?"

"Five minutes. Now go." Eppie almost had to push him out the door into the hallway. She could tell he didn't want to go, but he did because she asked him to.

She took the box out from under the bed and pulled the tissue open to reveal a beautiful blue nightgown—robin's egg blue, a bright gorgeous color that called to Eppie's spirit. She'd been told before the coma that she used to wear only bright colors, and now understood why. Bright colors reaffirmed life, reminded her of how much she should enjoy everything around her.

Eppie intended to enjoy this night quite a bit.

With a happy yip, she pulled off her light green dress and laid it on the chair in the corner. All her underthings followed until she was nude. The air coming through the open windows put a chill on her skin, raising goosebumps and her nipples. A ripple of sensual excitement followed, anticipation making her anxious for her man to return.

With only a few minutes to prepare, she washed up using the water left in the pitcher, then slipped on the nightgown. It was softer than a feather and so smooth it slid down her skin, echoing the excitement she'd felt a few minutes earlier from the breeze.

A tentative knock at the door startled her. "Ready?"

He sounded pained and as anxious as she felt. Eppie was more than ready.

"Yes, come in." She stood by the bed in a bright sunbeam.

Her voice was still hoarse from the day before, but it was better. It was enough to do what she needed to.

When he came through the door, he had his hand over his eyes, making her smile. "I wanted to be sure the lady was properly prepared for her gentleman husband." The southern drawl dripped from his mouth like hot honey. "I hate to keep a lady waiting, after all."

"The lady is properly prepared." She couldn't help the tremor of excitement in her belly when he finally looked at her.

Eppie knew there were few moments in a person's life that were so perfect someone would remember them in detail forever. This was one of those moments.

Shock and amazement blossomed on his face. His gaze moved up and down her body until it met hers. In the depths of his gray eyes she saw so much love, it made her heart miss a beat.

"You're the most beautiful thing I've ever seen," he whispered it with reverence and awe. "I can't even begin to express how much I love you, Eppie."

She opened her arms. "You don't have to say anything for that."

Micah swiped at his eyes, then shucked his clothes faster than she'd ever seen him move. "I can't wait to feel that against me."

She knew what he meant—the fabric was even arousing her. When he came into her arms, this time his kisses were slow and light.

"Oh, Lord above, you feel like heaven." He slid against her, rubbing his body where she ached most. "Surely I have found paradise on earth."

Eppie whispered hoarsely on a laugh. "Not quite, but we can make some of our own, if you're so inclined."

"I'm inclined all right. If I get any more inclined, we won't get very far before I have to start over."

"Kiss me." Eppie pulled his head towards hers.

He obeyed. Up and down her cheeks, her jaw, her ears, featherlight touches that left a trail of excitement as they went. By the time he reached her neck, Eppie was breathing in short bursts, her nipples aching for attention, her cunt damp.

Micah pressed his lips to each one of the bruises, silently apologizing for what she'd been through. Eppie understood why he blamed himself, and she also understood he was letting go of that guilt and moving on. This was the beginning of their new life together.

Before she realized it, he'd backed her to the bed and the mattress hit the back of her knees. She sat down while he knelt in front of her.

"I love that blue color on you, but there's something I enjoy more."

"What's that?"

"Me."

Eppie shook her head. "Stand up, Mr. Spalding. This time it's my turn."

He frowned at her. "Your turn?"

"Yes, my turn. Stand up." Her voice was fading fast and he knew it. She wasn't about to allow him to take the reins again. This time she wanted to.

With a doubtful expression he rose and held out his hand. She brushed it aside and focused on what she really was after. Eppie wrapped her hand around his cock, feeling satin and steel together. Smooth skin rippled beneath her fingers. He sucked in a breath and his balls tightened up right along with the muscles in his legs.

"Oh, that's what you meant. Your turn." He sounded as if he was having trouble speaking.

Good, that meant she was doing it right.

She tugged him a bit closer, running both hands up and down his length, pausing to fondle his sac. Even if she never saw, or remembered seeing, another man nude, he was a glorious specimen. Long, and wide enough her fingers just touched as she felt his girth. Micah had been gifted and so in turn had she.

When her tongue darted out to taste him, he groaned. "God, Eppie, you're going to kill me."

"That wasn't the plan, now hush."

This time when she tasted him, she put him in her mouth. Her tongue slid down, then back up, to swirl around the head. His hands landed on her shoulders as he hung on for the ride.

She squeezed the base of his cock as she took the rest of it into her mouth, or at least as much of it as she could. It was salty and so amazing, she found herself nipping at him. Each scrape of her teeth made him jump.

She loved it.

"I can't . . . take . . . much more," he huffed out. "Please, Eppie."

He was nearly begging, but she wasn't ready yet to give up her new discovery. His satiny skin grew slick from her mouth as the tip of him touched the back of her throat. She tasted his essence and knew he'd told the truth. There would be other times, and she intended on taking full advantage of them.

Eppie released him from her mouth with an audible pop, then reached out and licked the tip once more.

Micah must've been beyond the point of speaking because he pushed her back on the bed and yanked up the nightgown. She liked him like that, aggressive and sexual, and all hers.

His mouth descended on her pussy and lapped at her while he nibbled at her nubbin. Eppie slammed into full-blown arousal in seconds, bucking on the bed as his mouth, tongue and teeth brought her the most exquisite pleasure. She almost came immediately but was able to pull it back by clenching the bedspread and closing her eyes.

When he looked up from between her legs, an evil grin split his face. "Ready now?"

She laughed and pulled at his arms. "Now."

Micah climbed atop her and thrust his cock into her in one motion. Fully sheathed inside her, he stopped, and it was a good thing, because yet again she had been seconds away from coming. Micah made her lose control as she did to him. Eppie clawed at his back, her body trying to absorb the sheer bliss from their joining.

He moved slowly at first, pulling out, then back in with a kick. She picked up his rhythm and pushed her hips up as he pressed down. The heat from their bodies nearly exploded as they moved together.

Eppie forgot everything except the sensation of his cock thrusting in and out of her. Carnal lust had her scratching at him, needing him to be deeper, faster, harder. He obliged by picking up the pace until the first wave of her orgasm hit.

Then Eppie's mind ceased functioning. Waves of rapture splashed over her, pulling her into a whirlpool of pleasure so deep, she threw herself into it. There was never anything so perfect as that moment of eternal joy.

Micah called her name as she called his. He thrust into her so deeply, she raised her legs, feeling his seed spill into her, giving her life, himself.

Tears filled Eppie's eyes as the pulses of joy swept through her. Perfectly matched and absolutely one soul, at last.

Epilogue

Micah sat on the front porch sipping coffee, at peace, a hard-earned feeling he never thought to find in his life. It had been a month since Miracle had been rescued and life had become more predictable, exactly what he needed. Eppie had recovered completely and Miracle seemed to have suffered no ill effects that he could discern from her ordeal.

Even the people in Plum Creek had begun treating them as neighbors and not outsiders. Matilda Webster kept her distance after the incident on the street, for which Micah was grateful. She must've heeded Eppie's warning, or maybe it was Eppie's fist that warned her off. Small-minded people had no business judging others. Perhaps one day Matilda might see the error of her ways, but somehow he doubted it.

He finally had everything he wanted. In a week Eppie would be his wife. They had a daughter, good friends, and a place to live. There wasn't anything else he could imagine he'd need. Life was perfect.

As Micah enjoyed the feeling of being content, Daisy dug around in what was left of the flower beds. He decided not to yell at the dog anymore. She'd proven her mettle in the fight with Eloise and deserved a warm spot next to the stove for the rest of her doggie life.

Fall had already arrived in Colorado and the mornings

were crisp. His breath in the morning air told him a frost would soon be on the way.

Coffee halfway to his lips, Micah spotted two figures walking down the street toward the house. From where he was sitting, he couldn't quite see who it was, but he wasn't concerned. Homer Prentiss had picked up and left town, never to be seen again. Micah even heard the farm had been sold. There wasn't anyone else he could imagine would want to do them harm.

Feeling safe in Plum Creek, in his house, was a hard-fought battle. Micah was home.

Whoever walked down the street toward his house on a Tuesday morning shouldn't concern him in the least. When Miracle popped up beside him, a fierce frown on her little face, his heartbeat picked up a bit.

"Sad lady coming."

Micah sat up, startled as much by Miracle as what she said. "What sad lady?"

"Sad lady with eyes like you." She pointed a chubby finger toward the couple. "Sheriff coming too."

With that, his daughter disappeared into the front door, once again surprising him with her understanding of the world. What woman had eyes like him? There was only one person he knew of, and his sister was back in Virginia somewhere, lost to him more than ten years earlier. There was no way Sarah was in Colorado, no way she was walking up the street toward him.

As the couple got closer, Micah's stomach began to tighten, and the hairs on the back of his neck stood up. He could see the woman stood about as tall as Daniel, long brown hair swaying as she walked.

Micah's nerves started jangling with alarm and he stood, setting the coffee on the porch railing. He stepped off the porch and onto the walk. His throat dried up and he found himself unable to swallow.

How the hell Miracle knew who the woman was could not be explained, but plain as day the woman he saw coming toward him was his sister, Sarah.

Eppie fussed in the kitchen, rewashing dishes and refolding towels. It was the day she'd been waiting for, dreading perhaps, and it had finally arrived. She had a feeling Micah would be angry with her, but she didn't regret what she'd done.

Breakfast had been difficult for her. She made eggs the way he'd taught her, but had nearly burned the biscuits and the bacon was too crispy. He hadn't complained, and ate while he chatted with Miracle. The girl had been strangely quiet during breakfast, her chocolate brown eyes full of what looked like worry.

Eppie should have been spoken to her daughter after she finished eating, but Miracle would sometimes get into moods and then snap out of them a few hours later. Eppie had spoken to Doctor Carmichael and he assured her that Miracle was healthy. She would recover from her kidnapping in time.

The best thing Eppie and Micah could do was love her, accept her, and give her a safe home. Although some days, like today, weren't enough to keep Miracle from those dark moods of hers. Eppie was nervous enough about what she'd done and promised herself she'd talk to Miracle later and find out what was bothering her.

Right then, Micah was foremost in Eppie's mind. There was a hole in his life, one left by the sister he'd lost so long ago. While his childhood had been unhappy, it seemed the one bright spot in his life had been Sarah. Eppie heard the sadness in his voice when he spoke of her. Many nights after making love, they would talk for hours.

He spoke of Sarah with a fondness that made Eppie wish she had a brother who loved her as much. Apparently Sarah'd been a surprise to her parents and her older siblings six years after Micah had been born. From what Micah said, Sarah had been ignored by her parents; she was raised by him and his older sister, Veronica.

Too many times Eppie had been tempted to ask him to try to find Sarah, but she hadn't the courage to ask. Micah's wounds in his heart and soul were finally healed, and she couldn't deliberately reopen them.

However, she also couldn't allow the rest of Micah's life to go on without ever knowing what happened to the one person he'd loved as a child. As someone who loved Micah more than life itself, Eppie considered it her duty to help him, even if he wouldn't help himself. So she'd enlisted Madeline's help and together they'd tracked down Sarah and paid for her to travel to Colorado.

A knock at the back door startled her and she dropped a tin plate. It tinged and clattered on the wood floor, making her jump again. She glanced up to see Daniel at the door, one blond eyebrow raised. Eppie's cheeks heated in embarrassment, but she gestured for him to come in. He'd been a frequent visitor to the house, a new companion to Micah. They'd even gone hunting together a few weeks earlier. Daniel was more than a friendly face, he was a true friend.

Daniel came in and took off his hat, but he wasn't wearing his usual smile. She knew right then that Sarah had arrived in town and her heart leapt to her throat.

"Is she here?"

Daniel nodded. "I just left her on the front porch with Micah. He looked like he'd seen a ghost."

"He did. She was a ghost in his mind, one that haunted him." Eppie set the plate on the counter with shaking hands. Her stomach fluttered with nerves. It took every ounce of self-control not to run out to the front porch and see what was happening.

However, this was Micah's moment, his personal moment to reacquaint himself with his sister and truly accept that while his past was behind him, it was part of him. She couldn't take that away from him. He had to do it himself.

"Coffee?"

"I'd be obliged for some." Daniel sat down at the table and set his hat on the back of the chair. "Do you think they'll be all right?"

Eppie wrapped the towel around the handle of the coffee-pot and poured both of them a cup. After she set the pot back on the stove, she made herself sit at the table with Daniel. Her nerves were screaming for her to make sure Micah was okay. She was more than worried about him.

Miracle walked into the kitchen and pressed herself up against Eppie's side.

"Daddy's sad." Their perceptive child was right as always. Her dark mood seemed to be lifting as her concern for her father rose. She pointed toward the hallway. "Needs a hug."

"I know, honey, but for now we need to leave Daddy alone with the lady." Eppie pulled her onto her lap. "Did you say hello to the sheriff?"

She smiled up at the man shyly. "Hello, Sheriff."

"Good morning, Miss Miracle." He winked at her.

Miracle turned back to her mother and patted her cheek. "Lady sad, too."

It wouldn't surprise Eppie in the least if Sarah was sad, but perhaps together, she and Micah could break that cycle of sadness. Life was meant to be lived, not endured. She hoped her idea to find Micah's sister would have the desired results. If it backfired and she caused more damage to both of the Spaldings, Eppie would have to live with that.

It was a gamble and she bet on all their lives.

Eppie continued her conversation with the sheriff, discussing the weather and other inane topics while Miracle picked at a biscuit. They were all waiting and the anticipation was making Eppie squirm.

Miracle must've felt her mother's anxiety, because she

started squirming, too. They were a pitiful group, waiting in the kitchen. If Micah didn't come into the kitchen soon, Eppie thought she might start climbing the walls.

Finally, the sound of the front door opening had them all standing, anticipation making Eppie shake. She didn't know what to expect and that made it even worse. Was he angry with her?

Micah appeared in the kitchen with a woman at his side. She was tall for a woman, nearly Micah's height, and thin like he was. Her long wavy brown hair was liberally sprinkled with bits of red as if she'd been painted with sunset colors. Her eyes, however, were the giveaway—they mirrored Micah's so much it sent a chill up Eppie's spine. This was definitely his sister.

Eppie straightened her spine and smiled as Miracle clutched her hand.

"This is my sister, Sarah." His voice was hoarse with emotion and his eyes suspiciously damp. "Sarah, this is my fiancée Elizabeth and my daughter Miracle."

Sarah stepped forward her hand outstretched. "I'm happy to meet you."

"Please call me Eppie." She shook the other woman's hand, noting the calluses and a missing small finger on her left hand. Sarah had obviously worked to survive, as had Eppie. An instant connection was formed between them.

When she saw the smile on Micah's face, Eppie knew things were going to be all right. "Welcome home, Sarah. We've been waiting for you."

The other woman nodded, tears in her eyes. "I'm glad to be here."

Micah pulled Eppie into a hug so fierce, she felt the love from her head to her toes and everywhere in between. Miracle joined in by hugging their legs.

Eppie knew then her decision had been the right one.

Sarah was now part of Micah's life again. They weren't the standard, everyday type of family, but they had each other.

"I love you," he whispered against her ear.

"I love you, too." Eppie couldn't ask for anything more than what she already had. Her cup runneth over with joy, love, and life.

Need some INSTANT GRATIFICATION?
Jill Shalvis's new book is just the thing . . .

This was new for him. And oddly . . . stimulating. "I think I'm going to be okay."

Emma arched a brow. Daring him to admit the truth. "Annie told you," he said with a sigh.

"That you're on a volunteer search-and-rescue team and you were called out to save a guy who'd gone off a cliff on his rock climb? That said guy panicked once you had him halfway up the cliff to safety, knocking you down about fifty feet? Yeah, she told me. *You* might have told me."

Stone looked at Annie, who was suddenly very busy at the stove.

"Oh, and given the redness I see around some of your cuts and bruises, you do need the antibiotics."

"You said I looked good."

"That was a few days ago. You don't look good now."

She let him start sweating over that one for a beat, before she shook her head. "You fell off a cliff and you're scared of me?"

"Hell, yes."

She stood up and headed toward him, and he stumbled back a step, smacking right into the door.

Spencer winced.

Annie cackled.

"Careful," Emma said, still coming at him. "Your ribs." She reached her hand into her bag.

Oh, Christ. He pictured another needle and felt his skin go clammy. His stomach went queasy. This wasn't working for him, not one little bit. Not unless she was going to strip down for him again. "I don't need—"

Still looking at him, she pulled out . . . a prescription bottle. "Are you afraid of pills, too?" she asked innocently, when he was beginning to suspect there was nothing innocent about her at all.

Annie snickered again.

"I swear to God," he muttered in her direction.

Emma lightly smacked the bottle against his pecs, a fact he found interesting—was it his imagination, or did she touch him a lot?

More importantly, did she do it on purpose? It was worth finding out, and testing, he leaned into her, just a little.

Her pupils dilated.

Check.

Her nostrils flared.

Check, check.

If they'd been wild animals, their foreplay had just been conducted. Still testing, he lifted his hand and covered hers, still against his chest.

She stared down at their now entangled fingers around the pill bottle, then lifted her gaze to his. Her breathing had changed.

Quickened.

Test over, he decided, his own breathing changing as well. Because oh hell yeah, she was aware of him, every bit as much as he.

Which meant she was all bark and no bite.

That was *very* good to know.

No one can resist MIDNIGHT'S MASTER.
check out Cynthia Eden's latest,
out now from Brava . . .

"Throw her out, Niol. You want the vamps to keep comin', you *throw that bitch out.*"

The tapping stopped, and, because the vampire had raised his shrill-ass voice again, the nearby paranormals—because, generally, the folks who came in his bar were far, far from normal—stilled.

Niol shook his head slowly. "I think you're forgetting a few things, *vamp.*" He gathered the black swell of power that pulsed just beneath his skin. Felt the surge of dark magic and—

The vamp flew across the bar, slamming into the stage with a scream. The lead guitarist swore, then jumped back, cradling his guitar with both hands like the precious baby he thought it was.

The sudden silence was deafening.

Niol motioned toward the bar. "Get me another drink, Marc." He glanced at the slowly rising vampire. "Did I tell you to get up?" It barely took any effort to slam the bastard into the stage wall this time. Just a stray thought, really.

Ah, but power was a wonderful thing.

Sometimes, it was damn good to be a demon. And even better to be a level-ten, and the baddest asshole in the room.

He stalked forward. Enjoyed for a moment the way the crowd jumped away from him.

The vampire began to shake. *Perfect.*

Niol stopped a foot before the fallen André. "First," he growled, "don't ever, *ever* fucking tell me what to do in *my* bar again."

A fast nod.

"Second . . ." His hands clenched into fists as he fought to rein in the magic blasting through him. The power . . . oh, but it was tempting. And so easy to use.

Too easy.

One more thought, just one, focused and hard, and he could have the vamp dead at his feet.

"Use too much, you'll lose yourself." An old warning. One that had come too late for him. He'd been twenty-five before he met another demon who even came close to him in power and that guy's warning—well, it had been long overdue.

Niol knew he'd been one of the Lost for years.

The first time he'd killed, he'd been Lost.

"Second," he repeated, his voice cold, clear, and cutting like a knife in the quiet. "If you think I give a damn about the vampires coming to *my* place . . ." His mouth hitched into a half-grin, but Niol knew no amusement would show in the darkness of his eyes. "Then you're dead wrong, vampire."

"S-sorry, Niol, I—"

He laughed, then turned his back on the cringing vampire. "Thomas." The guard he always kept close. "Throw that vamp's ass out."

When Thomas stepped forward, the squeal of a guitar ripped through the bar. And the dancing and the drinking and the mating games of the *Other* began with a fierce rumble of sound.

Niol's gaze searched for his prey and he found Holly watching him. All eyes and red hair and lips that begged for his mouth. He strode toward her, conscious of covert stares still on them. He could show no weakness. Never could.

I'm not weak.

He was the strongest demon in Atlanta. He sure as hell wasn't going to give the paranormals any cause to start doubting his power.

His kind turned on the weak.

When he stopped before her, the scent of lavender flooded his nostrils.

She looked up at him. The human was small, to him anyway, barely reaching his shoulders so that he towered over her.

She was the weak one. All of her kind were.

Humans. So easy to wound. To kill.

He lifted his hand. Stroked her cheek. Damn, but she was soft. Leaning close, Niol told her, "Sweetheart, I warned you before about coming to my Paradise."

There was no doubt others overheard his words. With so many shifters skulking around the joint, a *whisper* would have been overheard. Shifters and their annoyingly superior senses.

"Wh-what do you mean?" The question came, husky and soft. Ah, but he liked her voice. He could all too easily imagine that voice, whispering to him as they lay amid a tangle of sheets.

Or maybe screaming in his ear as she came.

He cupped her chin in his hand. A nice chin. Softly rounded. And those lips . . . the bottom was fuller than the top. Just a bit. So red. Her mouth was slightly parted, open.

Waiting.

She stepped back, shaking her head. "I don't know what you *think* you're doing, Niol—"

He stared down at her. "Yes, you do." He caught her arms, wrapping his fingers around her and jerking Holly against him. "I told you, the last time you came into *my* bar . . ."

Her eyes widened. "Niol . . ."

Oh, yeah, he liked the way she said his name. She breathed it, tasted it.

His lips lowered toward hers. "If you want to walk in Paradise, baby, then you're gonna have to play with the devil."

"No, I—"

He kissed her. Hard. Deep. Niol drove his tongue right past those plump lips and took her mouth the way the beast inside him demanded.

Don't miss Shannon McKenna's latest,
TASTING FEAR,
out next month from Brava . . .

Liam sounded exhausted. Fed up. She didn't blame him a bit. She was a piece of work. Her mind raced to come up with a plausible lie. Letting him see how small she felt would just embarrass them both.

She shook her head. "Nothing," she whispered.

He let out a sigh, and leaned back, leaning his head against the back of the couch. Covering his eyes with his hands.

That was when she noticed the condition of his hand. His knuckles were torn and raw, encrusted with blood. God, she hadn't even given a thought for his injuries, his trauma, his shock. She'd just zoned out, floated in her bubble, leaned on him. As if he were an oak.

But he wasn't an oak. He was a man. He'd fought like a demon for her, and risked his life, and gotten hurt, and she was so freaked out and self-absorbed, she hadn't even noticed. She was mortified.

"Liam. Your hand," she fussed, getting up. "Let me get some disinfectant, and some—"

"It's okay," he muttered. "Forget about it."

"Like hell! You're bleeding!" She bustled around, muttering and scolding to hide her own discomfiture, gathering gauze and cotton balls and antibiotic ointment. He let her fuss, a martyred look on his face. After she'd finished taping his hand, she looked at his battered face and grabbed a handful of his polo shirt. "What about the rest of you?"

"Just some bruises," he hedged.

"Where?" she persisted, tugging at his shirt. "Show me."

He wrenched the fabric out of her hand. "If I take off my clothes now, it's not going to be to show you my bruises," he said.

She blinked, swallowed, tried to breathe. Reorganized her mind. There it was. Finally verbalized. No more glossing over it, running away.

"After all this?" His tone was timid. "You still want to . . . now?"

"Fuck, yes." His tone was savage. "I've wanted it since I laid eyes on you. It's gotten worse ever since. And combat adrenaline gives a guy a hard-on like a railroad spike, even if there weren't a beautiful woman in my face, driving me fucking nuts. Which puts me in a bad place, Nancy. I know the timing sucks for you. The timing's been piss poor since we met, but it never gets any better. It just keeps getting worse."

"Hey. It's okay." She patted his back with a shy, nervous hand. He was usually so calm, so controlled. It unnerved her to see him agitated.

He didn't seem to hear her. "And the worse it gets, the worse I want it," he went on, his voice harsh. "Which makes me feel like a jerk, and a user, and an asshole. Promising to protect you—"

"You did protect me," she reminded him.

"Yeah, and I told you it wasn't an exchange. You don't owe me sex. You don't owe me anything. And that really fucks me up. Because I can't even remove myself from the situation. I'm scared to death to leave you alone. And that puts me between a rock and a hard place."

She put her finger over his mouth. "Wow," she murmured. "I had no idea you could get worked into such a state.

He reached out, a little awkwardly, clasping his arms around her shoulders, staring into her eyes as if expecting her to bolt.

He pulled her close, enfolding her in his warmth, his power.

Suddenly, they were kissing. She had no idea who had kissed who. The kiss was desperate, achingly sweet. Not a power struggle, not a matter of talent or skill, just a hunger to get as close as two humans could be. He held her like he was afraid she'd be torn away from him.

Mr. Super-mellow Liam let's-contemplate-the-beau
flower Knightly."

His explosive snort of derision cut her off. She shus
again, enjoying the feel of his lips beneath her finger. '
not a jerk or a user," she said gently. "You were magni
Thank you. Again."

He looked away. There was a brief, embarrassed pa
"That's very generous of you," he said, trying to flex
wounded hand. "But I'm not fishing for compliments."

"I never thought that you were." She placed her own han
below his and rested them both gently on his thigh. Her fin
gers dug into the thick muscle of his quadriceps, through the
dirty, bloodstained denim of his jeans. Beneath the fabric, he
was so hot. So strong and solid.

She moved her hand up, slowly but surely, stroking higher
toward his groin. His breath caught and then stopped entirely as her fingers brushed the turgid bulge of his penis beneath the fabric.

Here went nothing. "I think I know what you mean, about
the hard place," she whispered, swirling her fingertips over it.
Wow. A lot of him. That thick broad, hard stalk just went on
and on. "Or was this what you meant when you were refer-
ring to the rock?"

His face was a mask of tension, neck muscles clenched,
tendons standing out. "You don't have to do this," he said,
his voice strangled.

Aw. So sweet. Her fingers closed around him, squeezing.
He groaned, and a shudder jarred his body. "I can't seem to
stop," she said.

"Watch out, Nancy," he said hoarsely. "If you start something now, there's no stopping it."

She stroked him again, deeper, tighter, a slow caress that
wrung a keening gasp from his throat. "I know," she said. "I
know."